Chava's Dreams
By
Robert Schrager

For Zippy, Samantha, Rachel, and Salyann

And thanks to helpful friends

Cover design by Chana Levi

ISBN: 9798693644908

Copyright © 2020 by Robert Schrager

כתר (Crown)

Chapter 1: Sinners at the City Gate; גבורה (Strength)

Chapter 2: Jezebel and Adam; תפארת (Glory)

Chapter 3: Loaves of Dust; יסוד (Foundation)

Chapter 4: Serpent; בינה (Understanding)

Chapter 5: Chava Knows Yehu; דעת (Knowledge)

Chapter 6: Blessed Man of Fire; הוד (Splendor)

Chapter 7: Two Kings and a Donkey; חסד (Kindness)

Chapter 8: Not a Prophet; חוכמה (Wisdom)

Chapter 9: Jezebel's Daughter; נצח (Eternity)

Chapter 10: An Eternal Sabbath; מלכות (Kingdom)

The Place

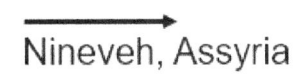

The Period

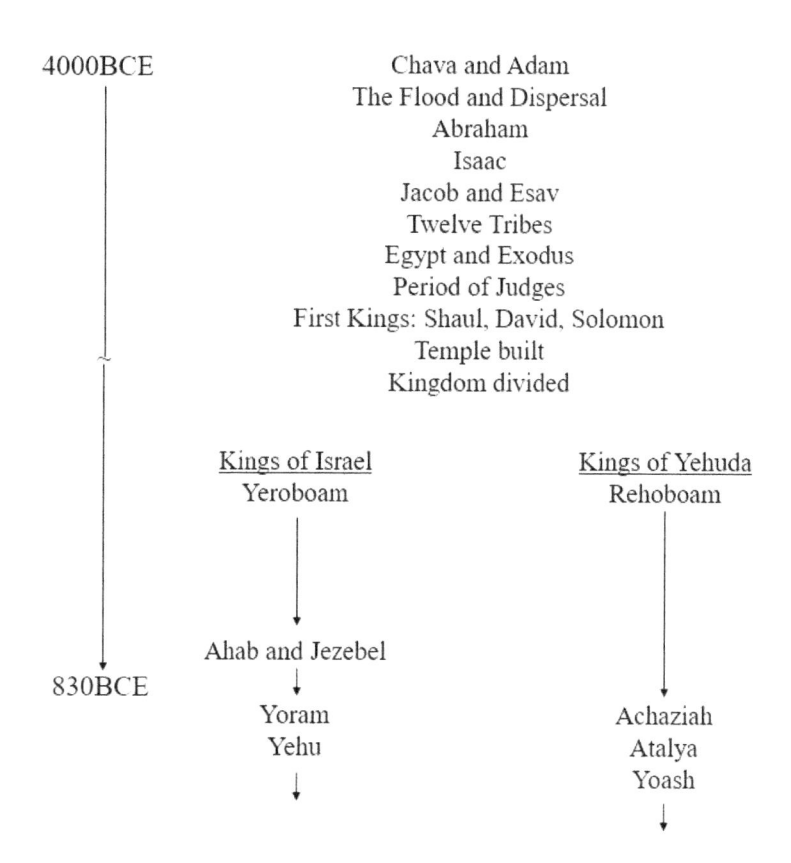

4000BCE

Chava and Adam
The Flood and Dispersal
Abraham
Isaac
Jacob and Esav
Twelve Tribes
Egypt and Exodus
Period of Judges
First Kings: Shaul, David, Solomon
Temple built
Kingdom divided

Kings of Israel	Kings of Yehuda
Yeroboam	Rehoboam
↓	↓
Ahab and Jezebel	
↓	
Yoram	Achaziah
Yehu	Atalya
↓	Yoash
	↓

830BCE

My story begins in the year 830BCE.
My dreams harken back to (before) and after 4000BCE.

כתר (Crown)

CROWN. Something from Nothing.

I hold a story.

Father leads me to act in ways that conflict with my sensibilities—rules to keep and break. Yes, He created me in His image in accordance with His will, but I'm left with impossible choices.

Did I do evil? Seek trite answers or consider additional questions.

Although I call Him "Father" or "Him"—He has no gender. He was, is, and will always be related to in terms of both masculine and feminine. Please attribute my descriptions to the shortcoming of language. May Her will and mine be eternally aligned.

This is the story of how I chose. I gaze on the infinite and tell my tale in present and past. For me, all time has happened, the entire epoch of man. I chose to live within the physical dictates of this world and cannot perceive choices and outcomes. I will tell why I left Eden; you will *know* why but may never *understand*. The teachers never explained, did they?

Listen to the testimony of the most beautiful woman on earth. It is I, Chava, who made her choice, so you can say, "I have a choice."

This story is about morphing; evil morphing from force to place or person; good morphing into the physical; Me as I morphed from the primordial garden to this physical world.

Long ago, there was a time and a place, when and where the evil force morphed into the corporeal realm. I will recount the archetype of the evil roost perched on a foundation of famine and Baal, that evil spirit who shall not morph into the physical world.

Before the beginning of the epoch of man, a primordial woman made her decision. This first female confronts the spiritual emanations unleashed on the physical world. For all time past and to come, I bear witness to my choice.

We go now.

Chapter 1

גבורה (Strength)

Sinners at the City Gate

Why do you stare at me? What do you hope to discover? No, I am not scared to tell you. I make my own decisions! Please stop interrupting. I will explain only because I desire to do so.
The story begins with a body of produce: Waste and blood.

    The children emerged from the house to watch their village line up to pay sacrament to Baal. Those present formed a line facing the statue. Each squatted and relieved their bowels in the face of the worthless god. The offensive aroma of human waste and fanatical chants mingled and hung in the air with the flies. Parents brought a child as an offering. They set the corpse upon the fiery pyre after a slice across the throat. Servants of the priest harvested the ashes. The worshippers coated their bodies with a morbid slurry composed of ashes, roots, and herbs that were ground together and mixed with oil.
    This village, an island of morbidity surrounded by tranquil farm and countryside on a brisk harvest evening, seeped with angry soil. I was mesmerized by the stark contrast, for earlier in the day, I strode with joy on fertile land where every beast, bug, and rock sang a happy song.
    Soft green and cool blue had yielded to sticky red and putrid brown.
    Most of the little ones ran away from their possessed parents. Others hovered, paralyzed with fear. The helpless brood grasped at the only caregivers they ever knew, with a hope that their father's returned to sanity. A Baal cult controlled the elders. Assyrian's practiced idolatry, but this extreme ritual cult enslaved the people of the land.
    From a distance, I watched the settlement to avoid detection. My beauty, fatal to behold, cloaked my will. I glimpsed a child running from the settlement. She ran past me. As the pursuer encroached upon my position, I leaped from behind a boulder and smacked him on the

forehead with my staff. He collapsed unconscious. The girl halted thirty paces away from me and glanced back at the hunter who laid unthreatening. I kneeled and beckoned her to come, but she froze until I revealed my face from the cloak hood. Happenings of her mind were easy to read. People saw me as an unthreatening, gentle young lady because I concealed my ancient beauty.

Relief washed over the homely girl as she approached.

"What's your name, girl?"

"Why do you ask my name? Who are you?"

I smiled.

"I'm Chava. There is a lot to know from a name. If I know who you are, I can help. That is your father, correct?"

"I'm Simta. Thanks for stopping him."

"Very well, it's Simta. That's a pretty name. When did the Baal priest come to the village?"

"He arrived one moon ago, at the beginning of the harvest. The priest and his servants instructed the men of our village to gather roots and herbs for their rituals. They arrange a nightly ceremony when the people return from the fields. These ceremonies changed our parents. In the morning we wake, and everything is normal as we go to the fields to work. Every evening is death. In the morning we hope it will be different, but it's not."

Simta sobbed and tried to catch her breath. "Our parents swallow the sacred drink, squat in front of the Baal, and take us."

Sad, but my patience approached its limit, which happens when one has listened to victims for thousands of years. Mankind grew immune from too many tales of child sacrifice.

Simta told me the pleasant past of the community and friends lost to the Baal menace. Oh Simta, such a smart girl, but she was bothersome in speech and smell and descended from a pathetic line of exploited people.

Sunrise would be soon. It was time. "Simta, wake your father. Let us go to the village."

I spoke to Simta's father of the priest and servants; of how many and where they slept. Then, he spoke of the wheat, and I cursed with anger and vengeance at those despoilers of the primal grain. Their plan was to pilfer the village plenty. Priests! Parasites fanned across the land at harvest time to ensnare and abscond communal livelihood. Whoever remained after the harvest became chattel—a reaping of wheat and humanity. Simta and her father understood this priestly crew and their devious intentions, but they had no will to object.

What did they know of me? A beautiful young woman; perchance twenty years old with no companions or family. I am dressed in a cloak of alien fabric and carrying a long staff. This confused him, but his initiative had vanished. A thought of protest bloomed and withered as I commanded him to return to the village.

I said, "One cannot flee from community. Wicked priests with worthless gods rule the night no more. A banishment of travesty, a scourge I'll not ignore."

"Simta, go with father to your house and wait for the noise to cease before coming out."

A putrid fog of dew and smoke hung in the air wreaking of wet death. Nothing provoked my emotion. Things were as they would be according to the dictates of His majesty. It was a despicable reward not warranted or understood by meek souls. I could help now, but they would always be vulnerable to exploitation.

Servants of the priest slept in heaps on the floor of the village hall. The priest examined me as he sat in a chair at the far end of the room.

I cast off my hood and ordered, "Depart at once. Go!"

The priest stared with shock and became overcome with weakness as a sharp pain behind his left eye nullified his autonomy. One servant approached me from the side. I tapped him on the forehead with my staff and he dropped. The priest beckoned the servants to collect their belongings and flee the village.

Upon the left eye is a portal to live or die. From the organ that sees lays a path to the place of dreams. On that path, a woman called Chava controls their liberty.

The procession, priest and servants, departed without fanfare. The villagers emerged from their houses, watching the charlatans' departure. I added wood to the fire of the town square to incinerate the Baal statues. The villagers led the destruction.

I snuck into the grain storehouse to inspect the harvest. A regiment of sacks stood like soldiers inside the peaceful room. With my dagger I ripped open a sack, then thrust my hand deep into the interior. In an instant my skin tone transformed into the tan color of the wheat kernels. I cupped my hand and withdrew it from the sack, inverted palm, inspecting kernels of flesh as they descended.

Thus, the story begins with this trivial incident in the Assyrian village, land of Ashur. The village tale is brief. The place itself is of little importance—the battle I wage is existential. It's not only the worship of idols and false gods, but the methods used by the elite to advance their interests at the expense of man's spirit.

"But let justice roll on like a river, righteousness like a never-failing stream." This is the message Amos carried throughout the Shomron, the Northern Kingdom. Amos was an illustrious man who moved the masses and made history with new words. Some people listened and acted upon what they heard. For most, the daily flow of life interfered with the never-failing stream of righteousness. The burden Amos carried was the same as every prophet.

These men had hearts of flesh and veins flowing indestructible truth. Amos carried that crucible of truth from town to town even though the people had ears but would not hear. Their ears had become like the ears of the stone statues. Ears of stone and wood did not dissuade Amos. At the risk of his life, he rolled like a river, like a never-failing stream. I followed Amos throughout the Shomron until the people set him to flee. Such a pity to lose Amos, the prophet of the righteous deed and word. The people had slid too far, they forwent redemption, but I could not stop listening. And he would not stop preaching. I urged him on from the audience. He saw me in the crowd and smiled a secret smile. I'll tell you of Amos the small boy. But before, this happened…

A force pulled me on travels from Ashur to the Kingdom of Israel. This, the Northern Kingdom, had split from Yehuda generations ago. At last I dwelled on the outskirts of a settlement and attempted to be a member of a communal society, if only to comprehend their behavior. After a few years I'd move to another community to avoid routine. This went on for many years. It was an enjoyable time, but troubles grew from a seed of strange worship and corpulence. Generations had passed since the Northern Kingdom split off from Yehuda; misguided progeny ebbed away from the spirit of Jerusalem. The yearly pilgrimages ceased, as did observance of the ancient laws and customs. This Israel, the Northern Kingdom, had scant memory of the grandeur of Solomon. Strange worship, new and old, flourished and filled the void. Let's begin.

***

There will be horror. Do not flinch. Hope shall follow.
STRENGTH. A left hand, red hand, squeezes tight, applying strict judgement.

The words of the prophet Elisha went forth. A famine was in the land in those days as I approached the city of Shomron. The Aramean forces of Ben-Hadad laid siege on Shomron, seat of the Northern Kingdom that was Israel in that time. Dusk settled when I encountered four men outside the city gate, one old and three young. The four had attempted to stay hidden, but I startled them.

Shomron and the surrounding countryside boiled in the dry heat. All was reddish brown, and even the sky and clouds took on that forlorn hue in the absence of rain and dew. There was no escape from rusty dust emanating from Sinai.

The aged one spoke with self-exacerbated brown teeth, "Who are you? How did you journey here alone? It's no matter. All of us will die."

I sat across from them and responded, "I come from the north, a widow bereft of small children, family missing, destitute, and abandoned. Have you no bread? Why dwell outside the city gate? Guessingly, I say to thee, why shall men sit, not flee? Is known now, though you never told me, sinners are thee! Transgressors! Thy skin is stained with guilt!"

Could it be that this rusty earth and sky shall not claim their white flesh and brown teeth? Perhaps they are lucky men.

The old one spoke, "Listen to me little witch, Shomron is under siege, no food exists to share with a wayward woman prowling the night. Quiet your voice lest you rouse guards, or worse, the Aramean invaders. Have you no food? Why do you tarry here? Move away from us, odd woman."

Their breath filled the air with a most peculiar smell: date honey. Brown? Yes. But the sweet aroma lingered in stark contrast to their putrid white flesh and desolate surroundings. The honey dripped past my nose and assaulted my eyes with a sweet char.

In a rage, I screamed, "How does this sinner order me to leave? Shall an afflicted outcast with no claim on the land tell a poor woman to flee? Explain how this group of four earned these abominable afflictions? Detestable men!"

I laughed with merriment at their ridiculous dilemma. They had thought their predicament could get no worse until I arrived.

"Lower your voice and stop laughing," this, the old one stammered as his starved body stood prepared to pounce me.

I poked his belly with my staff, laughed, and said, "Sit!" He dropped to the ground and struggled to catch his breath. "The rest of you stay seated with your father." They obeyed the order with deafening glares of apprehension. "That's your father, eh? Why so sad? Nothing to say to a poor widow?"

A flash of insight occurred to me. "Now I understand who and what are thee: a prophet! Yonah has replaced you as Elisha's disciple. Now, tell how you gained these afflictions of the outcasts?"

The four remained speechless, defeated. On one side was starvation; on the other side was death at the hand of the enemy. There were only two sides—so they thought.

"Two sides you see, but you'll summon three."

***

I laid on the rocky ground, shut my eyes, and dreamed of this man, the father of the three, a man of importance: Gechazi. He was the most prominent disciple of Elisha; a man that was well learned and of fine intellect, but deficient of heart and faith. Elisha tried to pass the staff to him for resurrection of the Shunammite woman's child, but Gechazi was unsuitable. Gechazi's lack of faith spawned failure. Failure reinforced his base nature. He grew concerned, obsessed, with his own station in life. Resentment of Elisha's eminence blossomed with the realization he'd never achieve such status. Gechazi dissuaded other disciples from coming to Elisha's lessons, causing his situation to become more severe. Gechazi extracted payment from the Aramean that Elisha cured of afflictions. He received payment in money but was cursed measure for measure with the same affliction of the Aramean.

I awoke.

***

I glanced at the four men and shouted, "The Almighty has cursed the city wherein dwellers eat the fruit of their womb. Does the king, Yoram, adjudicate over dead babies?" The four men were speechless as I continued, "How can a man feign ignorance on matters recognized within every soul who dwells in Shomron, the cursed city?"

***

Settling to sleep, I entered the city gate through a dream. Mid-morning: the streets were silent and the markets unattended. There was no dignified food to buy or sell. The dynamic machinations of Shomron had seized. The pallid stasis of starvation hung in the air—a fog even the sun refused to burn away. Famines are slow painful destruction, but there had never been a famine of this severity. The dream pulled me along the streets of sadness. Despair seeped out of houses through cracks in the bricks, doors, and windows. The ephemeral brown fog of famine, judgment from Above, could not be breached until He obliged. Until then, blood and fat exhaled across starved lips.

I entered a courtyard of four houses and walked up the steps of the closest house to the balcony. A young woman lay on a couch clutching a deceased baby boy. This skeletal form shivered under several layers of clothing and blankets. Her face, in the changing light, took on a facade that oscillated between flesh and skull. The flowing river, within the branches of blood vessels on her forehead, pulsed with every heartbeat, undulating between life and death.

"Mother. Lay with me."

The starved woman spoke. This startling predicament confused my soul and shouldn't be since I entered her world through a dream—none should see me, but her soul requests I lay with thee. She was far removed from normal consciousness but saw or sensed me still the same. With surprised fright, a portent of evil, I considered what to do. With excitement, without a decision, I laid next to "my daughter." A comforted groan breached her lips as I stroked her head and thin hair. I nestled against her bony frame. She flinched in pain as I placed my left hand on her shoulder. What power remained in this frame of skin and bones needed preservation for basic life functions. There was power from the primordial realm that allowed her to stay in this husk, in this world. It was perplexing for a woman from this same primordial realm who knows the heart of her children to see this woman and know how this sinewy waif sustained. With a clasped shoulder, a breathed breath, could I become this skinny girl? I had to discover her.

In half embrace with the young lady, I drifted into a deeper dream. I was her, this woman—my daughter—perhaps ten years prior, in happier times. In an instant a life blossomed and withered: a marriage, famine, husband's death, and painful loss of the infant. In outrage, I assaulted the dream world for the allusive secret but woke alone, unanswered, on her couch. The woman stood staring over the balcony. Another woman, clutching a swaddled infant, ascended the staircase.

The woman I laid with, the thin one, placed her baby on the couch. She took the other woman's baby, placing the corpse on a nearby table. This "other" woman, in form and function, appeared oblivious to the famine. She was better fed. Had she been more affluent? No matter, there was no food for money. Why do I uncover two mysterious women in this starving city?

"Mara, yours now," the thin one said.

Mara agreed, "Mine now, yours tomorrow at nightfall."

The thin lady dismembered the infant corpse; purged offal from the tiny intestines, cut limbs into small pieces, and placed the contents into a clay pot. Guilt welled in my soul for voyeuristic watching's as she absently scratched the back of her head and thinning hair with fingernail bits of coagulated debris. And the stew simmered.

What mattered if one had silver? The common denominator of hunger had erased degrees of status and affluence. They were two young ladies at a grisly supper plotting to grist the remaining bones on the morrow. The horrid deal: each to prepare the others' babe. Cursed be the prophet that brought His rebukes to this world. Oh Father, how thy prophets are tormented.

I followed the larger one, Mara, as she descended the balcony steps and walked along the road. On the way her stomach protested the illicit supper. Even the livid earth groaned objections at the vomit splash. The fruit of her womb was consumed and wasted in futility. A deal was struck for Sara's baby on the morrow. And that is how I learned the name of Sara, the mysterious skeletal lady; from Mara's thoughts, as debris dribbled from her mouth.

One woman is Sara: a mysterious emaciation. The other woman is Mara, opposite in form and function.

I followed as Mara entered a house containing five men.

One, a red head, spoke, "As four partners in the grain broker business, we could extract huge profits from the time stocks began to dwindle. We hadn't been operating in the city for long. Since we were not recognized, we had plenty of potential customers."

I listened to him and thought, customers or victims?

And then, as if he read my mind, one man asked, "Customers or victims?"

Red rolled his eyes and continued, "Customers." Red appeared to be the talker of the group. He had an effeminate and easy way with speech and the ability to arrange a confidence scheme. They took turns telling their story. Each of them spoke uninhibited on this day—possibly their last day on earth. Death by famine or war was inevitable.

"I'd visit a bakery, twice a week over a period of a month to buy flour," said Red. "I'd go in the early afternoon when things were quiet, and I had the master's attention. We'd speak, and I'd purchase small quantities of flour to present myself as an ordinary customer. When the time was ripe, we'd move to the next step."

I closed my eyes and projected my mind into his narrative. I existed in the present, in the past, seeing Red and the baker talking to each other while the shortest of the other four men entered the bakery.

"Thanks for the flour, Shimon. In a few days, can I buy more?"

"My pleasure, Joseph. I'm not sure. Wheat is getting tougher to get. I suspect a portion of the crop is impermissible; it isn't old wheat. Also, I cannot imagine how we will cope when the land rests next year. With no stock and harvest for the next year, a miracle is essential."

Red, who calls himself Joseph, appears as a disarming actor. Shimon the naïve baker treats Joseph, a man he doesn't know, like an old friend.

The short one spoke, "Sorry, I couldn't help hearing. I'm Yonaton. A colleague of mine is bringing a huge shipment of wheat from afar. I control the power to broker a sale for him."

I lifted myself out of the dream in disgust. The details didn't matter. I objected to hear more of the conman and his stories of tricking people with flour, with wheat! What a waste. They neglected every warning. Thus, they reached the impending demise; a famine of such severity and nothing to eat except human flesh. And they persist in glorifying evil schemes!

The men sat and talked. Joseph approached the sole woman in the room's corner and said, "Where were you Mara?" He gripped her under the chin, squeezed her mouth open and sneered, "Where did you get the food?" He continued, this time with contrived empathy, "You didn't wait for me. I planned to prepare the baby. You didn't share with your brother!"

"There is a lone woman who has a baby," said Mara, appealing to her brother, the patriarch, "I'll show you where; we will share. A simple, easy task—the mother is unguarded and weak." Mara spoke with fear and urgent pleas that only Joseph could command.

"What? Who are you talking about?"

"Sara. It's Sara that has a baby."

"Oh, Sara lives in the courtyard across from that blacksmith." Joseph grinned as he registered Mara's acknowledgement then departed.

I followed Joseph to Sara's house. He looked around the courtyard and took his time to avoid detection. Joseph creeped over to Sara's house and negotiated each step of the balcony staircase without a squeak. From the top step, Joseph crouched and peered onto the balcony which looked empty save for the tiny swaddled corpse on the couch. Joseph grabbed the baby and started to descend the steps, slow at first, picking up speed as he expected his escape. At the bottom of the steps Joseph glimpsed Sara and the Blacksmith from his periphery. A quick instant later, the Blacksmith buried a hatchet in Joseph's skull.

***

Bolts of lightning flashed. I gasped trying to catch my breath and sank into a dream receding thousands of years into the past on a familiar field. The sun dimmed against turbid, wrathful rain. I saw my children, Cain and Abel, thirty paces away. Cain took a rock and smacked Abel's head. I screamed and ran to Abel. I kneeled to the earth of Adam's birth and cradled Abel's cracked head in my hands. Red juice trickled out of his fractured skull and streamed down the side of his face. The terrain shook with an accompanying burst of lightning and a loud thunderclap when the first drop of blood hit the wet soil. I shuddered in anguish and screamed until I breathed no more. My soul began to ascend as pomegranate seeds began to trickle from the split skull I held in my hands. The seeds hit the earth, and I could breathe once more. The soil swallowed the seeds with greed. The ruby-red seeds sprouted into a garden with hundreds of trees. The roots propagated into the soil and into the hearts of mankind. Branches and leaves shot toward the highest heaven, where they'd absorb the heavenly glow and synthesize the nutrients bestowed on the sons of man.

***

I woke up, thousands of years later, with a loud gasp. I lay across from Gechazi and his three sons. They stared at me in surprise as I caught my breath. No time for additional dreams, but some time before sunrise to antagonize them. I threw pebbles at the boys. "Damn woman, leave us be!"

I laughed and said, "Be quiet boy, lest we rouse the guards or Aramean forces."

The poor men lay in squalor as their strength ebbed away. I ceased annoyances and prayed for salvation until a thought occurred.

"Gechazi!"

He half opened his eyes and fell back into a stupor.

Again, I said, "Gechazi," but this time I threw pebbles at his face. He refused to wake until one pebble struck his snaggle tooth.

"What do you want woman? Leave us be!"

"If you want me to leave, please talk to me. Answer my questions."

"What do you wish to know?"

"Why are you sad and ungrateful?"

"Why? Look at me! My skin is diseased with His wrath. I was forced out of the city to starve or face the Aramean horde. I was Elisha's disciple, an important prophet, but Yonah has assumed my status and position. I am nothing but a despised outcast left to die!"

I said, "How do you not perceive the truth of the matter? As a prophet, you appreciate that little context exists in a single situation devoid of past and future probity. You are a fortunate man. Lucky Gechazi!"

"I answered your question. Please go, lest you further torment me with fantasies of my blessed luck."

"This seems a curse of evil and dire misfortune, but the Almighty has protected and preserved thee above the limits of love. Oh, lucky man, the boy you did not resurrect, Yonah, assumed your position and mission. You, the lucky one who wastes at the gate, not the boy who shall flee on sea! You shall not understand this sliver of wisdom, but I pray thee not envy pitiable Yonah, for you are most lucky to avoid his fate."

I extended my hand to Gechazi and said, "Rise lucky prophet." Through pain and tears I helped him stand.

"Prophecy for your sons and the people of Shomron. Sing with me the song, and let the past collide with the present in waves of wrath."

We sang the "Song at the Sea" with as fervent a joy as a recently freed slave, until we reached the turbulent verse: "Pharaoh's chariots and his host hath He cast into the sea, and his chosen captains are sunk."

An excitement stirred within me as I perceived the impending respite from this most severe famine. With laughter from the world of formation I spoke to the lucky man.

"Gechazi, lucky man, do you and the boys want breakfast? The specter of Pharaoh's chariots has set the enemy horde to flee! We go now."

The ragged four walked without fear to the Aramean camp. Praise be, the camp is abandoned! Not a single troop among the spoils. The four rushed to an officer's tent gorging themselves on fresh bread, olive oil, dried fish, and wine. They ransacked tents for treasure and buried the booty nearby. A miracle! The mighty force had forsaken the entire lot of provisions. Even donkeys and horses, with bemused eyes, stayed tied. Apparently, the decision to flee had occurred in an instant. The Aramean force had no time to tarry. The happy four, with their newly acquired wealth and well-fed stomachs looked at each other with unease and began to discuss this unforeseen predicament.

"It will be impossible to keep this a secret. The city officials will be roused by the quiet of the Aramean horde. They'll send spies on a reconnaissance mission to assess the Aramean camp, which they'll find vacant except for us. They won't be lenient. Our status as outcasts is dire. A simple choice. We can inform the city of the abandoned Aramean camp or wait for it to be discovered and face prosecution for neglecting our brethren."

Gechazi said, "We shall save Shomron."

He was a powerful prophet, capable of summoning an Egyptian specter, who went astray. The prophet who lived a life subordinate to his contorted rationalizations. The needle of his moral compass moved between fear and greed, navigating his decisions. But wasn't this good? Without fear and greed, the animal instincts, how could we survive? Imagine mankind's advancement without bittersweet reckonings.

The city would soon receive respite from the awful famine, but I grew curious with the people I had observed. I must become acquainted with Sara and Mara. Evil had identified and targeted these souls for a specific reason. I laid in an Aramean tent and dreamed another dream of those woman.

***

I floated into the city of starvation and entered Sara's courtyard and up the steps to her balcony. Sara sat alone, peering over the balcony onto the courtyard below. A fire sputtered its remaining flame while a skinny cat, with a morsel snatched from the pyre edge, burst out the front gate. This was the morbid end of Joseph's life, brother of Mara, a lifelong conman. Sara sat alone, digesting her meal.

Sara glanced Mara crossing the courtyard and appeared to tighten with every thump of the staircase.

"Where have you been, Mara? I supposed you'd come here earlier. The baby is no longer available to share with you."

Mara gazed at Sara and asked, "Have you seen Joseph?"

"No Mara, I didn't see your brother, but look there, liver to share."

Mara walked with mouthwatering determination to the table. She choked on newly produced saliva, grabbed a knife, and sliced off a generous piece of the charred liver. Mara took a bite and glanced at Sara with a blank stare. Sara shot back a brief smile that transformed into a fierce scowl and said, "You go now!"

Mara stormed down the stairs clutching the remains of the liver with anger for being cheated out of her half of the deal, Sara's infant. Someone broke a deal! She had fulfilled her end of the bargain and was swindled in return! She continued to eat, indifferent to the covetous glares of starved citizens, as she walked home. More than that, reckless Mara provoked inquisition about her background and the origin of the food. I watched Mara eating without care of the impression made on starved bystanders. This was Mara's nature. She carried misfortune from place to place and greeted evil with relief.

Was Mara relieved with the demise of her brother, Joseph? Yes, but she was orphaned of abuse that had been a stable presence in her life since childhood. As she swallowed the remaining bite of liver, she pondered, which of Joseph's gang might try to pimp her out. She laughed and cried at the death of her brother while enjoying liver textured undertones of the menacing master of immiseration. Nobody played the game as well as Joseph; brother, pimp, and lover. She wanted justice for her loss; the baby that was owed her! The King will adjudicate over the bargain of the babies.

This was the horror I spoke. Hope shall follow.

***

I awoke in the Aramean tent and overheard the four outcasts rummaging through the abandoned enemy camp.
Gechazi said, "It's time to inform Shomron that the Arameans fled."
"Father, where is the woman?"
Gechazi said, "What woman?"
No surprise that little boys forgot their mother so soon.

Chapter 2

תפארת (Glory)

Jezebel and Adam

Were you expecting something other than the story? What part do you expect to play? You forever try to insert yourself into the narrative! Yes, it is a horror, but hope shall follow.

The four approached the city gate and yelled to the guards on the watchtower. The exchange between the guards and four outcasts would endure until one side capitulated. For none shall believe that the mighty Aramean force fled. A few guards, consigning themselves to the fact that these four were here to stay, opened the gate and escorted the four into the city.

With calm amusement, I sat some bow shots away from the city gate and waited for a scouting party. This was the logical progression. The four repeated their report several more times until reaching a legitimate authority. As a matter of procedure, scouts would then investigate the abandoned Aramean camp.

This occurred in due course. Ruffians pilfered the Aramean camp under the control of the king's regiment; given the impossible task of keeping order among the stampeding masses. That day, as Elisha prophesied, one seah of fine flour or two se'ims of barley fetched one shekel at the city gate.

I walked through the city gate of Shomron. The crowd and noise diminished, but I wanted to sense how the inhabitants coped with this new blessing. An enormous stockpile of food materialized in an instant. A plan of divine perfection. The invading Aramean force stripped their own lands of food and resources and deposited this bounty on the doorstep of their foe, forgoing thanks. A marvelous echo bounced along the city streets reverberating sounds of refreshment and relief. A tenuous grasp of positive spirit belied what I recognized; that Elisha's prophecy—and the miracle—would soon be forgot. As usual, I cursed my cynicism and tried to maintain faith in the people. If I couldn't be grateful, how could they? I squeezed the ancient bones of my hands into tight fists as if I could exsanguinate the remaining drops of scorn. No question, I could not stay in Shomron for much longer.

The striking woman walked with indifference. Who could mistake the buxom frame and big red hair for anyone other than Mara who walked coquettish while chewing a crust? Was she unaware of the effect she inflicted on men whose eyes burned holes into creamy flesh and magnified her radiance? The famine was a minor obstacle in her life. The vixen walked oblivious to the wreckage left in her wake; never to dwell on past mistakes and tragedies. This detachment was a strength or gift Mara possessed; putting the past behind with little care for the future. Anger and sadness were alien forces. All that happened between her and Sara washed away. If she saw Sara now, she'd greet her as a dear friend.

A chuckle burst out of my stunned mouth as I observed Mara enter a study hall to hear a prophet explain the laws of the Sabbath. This Prophet possessed a special ability to connect to the entire audience, from unlearned simpletons to the most advanced scholars. He was a visiting prophet from the outskirts of Shechem.

Two organisms were waging spiritual warfare in the womb that was Shomron. Jezebel inspired the people to worship Baal. Would a viable opposition prevail? The standard bearer was Elisha. Too many unanswered questions and contradictions. What was the secret of Mara's holiness and immunity to Baal?

I sat in the back of the lecture hall with Mara. With dignified composure she departed once the lecture concluded. How odd and amusing that this red headed tramp was so attracted to the laws of the Sabbath.

I stayed in the lecture hall, staring at my feet, gazing upward to see the Prophet and his son standing in front of me. The hall was empty except for the three of us. The Prophet was a distinguished looking man of fifty years old. The Prophet's son was tall and thin with a face certain to appear boyish well into old age.

They introduced themselves and obliged in polite conversation, but the Prophet and I already discerned much of each other. For one, I identified he was a holy man, learned and subject to bouts of insanity—saintly and dangerous.

He waved forward and led the way. "Come let's walk while I explain. We live in a village on the outskirt of Shechem. I'm here to gather food provisions and…" He trailed off, lost in thought, and began again. "Yes, I foretold that the Arameans must flee and leave behind a vast storehouse of provisions. Tell me, that woman with the red hair, do you know her, might she be a suitable wife for my son Joseph?"

We smiled at each other. In an instant he recognized my identity.

"Mara is the suitable wife for Joseph."

The Prophet spoke to me as a servant. "Bring the bride to the village before the new moon."

The Prophet promoted me from aimless wanderer to a helpful servant, and he awarded me with a peculiar mission.

He continued, "Please take care of this young couple and act as their servant. As you realize, our two kingdoms are going through drastic changes. These two will need your help. Well, here we are at the gate, loaded and ready to leave. Have a safe trip."

Blessings be, we'd look forward to the wedding of Joseph and Mara. Joseph, a budding scholar, son of an esteemed prophet. Mara the good-time girl. These two were similar at their core. Only environment and circumstances manifested a guise of dissimilitude. Mara's pure faith guided her through life's happenstances. She'd be a dutiful wife. A woman who'll understand the illusion of choice.

I returned to Mara's neighborhood and searched for lodging. The unexpected Aramean bounty inspired masses of hungry visitors. I found a suitable inn and payed a generous advance to secure the lodging. We'd need to buy provisions for our journey. What concerned me was the role of caregiver I was to assume. As the Prophet said, "these two will need your help." These two: the young couple and the two kingdoms. I'd need practice, and patience, listening to the wise Prophet. Did he believe I'd save the two kingdoms, Israel and Yehuda? No prophet strove to amuse—speech contained the simple and deeper meanings—but he teased me as if he knew my mission. This was how he connected to such a wide audience. Having listened to these sermons firsthand, I experienced that the message lost its soul if rearticulated or transcribed.

Night rolled into the city. The markets closed. I stood ready to fetch Mara and bring her back to the inn. I shut my eyes welcoming darkness. With a meditation on Mara, the darkness etched away to reveal different colors. We created the painting through removal rather than application. This art was a precise map of the city. Opening my eyes, I projected the painting in each direction then let my legs carry me to Mara. It wasn't necessary. I could find her easy enough through pure physical methods, but I craved the loveliness of spirit birthing action.

Moments later I entered a sticky tavern that smelled of stew and vinegar. Mara was sitting next to a man, old enough to be her grandfather, who plied her with meat and wine. Mara's booming laughter permeated the establishment and infected the illustrious patrons with a contagion of mischief. The fiery girl tricked the rabble, including her sly suitor, the old man. The bartender and waitress gawked with distressed annoyance as the party sputtered to its feeble conclusion. Mara's companion lurched sideways to plant a sloppy kiss on her cheek, but Mara pushed him back and let out a hysterical laugh as he hit the floor. The whole tavern erupted in laughter. People threw bits of food and refuse at the pitiful man as he struggled to stand upright. Mara rocked back and forth with bewitching laughter. Two men on the other side of the tavern scuffled with each other. Blows followed until the entire tavern ran riot. Seizing the chance, I scooped up Mara and dragged her out the door. She feigned protests but appeared to welcome the change of scenery and cool damp air.

With looped arms, we marched toward the inn I had reserved. Mara wore a perpetual broad smile on her face the entire evening. It appeared she misplaced the ability to form other expressions. What else could I do but return the smile? Mara asked several questions during our walk to the inn which I, her servant, answered.

The open shutters clacked a boisterous welcome to the stormy breeze and intermittent rain. Morning light struggled to penetrate the musty room. I lit a lamp and arranged herb tea and breakfast for Mara. She arose early and went to the bathroom. With that same smile she returned to our room attacking the tea and food. Her demeanor was contagious. All were joyful when Mara was well fed and miserable when she hungered.

"Who are you and why am I here?"

"Mara, my name is Chava. I spotted you at the Prophet's lesson yesterday. After you departed, the Prophet inquired if you are a suitable marriage partner for his son. I told the Prophet that I am your servant, and you're available to be wed. I promised to bring you to their village, near Shechem, for the wedding, which is to be on the next new moon. Let us prepare for the journey."

Mara stared at me with a blank face as she chewed on the remains of her breakfast. She swallowed the last of the tea, stood up, and looked out the window at the puddles on the empty street below. She faced me with an incredulous expression on her face. "Chava, why did you tell him this? How do you force a plan on my behalf, understanding nothing of me? We are complete strangers. It's… You're crazy."

I didn't need to exert control over her. The truth was plenty. "I understand you, Mara. I observe people. This awful famine hasn't ceased. The city is in terrible danger. You lost your brother, your only relative, and you have no future here. Mara, I comprehend enough to tell you that this is a chance to have a purposeful life, marry a scholar, and flee this madness."

"How do you know my brother Joseph? What happened to him?"

She decided. I could sense the telling inflection of speech when she bemoaned the name "Joseph." Still, it was obvious she expected me to belabor the point.

"Mara, you have no connection with Shomron. You recognize a higher purpose in life and move to live a life of purpose. Why is this even a choice?"

The decision occurred even though she craved the suffering I endured by perpetuating in this pedantic exercise to persuade her. No problem, I could play worse than bitter Mara.

"Mara, mourn Joseph's loss and bid the terrible famine good riddance. Life will not get easier in Shomron. The past will torture this generation. Leave the past of Shomron. Fashion the changes you need to alter course. Mara, where do you expect the current path to lead? Conscience will haunt you. Dream with your dreams, not your conscience. Either that or rot here in Shomron. What's your choice?"

"I need to pray. I'll come back here with my belongings if I so decide."

"Mara, I'm sure you'll reach the right choice. The Prophet's son; his name is Joseph. The same as your brother."

Mara walked out of the room stone faced. I peered out the window studying Mara scurry along the damp street. The news was abrupt, and the plan was life altering. Once the shock subsided, she'd welcome the decision. For now, she was numb and fearful.

***

I closed my eyes and fell into a dream. Mara walks along the city streets and enters a house of prayer as I drift past. The force pulled me to the place where I first saw Mara, across the city toward the courtyard; Sara's courtyard. A lifeless place. I floated up the steps to the familiar balcony and spied Sara sitting on a couch staring straight into my eyes. I drifted out of her field of view as she maintained her fixed stare on the same spot. The same place where my eyes were a moment ago. Could she see me? I moved to Sara's periphery and remained motionless staring at her for long enough to realize nothing would occur. Sara let out a soft laugh, rose, and peered over the balcony. Sara, with her boney posture was Mara's physical opposite. Sara gazed at the spent fire in the center of the courtyard and hummed as her view shifted to a nearby Ashera pole.

Humming, an alien song, grew louder and faster as she communed with the pole below. The pole, the mother god, consumed Sara. Someone carved the pole into a figure of feminine beauty. The hair was symmetrically parted in the middle, which framed a triangle on the forehead. This triangle matched the inverted triangle below her waist; palmed hands whose arms triangulated from elbows to the life source— the female organ. Triangles outlined the shoulders to waist and hips to feet. The head, eyes to nose, the abomination triangulated. The symmetry provoked worship of the female form as a god representing fire, water, and earth. Air, the fourth element, surrounded the pole. The three points of the triangle thus being represented by the triangular symmetry of the goddess. This was the antithesis of Father.

Initiates of the Ashera faith were women, sworn to secrecy, targeted, and recruited on the eve of maturity. Those targeted were at the most vulnerable period of their lives. Sweet young ladies plucked from unsuspecting families. By the time the parents discovered what their girls were doing it was too late to bring them back. The attraction was compelling for a young lady on the verge of becoming a woman. With enthusiasm, questions and fears were put at ease within their new fellowship.

The pole was an alluring aspiration for these girls. Worship of self, softened self-doubt. And why exert effort on the unearthly pursuit of heaven when the physical domain was more accessible and fleshier? The poles established firm root in the fertile ground of the cities. That is where communities became detached from the land in pursuit of mercantilism. The city dwellers spent more time on intellectual pursuits and exploration of new ideas and technologies. The country dweller with her toil of the land took solace in pursuit of heaven. Without the noise of the city, she heeded the blessings bestowed on her and retorted with psalms.

As I gazed at the triangle outlined by the nipples and belly button, I thought of Sara the city dweller and Mara the soon-to-be country dweller. Tragic oblivion greeted Elisha's prophecy of His miraculous bounty served at the city gate. Looking at Sara, I screamed, "It was not your pole that fed the city!"

Sara strolled toward me until one pace stood between us. Her breath probed the cool air. Sara gazed at the pole and said, "I eat the dust of the earth."

I responded, "I see how the toes of the goddess graze the dust of the created earth. This pole is not your master. Human hands will destroy something fashioned by human hands. Spirit is infinite, your pole is finite; a trinket."

Sara and I were in different states of consciousness. I was dreaming. She couldn't hear, even if I hoped otherwise. "Sara, the pole will not oblige, will you hear?" Sara walked to the couch and laid down. In an instant she was sound asleep. I climbed in and nestled against her backside placing my hand on a boney shoulder. Sara sighed, "Mother".

***

Tears welled up in my eyes when I woke. These are the consequences of my choice. Thousands of years to witness my children suffer. I made my choices, and they made theirs. But like any mother, I interfere.

Darkness settled but Mara did not return. I left the inn and went to a nearby market to purchase some groceries on my way to Sara's courtyard. This time I was conscious, singing as I strode through alleys observing people returning to their homes at days end in this altered city. Food is miraculous but miracles have a shelf life. For the famine-racked leftovers of Shomron I'd pray there'd be no expiration of either food or miracles.

The hectic city; too grueling a change for me. I had grown accustomed to solitude. Sometimes I'd stay for fifty years in a serene cave without talking to a soul.

The walk adjusted me to the task at hand when I arrived across from Sara's courtyard.

The Blacksmith, armed with an axe, stood in front of the gate. I walked his way wearing an amused smile and asked, "Can I come into the courtyard?" He started to speak but turned mute when I stimulated a sharp pain behind his left eye. The burly appearance changed from pain to fury as he stormed into the courtyard. I slipped in behind the Blacksmith and remained on the fence line. Sara and the three acolytes circled the blazing fire. They glanced with a startled expression as the axe-wielding blacksmith lumbered toward the Ashera pole. The Blacksmith raised the axe high above his head and swung through the center of the pole, bisecting the triangle in a rage of geometrical wrath, then fell to the ground asleep. With enormous effort I stayed composed amid laughter's assault on my precious soul.

Reddish brown gave way to yellow…

GLORY. It was a delightful gift from parent to child. Balance between discipline and compassion. Symmetry.

I approached the shocked group of practitioners. One girl scurried into the corner. The other girls sat in disbelief, except for Sara who wore the empty and tired expression of defeat. I said, "Hi, I'm from the neighboring courtyard, and we have food to share. Can you girls help prepare?"

At supper I prattled on with manipulative distraction. The Blacksmith lay asleep on the ground for hours, only stirring when I finished braiding Sara's hair. My throat tightened as I thought back to the first time Father braided my hair. With this, my final act of the evening, I arose, wished peace upon them, and departed.

The Blacksmith stumbled to his feet as I departed the courtyard. Laughter crossed my lips at the memory of his lumbering frame smashing the Ashera pole.

I reflected on my purpose in Shomron as I walked back to the inn. The present held many obscure and unanswerable questions, and, a plan for Mara and Sara. Did the Almighty guide me here to fulfill His plan for me and them? With certainty. Otherwise I'd dwell alone in a cave or on the outskirts of a community. Instead, I'm here in Shomron, but not much longer.

The inn was quiet at this late hour. Mara slept in peaceful bliss while I sat in the dark plotting the future. When dawn broke, I greeted Mara with hot tea and breakfast, for I was a competent servant. Although I perceived she was agreeable to the plan, I asked, "Mara, did you decided on moving to the village near Shechem?"

Mara remained silent for sufficient time to build drama. "I do things the normal way and this isn't normal, is it? He has a will and means to provide for me? Who knows the history of this family and the man I'm to marry?"

"Mara, I need to go out. I'm in a hurry, and I can't decide for you. Decide."

"What's the bride price?

"It's your weight in silver, Mara. Here's money for lunch. Eat, bring your things, and wait here for me."

Mara stood speechless as I ran out the door. I covered my head with the cloak hood and sped toward the city palace. With stealth, negotiating the back alleys to avoid identification. I planned my route with everything considered, stowing away a change of clothes and weapons at strategic locations.

Later in the day, witnesses reported to Jezebel that the perpetrator wore a gray cloak. "He," they assumed it was a man, stormed into Jezebel's temple and hurled a spear at the alter that pierced the Baal statue. Crazed, he drew a sword and smashed the temple decorations as people scattered screaming. The temple guards weren't trained to guard. They stood paralyzed with fear. The sanctuary emptied as the man smashed a treasury box and scooped up the coins into a sack.

That's what they reported. The main sanctuary evacuated except for a baby boy sitting in a crib next to the alter. I threw my sword to the ground, picked up the baby boy who I tucked under my cloak, and ran out a side entrance of an adjacent alley sneaking into a nook where a change of clothing lay hidden thereby transforming from vigilante to a young mother shopping with a baby. I put distance between myself and the palace compound as I walked to Sara's neighborhood. Nobody had identified or followed me. I cradled the infant in a sling on my belly and sang to him. My shoulders slouched from the chubby boy who was healthy but uncircumcised. I needed to do this soon. A few more items on the shopping list. A gift for Sara. The boy would give her purpose. He'd take care of her and grow in leadership.

The mission had infected me with a brutal contagion of rectangular misery. Four cornered walls, houses, courtyards, and cobbled stones underfoot had crushed my bones into powder. Woe is me, cornered in this city.

I concluded my shopping and entered Sara's courtyard.

"Good morning, Sara. I enjoyed spending time with you and the girls last night. I brought more food. Where shall I put it? Also, I brought you an orphan boy to care for. Please sit and hold him while I boil water."

Sara's eyes lit up as she embraced the child. She glowed with life as the boy tugged her out of the abyss. "I'll take care of him. What's his name?"

"Sara, you shall name your own son. Place him on the couch. Go wash yourself and put on your finest clothing while I prepare."

I laid a clean cloth and bottle of strong wine on top of the table. Never minding I bore witness to the butchering of Mara's baby on that same table. The knife lay submerged in a vessel of hot water. Bandages and tools were at the ready.

"Chava, will you do the circumcision?"

"Yes, I will, or do you prefer the Blacksmith conducts the procedure?" Our eyes connected with laughter at the brutal prospect. Welcome Sara, to the world of the living, I thought. Sara looked beautiful.

Sara liked ceremonies. She'd like this one. I whispered, "This is for you and the boy." I instructed Sara to sit in the chair and hold the boy. I said a blessing, cut, peeled, bent down, and sucked blood from the wound. I rose erect and handed Sara bandages. And then, a drop of blood rolled off my lip and hit the floor with a thunderous crash!

***

After another loud crash I opened my eyes, no longer on Sara's balcony.

I stood on the edge of a muddy field. The wind and rain beat black clods of earth. Lightning lit up the field and sky with accompanying cracks of thunder. I stared off in the distance and spotted a form in the field. As I walked closer, I glimpsed the form moving. It was a man shoveling rows for planting, but the figure remained slyly delineated from the earth. It was as if the earth was shoveling itself, but the form was man. The figure worked with logic and power clearing one row and crossing back to work another.

This was the man I knew, formed from living earth that worked the earth. The figure stopped, turned around to face me, and opened his mouth to reveal strong white teeth. We returned smiles as the rain washed the soil from his body to reveal Adam's massive torso. His chest heaved in and out with each breath while the legs stood planted like two mighty trees. I said aloud, "My love, all you want to do is work." Adam laughed a booming laughter that unleashed furious lightning bolts and explosions of hurled earth into the air. Suddenly, the laughter ceased, and he returned to work. Again, the ground was indistinguishable from his frame. I laughed as a lightning bolt carried me back onto Sara's balcony.

***

I spit out the remaining blood from my mouth and rinsed with wine. The baby suckled a wine-soaked cloth as Sara gazed in his eyes and again asked me the boy's name. Before I could respond, Sara said, "I name him Adam." The look in her faraway eyes assaulted my nauseous stomach.

"Adam is a suitable name. Good choice, Sara. I brought you food and other supplies. See here, I'll give you money when you need something, but you and the boy shouldn't leave the courtyard. Send the Blacksmith to fetch what you need. I must explain important matters to you. Shomron isn't safe. Difficult times are coming, and it'll be dreadful to raise the boy here. As for last night, I planned the spectacle. I possess powers of influence, which I employed on the Blacksmith to destroy the pole. Not everything can be explained now. Please put your future in my hands. Prepare yourself and meager belongings to leave with little warning. Are you listening to me? Why don't you speak?"

Sara stared back at me blankly. I looked at her, gesturing with open palms and wide eyes to show I was expecting her reply.

"Chava, I saw you twice in dreams. The first dream was a few days ago during the famine. The second dream was yesterday. I never sought to consider my destiny or discover meaning. But you are the only person I dreamed about in years. Not even family members I lost. Today is my first day of joy since my husband passed away. My body shivered when I named him Adam. I don't know where he came from, but danger lurks. Never mind asking you a detail for nothing gained. Not knowing is safer. I'll be ready to go whenever. It matters not where."

"Sara, let me interrupt. Decide with commitment and apply self-respect to your destiny. I don't want to offend your sensibilities, but you coped in this mode since childhood. What do you want for Adam? When you look at the boy, hope strong and you'll see him bloom like a mighty cedar."

Tears were flowing out of Sara's eyes and her face became contorted in sadness and rage. After some time, she gained control of her breathing and said, "You recognize me, you think, but nobody gave me a chance." She continued, struggling to compose herself. "From as far back as I can remember I was unwanted. The other children didn't want to be with me. My father and brother died when I was young. We were forcibly evicted from our home. Mother worked at an inn under severe harassment. We lived in a room in the yard that was hardly fit for an animal. The master of the inn visited in the evenings to molest my mother while I huddled outside in shame and despair. Many nights I forwent sleep and did my chores in dazed misery. I tried to help my mother with the cleaning, but most often fouled things up. The master's wife hated me for everything I did but mostly for being my mother's daughter. I carried scars from her beatings. What's worse, I was not yet a woman when the master's boys pursued me.

"One evening the two boys cornered me in a storage room. I cut one in the face and fled to Shomron. This house and courtyard belonged to my husband. A miracle, happiness found me.

"I arrived in Shomron, found employment at a bakery, and married one year after my arrival. My husband, Shimon, was the master baker. During that time Shimon identified a property to rent and opened his own bakery. I became his wife. Customers frequented the bakery, and we lived content. I kept my secrets and disgrace hidden and bore guilt for abandoning my mother. True contentment and happiness always out of reach. Shimon and I tried to conceive. At last, a year ago, I gave birth to a girl with gratitude for the blessing and thought my luck turned. But the good times didn't last. The famine creeped in, and the wheat creeped out. That fiend, Joseph, swindled Shimon out of our savings with a deal of wheat."

My skin flushed with golden rage at Sara's tale. The wheat!

"Shimon died heartbroken. Recently, our daughter died of starvation. That's my lot. See, I stopped crying. I don't realize how to answer you, but you're wrong! I tried to build a life here with Shimon. I wasn't grateful for the inevitable misery. But now, I'll nurture this baby boy—a new life for him and I. I'll take the chance to live and care for Adam."

Sara continued, "He's only two months but weened. I'll stew the vegetables you brought. Don't tell me where you got him. This boy was consecrated to Baal. Jezebel will be furious and dispatch guards to search the city. Chava, did you think of this? What prevents guards from searching here?"

"Don't worry Sara. Yes, the guards will conduct a search. Before they think to search here, we'll leave town." I reached into my pocket and pulled out a small sack of candies. "These are potent. Give him one if he becomes inconsolable. Only one. It'll put him to sleep quickly."

"Chava, what are the plans?"

"We'll be going to a village close to Shechem. Pious people inhabit the settlement. A valley nourishing the spirit. The village is isolated, and nobody bothers the people."

I held back other information to allow Sara a chance to adjust. We stayed busy with chores and spoke little. She asked my history, and I answered as usual. "I am a widow bereft of small children." I tell that to many who ask. Here, a song to forever remember:

I am a woman, bereft of small children
They left their mother to seek for their own
A new horizon, with no tender embrace
The mother who loved them, they suffer no trace

He blessed us to birth children. From the moment they exit Chava's womb, they take the long march to their tomb; that is, the ground of Adam.

The next few days were routine. I spent most of my time visiting Sara and Adam. As for Mara, I saw her for a brief period every morning. Our party was stable and ready for the journey. A few days before our planned departure I informed Mara that Sara would join us on the journey. In turn, I provided Sara details of the forthcoming marriage between Mara and Joseph, the Prophet's son.

Of course, they knew each other and shared a grim history, including betrayal and murder. Joseph, Mara's brother, swindled Shimon, Sara's husband. And Sara coerced the Blacksmith to murder Joseph. They wondered how I knew their secrets and felt violated as if I burgled their riddles.

Mara and Sara executed coldblooded choices to survive the famine. This was their bond and foundation. Could one ask another, what did you do and what did you eat during the famine? Sara and Mara didn't need to ask each other gruesome questions of Shomron's great famine.

And so, us three woman and baby Adam lounged away a cool evening on Sara's balcony. Mara and Sara sat at a table having supper. I laid on a couch with Adam who was exploring the world around him.

I perceived with closed eyes the hammering of the Blacksmith. The hammering ceased when I opened my eyes. I shut my eyes and dreamed; the hammering grew louder as I drifted to the Blacksmith's workshop. His banging was here, but not him. I followed yellow-glow footprints out of the gate. Ahead! I spotted the Blacksmith until he came to the temple next to the palace. For what reason did he visit the temple?

Betrayal.

I awoke and said, "We go now."

Chapter 3

יסוד (Foundation)

Loaves of Dust

The Almighty directed me. There's a larger purpose. I'm an obedient servant.

"We go now."

Mara and Sara froze in place with wide-eyed stares.

"Girls, the Blacksmith is out to collect a bounty. Don't panic, but we need to act quick. Mara, take one of Sara's bags and go to the stable to fetch the donkey. Afterward, go to the inn and load up the beast with our provisions. Head south toward Shechem. Sara, take your other bag and travel to Shechem. Go slow. Mara will catch up to you. I'll take Adam."

The girls moved aflutter as I tucked Adam under my cloak and hurried to the western gate of the city. Mara and Sara would leave through the southern gate.

I arrived near the gate, covered my head with the cloak hood, and carried Adam for all to recognize, making this gate the point of focus by the guardians of Shomron. With aggressive pushing, I shoved my way through the city gate causing as much commotion as possible. All eyes were on me as I burst forth. One man, a soldier with a confused look on his face blocked my advance. I laughed then shouted, "Do something, boy. Don't stand idle." The soldier halted hypnotized as I advanced and swung my staff hard on his shin. He plummeted to the ground screaming in agony as I languished with guilt for breaking his leg. Oh, the absurdity! I slipped into a dream but pulled myself out when two guards approached with swords. Without hesitating, I cracked each head and fled.

Once out of sight, I circled around, heading south to catch up with Mara and Sara, then tucked behind a big boulder. With eyes shut my consciousness rose upward, above the city and flew south across rocky countryside until locating Sara and Mara. I planned to overtake them by traversing this ridge line.

With open eyes, I creeped up to inspect my surroundings and continued circumventing the city, proceeding southward. An hour later I spotted Mara and Sara walking together with the donkey and caught up with instructions to stay with each other as I walked ahead. Although it was dark, there were still other travelers on the road, but the majority traveled north, to Shomron. Travelers returning to their homes from Shomron with a laden donkey was not an unusual sight.

As we walked south, I recalled how we arrived at this point. No, I thought not of I and my companions. I mean, the split kingdoms.

Once there was a kingdom united under one king. The people cried out for a king. They said, "Let's be like other nations." Shaul was anointed. After Shaul came the Davidic line. The line went David, then his son Solomon, and his son Rehoboam. Rehoboam ascended to the throne and instituted exorbitant taxes. A revolt, led by Yeroboam, resulted in a split kingdom; the tribes of Yehuda-Benjamin split from the ten northern tribes. About one hundred years after the kingdoms split is where I now dwell, walking to a village near Shechem in the Northern Kingdom, known as Israel. Shomron is its capital. But I mislead. The split wasn't the result of exorbitant taxes, but rather, the influence of Solomon's foreign wives.

We walked half a day south of Shomron when a strange man startled me. This ancient apparition stood on the roadside wearing nothing on his starved body other than a tattered loin cloth. The chill evening air didn't bother him. The man moved his bulbous head as if tortured. Big eyebrows slanted downward and drooped over his widespread eyes. A contorted mouth mumbled and screamed incoherent gibberish, but he seemed to utter my name. It was my name! What was said, known? Mara and Sara caught up. We gawked for a moment before continuing.

Down the road we spotted the Prophet in the dim morning light. The Prophet cared not that our party contained an additional woman and baby. He led us off the main road, eastward on a single-lane path. After a few minutes, the path opened to a lush green valley that contrasted to the brown landscape of the external environment, an embarkation into a different reality. The sun peeked over the eastern ridge of the valley and scattered purple rays of light through the morning fog.

FOUNDATION. A purple valley.

We glanced around and noticed the Prophet had vanished. Furthermore, the pathway leading to this valley was cloaked in obscurity.
Alone and trapped.
Steep mountains encircled the environment. We walked across the emerald grass, enchanted by its fertile beauty. Fruit trees and various crops abounded. Balmy scents competed for our attention. A tranquil river straddled a field of pristine wheat. Each stalk emulated the other. The wheat swayed in unison as if welcoming us. When the wind picked up, it whistled through the stalks and sang. Several houses, a village, nestled on the edge of the wheat field. Retarded goats and chickens wandered nearby. Noise emitted from the biggest house, a barn.
"Girls, stay here while I go inside the barn."
Inside stood the Prophet and Joseph. The Prophet said, "Mara's house is opposite the barn. You others can dwell in one of the adjacent houses."
The houses included soft beds, tables, and chairs. We sat in Mara's house and shared a breakfast of fruit, yoghurt, and barley bread. The pendulum swung from hunger to exhaustion and soon all were asleep, including little Adam.
I went to investigate this new world. It seemed unpopulated other than us and the Prophet and Joseph. The surrounding countryside abutted mountains that encircled the perimeter of the valley. The path was the only exit. Without a doubt, Mara and Sara wouldn't be able to discover the way out.
The village stood in the central valley. Two streams joined on one side of the village and exited as one stream on the other end of the village. The stream emptied into a large stone-lined pool. The water was crystal clear. Fish were visible in the transparent water as they darted above the stone-paved bottom. At its deepest, I guessed the pool was twice that of a man's height. The pool was a few hundred paces long and one hundred paces wide. This first pool spilled into a second pool, which

was the same dimensions as the first pool. A bridge extended over the two pools at the point where the first pool ended, and the second pool began. The end of the second pool spilled over into a third pool, which was much smaller than the other two pools. This third pool was ten by twenty paces. From here, the water entered a channel to power a grain mill then disappeared into a subterranean stream.

I walked to the secluded third pool, shed my clothes, and eased into the cool delightful water, swimming to one side and coming to rest on a submerged rock shelf. Just then, I detected the tickling sensation of fish nibbling on my feet. At first, it alarmed me, and the fish scattered as I jerked my legs. When I disciplined myself to sit still, the fish nibbled on my feet undisturbed. The sparkling pool tempted an extended stay before returning to our lodge to retrieve the girls for their baths.

I took leave of the girls, grabbed a rope, and wandered toward the valley's forest. At the forest edge a large deer emerged and walked straight toward me without fear. Her big eyes stared into mine with noble defiance. With a rope cinched around her neck I led our way back to the village. "In a stall you go doomed deer."

At the other end of the barn was a large room containing milled spelt and barley. No wheat. A large clay pot held a slurry of spelt, a hungry creature. I added water and spelt to the pot and stirred the mixture: preferment for the wedding. Sara would help me tomorrow. The laughter of Mara and Sara echoed throughout the village; a welcome change from Shomron.

An outdoor kitchen stood behind the barn. The valley and the village were like a set table with all items in their proper place. Wherever you thought or wished something to be, that's where it'd be. In the kitchen the firewood, clay pots, and utensils were exactly where I would've put them. The valley and everything here were like a distinct consciousness.

I closed my eyes to contemplate this valley. The first to enter my mind's eye was the wheat atop the hierarchical pyramid. All the blessings of the valley, transmitted with His right hand, blossomed from these kernels. One *understood* and *knew* that this wheat wasn't for harvesting. The light-brown stalks pulsed with life and *wisdom*.

The streams of the valley did not water the wheat but emanated from the wheat. An earlier reconnaissance of the valley revealed the wheat shifted position as if following my journey. It was almost imperceptible, but the field shifted as I moved about. The valley was difficult to enter and depart. Twice I circled back to the obscure path we entered and struggled to uncover it.

The woman finished bathing and were sitting under an ancient oak tree while I continued to walk around the valley. It wasn't possible for me to sit with them. The valley made me restless, so I walked hither as the wheat followed.

I glanced Joseph coming out of the wooded area, but he paid me no heed. I sensed that Joseph was the only person here, other than Adam and us girls. What of the Prophet?

With sun descent, a long-lost urge, a desire not discerned in years. In this strange place shall I dream of sleep and food? With peculiar hunger I spotted a fig tree and helped myself.

I finished eating at sundown; a pitch-black moon-waned night. My skin tingled from airborne chafe as I walked to the village, but the wheat interfered with the path and led me astray; encircled, trapped by the intelligent stalks. I stood in a circular area of grass ten paces in diameter, wheat encircling the perimeter. A path opened in the distance and moved toward my circle. The path encroached and a large snake entered. The wheat held the snake and me in the circle with no escape. I sat in the center. The snake moved along the perimeter, getting tighter, until the snake, now immobile, formed an inner circle from head to tail. The sweat on my body hardened or froze as icy air descended and the snake transformed into a frozen statue. I extended my finger, and the snake, coated in purple frost, shattered at my touch and crumbled to dust. Suddenly the weeping wheat receded. Yes, the wheat itself mourned the demise of the snake.

I stood up and walked back to the village, entering the nearest house, the nearest bed, and fell into a deep sleep.

I woke in confusion until the memory of the past day returned. When had I ever slept so deep? Not in ages. The house was empty, so I ventured to the pool, following the booming laugh of Mara. I approached the two women.

"Sara, where is Adam?"

Sara looked up and smiled at me from the pool, "He's with Joseph. I met him this morning. He's been taking care of the boy. We've been waiting for you to begin preparations for the wedding."

"Yes Sara. Let me wash then I'll meet you in the barn. Mara, stay out of sight this afternoon. It's best if you stay in your house. Girls, you recognize this valley is special. Take your time to understand the environment. And I don't think it's a good idea to wander around the woods or meadow in the evening. Did you go to the woods?"

Mara laughed, "Oh, the valley is special is it? It's a heavenly orchard."

Mara stood in the pool submerged to her neck with a strange squinty-eyed smile on her wet-red-hair-plastered-face. Was she rubbing herself?

My throat tightened, and I said, "Mara, you're about to get married."

Chores abounded, we possessed little spare time for talking. The pool's delightful wheat-water was difficult to depart. With effort I got out and dressed. Sara and I walked behind the barn to the outdoor kitchen. We rounded the corner with a start when Joseph appeared standing in front of the butchered deer hanging upside down by its hind legs. Blood dripped from its nose to the ground. Adam sat nearby looking with curiosity at the red puddle. Devoid of pleasantries, Joseph spoke.

"I'll roast her", Joseph said as he pointed to a large open fire. He didn't look at our faces. "For the bread, you'll see I started a fire in the oven."

Joseph was struggling to talk to us. An interruption to lighten his burden.

"Joseph, Sara and I will take care of all the food except the meat. We'll find what we need. Take good care of the liver, it's Mara's favorite part." Sara swallowed and looked away. Do you think I expected those two to forget the horrors of Shomron so soon? Not me, my consciousness stretches back thousands of years.

Joseph continued, "I never ate deer. Only little chickens and an occasional goat. I saw you yesterday when you fetched the deer. You never killed, Chava? You realized I'd slaughter her?"

"Yes, Joseph, I've killed, but I knew you'd slaughter the deer. It's your wedding."

Me, a killer? I rarely slaughter animals. She came with me to the slaughterhouse, so it means I'm a party. I looked at the dead deer then turned to face Joseph and said, "I'll get started on the bread."

I walked inside the grain room and added a large amount of water, spelt, and salt to the mixture I prepared the previous day then carried the dough mass outside for kneading.

Joseph looked up and smiled at me while he finished skinning the deer.

Adam sat by and watched.

Sara grabbed a basket and scurried off to harvest vegetables.

As hard as I tried, the dough mass wouldn't cooperate. The knead didn't stick together, but I refused to add additional flour, and the dough stuck like shine to my fingers. I raised my forearm to wipe the itchy sweat from my forehead. With frustration I quit kneading and made flat patties, which I placed on a table nearby the oven after separating a piece to burn. The flat loaves could rest before baking.

I'm the original baker, but this coarse spelt was a disaster. Dejected, I cleaned my hands and washed my face with a damp cloth.

A cloud of burned fat struck my face as I walked to Joseph and the spit-skewered roasting deer.

The sweaty man spoke nonstop to Adam about different religious laws while tending the sizzling meat.

The little baby gazed into Joseph's eyes, heard the sounds, and breathed the sizzle.

The fire raged, and the deer needed frequent turning. Joseph asked if I could attend to the deer while he slaughtered some chickens. I responded, "Fine, I'll tend the meat. But isn't it enough? Why do you need to prepare chickens? And why are those birds so scrawny?"

Joseph started to go to the barn but rushed back when Adam began to cry. Joseph said, "Many people are coming to inhabit the village."

"There's little meat on those chickens for feeding *many people*."

The afternoon continued with food preparations for the new people—ten young married couples. All were childless, but some were pregnant.

Joseph showed each of the couples to their own house and the village became populated.

The Prophet had led them to the village along the same path we traveled the previous day. I spotted the Prophet as he entered a large building on the outskirt of the village and followed him inside. He sat at a large desk peering over a scroll at one end of the stark room. Open shutters permitted purple light to stream across the dusty room onto the broad desk. The Prophet spoke with shifted gaze.

"Come forward. Here is the marriage contract if you'd like to review it. You wonder about this place, but you'll comprehend in time. For now, these people are safe from the turmoil in the northern kingdom. Although I brought them here to preserve some remnant, it'll fail, but they need to be here until..."

I interrupted, "Why, what's happening?"

"Elisha anointed a new Aramean king. How, or why, Elisha inserted himself into Aramean affairs I have no idea. But this king, Chazael, will wage war upon us and many will die. I organized this community to preserve a remnant. The Almighty alters the laws of nature in this valley, but it shall not be so forever. I understand you're ill at ease with the reality here. It's possible to leave whenever you wish, Chava. If we need you to return, I'll send word."

"Master, I don't plan to stay long. This place is idleness for me. I know you wanted me to serve, but they'll be fine themselves. I'm done caring for children."

"Chava, where is it you'll go? For what purpose?

"Master, Shomron and Yehuda are bordered by Egypt, Edom, Moab, Ammon, Aram, Assyria, and Sidon. Even though hostilities exist between Israel and these nations, at one time, long ago, we were one family. I bear witness, sojourning throughout these nations and have seen their wonders. What you know of Sidon, grandson of Ham, is the evil Jezebel. It's true, Sidon is rife with idolatry. Is not Yehuda and Shomron?

Sidon has seafaring technology. I voyaged the sea on one of their mighty ships and gazed at the immense rock. It is I, Chava, who dwelled in the great city of Nineveh built by Ashur, grandson of Noah, after he fled the rebellious Nimrod. These nations are my family, and they'll protect or destroy according to His judgement. Now, Assyria, is our earthly protector. To the north of Assyria is an alien horde. The might of Assyria keeps the northern horde in check. This northern horde are beasts of men—not of my flesh. I traveled those inhospitable flatlands and lived among the beasts that dwell there. It was a land extending to the ends of the earth where fierce warriors live, experts with the horse and bow. The baby boys go straight from the womb to the saddle. It is the Assyrians that protect you from this menacing horde."

The Prophet interrupted, "The Almighty protects the Assyrians. This family you speak of is a threat to Yehuda and Shomron. Look at the destruction by Jezebel, a solitary woman from Sidon! Chava, those people are not my family."

"Yes, Master," I smiled and motioned him to glance out of the window. "Look at the threat."

On cue, we spied Joseph and Sara laughing together—an obvious attraction. The village aroused human passions.

The Prophet said, "Joseph can marry her a year from now and care for two wives."

"Wait one year? He'll be sneaking her into the barn within one week. Go throw some cold water on him.

"Master, Mara and Sara share a complicated history. Wisdom cannot forestall the complications. And this village, it's ideal for a love triangle. The houses are too close together. These are young people with strong passion."

We paused speechless until I broke the silence. "Master, perchance the biggest threat looms in paradise."

The Prophet refused to look at me. Now I understood the heightened sensitivities that people experienced in this valley. I didn't harbor lust like they did, but I had cravings for food and sleep. Cravings that were not my own. That's why the Prophet didn't stay here for long periods. The valley gave its blessings but seethed its discontent in our souls. Lust was stronger here.

"Master, I'll establish rules."

I walked around the village and gathered everyone together except for Mara who I instructed to listen from the confines of her house. It was here I established the rules.

"Blessed are we to dwell in this protected valley. His wings safeguard us, but we need to erect physical fences. Each married woman will dwell in their own house; you ten and Mara. There is a large house for all the men. They'll sleep there when not cohabiting with their wives. Woman and Man shall stay separate. No conversing between man and woman unless it is your spouse. Women must travel in groups of two or more. Men aren't permitted in the barn and grain room. They can enjoy the bathing pool only in the afternoon and evenings. That's all. Let's prepare for the wedding reception."

After the initial bewilderment they stirred into motion. Sara approached and said, "I am not married".

I smiled and held her close saying, "We will enjoy Mara's evening. You and I will share a house together. I do not plan to leave until someone marries you."

Sara interrupted, "When? To whom?"

I pulled her closer, "You'll know. Stop asking and get to work on Mara's reception. Instruct the men to erect the wedding canopy while the woman bathe."

The preparations were complete. Our ears perked by the booming songs of the men from inside their house. All of us women sat across the bridge between the first and second pool. Mara sat in a large chair in the center. Torches lit up the entire village. The Prophet probed me from a distance, and I nodded to proceed. After a few minutes the singing and screaming became louder, and the men advanced. Mara's wide smile beamed through her veil. My skin tingled as our circle opened, allowing Joseph to approach and unveil Mara. Joseph pulled the veil over Mara's face and let it drape onto the back of her head. Their faces were mere inches from each other, two lovers in a dreamy gaze, when one man shrieked and dragged Joseph away to the group of men dancing in a circle. The Prophet approached Mara, laid his hands on her head, recited a blessing, and departed with the men in the direction of the canopy.

I reflected with joy and cynicism, "Congratulations Prophet on the first wedding in this ark."

We waited for Mara to gain her composure before continuing. I held Mara's arm as we walked to the canopy and assisted her as she marched around Joseph seven times then stood off to the side.

The environment on the dais stifled my breathing, so I departed past the crowd and stared from a distance.

The Prophet's lips moved, but no voice was articulated.

The site of the canopy, white light, streamed with hypnotic rhythm. Smiles of the betrothed beamed forth and were returned on high by my own daughters in the lofty heavens.

After the ceremony, Joseph and Mara were led to their house for private time. Two men stood guarding the house while the others sat at tables and enjoyed the meal of roasted deer and tiny chickens. It repulsed me to see people eat meat. How my skin crawled when I recalled the gentle eyes of the deer as I led her to slaughter. I grabbed a loaf of the spelt bread, which I ate while wandering around the village. The dense and sour bread did more than insult my mouth. It was a sign of disharmony with man's relationship to his Creator.

He makes bread sprout from the earth. I grasped this better than anyone. I was the first to eat His bread. Later, I practiced making bread myself. Oh, the fear of making my first loaves!

In those early days, we plowed and sowed the land and protected the first sprouts. This was the six days of work. There was stooping and ripping thorns and driving off pests who tried to steal our produce. We reaped and cried for joy at our meager success. I thrashed, winnowed, and stored the kernels then milled what I needed into fine flour. The first time I mixed the flour with water, Father put me into a deep sleep. I awoke to see the mixture had transformed. It grew and was full of bubbles. Perplexing. Was it alive? If so, how was it permissible to eat? I sat in contemplation and recalled a song, a verse of Adam's, "Thy thoughts are very deep."

I sang that verse until realizing we reserved wheat kernels for planting for the following season. Thereafter, I separated part of the living mass and reserved it for the next baking. This, I kept for centuries and passed on to my offspring. It has done more than endure. It has changed into different forms and spread to the ends of the earth. I thought these deep thoughts while I held a piece of the spelt bread crumbling in my hands. The smell was enticing. This wasn't my first bread, the original bread. The elemental life forms in this valley differed from the outside world. A unique smell and taste. I threw pieces of bread into the large pool. Fish cruised the water picking off the crumbs. Oh well, at least the fish enjoyed it.

I walked toward the fervent songs. The men danced round Joseph on one side of the lawn while the women danced around Mara on the other side. I sat nearby in a hidden corner basking in the merriment.

The rules were announced earlier. Although I had no plan to police the community, I'd still insert my authority in the presence of obvious misbehavior. Everybody seemed to enjoy themselves. I sat watching for a couple hours as they paired off to their houses. I put my arm around Sara and led her to our house. Adam was sleeping in a sling on her belly. And so, we concluded our first full day in the valley.

Again, I slept and didn't wake until sunrise. Nothing remained for me to do in the village, but care for Sara until her marriage. I could envision Mara and Sara being co-wives if propitious conditions were contrived, but I needed Mara to believe it was her proposition. The co-wife arrangement was prone to divisiveness since it disposed the wives to compete for their husband's affection. If Mara arranged for Sara to be her co-wife, the family would have better prospects for harmony. Outcomes aren't controlled by me, but I was ever capable of causing interpersonal complications. And how was I to assuage Sara's neediness? Indigent of spirit, a waif with an inexhaustible appetite, how much longer could Chava tolerate them? Yes, me, Chava! Oh, how my spirit longed to flee.

A puzzling revulsion of Mara and Sara; from where did it emanate?

I took in the crisp morning, strolled along the outskirts of the village, and thought about Sara. At that moment a noise descended. Above, a huge vulture flew across the valley and landed on a tree branch at the forest edge. The surrounding people, the newcomers, none of them spotted the vulture. The predator perched motionless on the same tree as I approached the winged beast. With gaze fixed on the vulture, in a blink it vanished. This distressed me. Natural laws were not the same here. Some aspects of nature were omitted from this purple place. A *thing* needed to fill this "lack". An absence couldn't remain unfilled. A fee is owed for this lush life devoid of natural order, a tempestuous void of temptation.

It didn't matter how long I scanned the tree line. The vulture had fled. I turned around and everything seemed quiet in the village. From a distance, I spotted Sara staring at me. Our eyes locked, then she lowered her head and walked into the barn. With curiosity I followed her into the grain room. Sara stood with her back turned to me. It appeared as if she was adding water to the clay pot. The deft hands added salt to the spelt flour and began mixing.

Sara said, "What visions emerge from the forest?"

That voice was different. What has the valley wrought?

"I saw a large vulture. The bird flew over the village, glided across the valley, and perched itself on a tree. I approached, and it vanished. Did you see the bird?"

"No, I didn't see the eagle. Come look, is this too much water?"

"Sara, it looks fine to me. Do you need help to knead? It's too much dough for you to handle."

"No, I can manage. But will you prepare the oven?"

I walked outside to fire the oven and gather kindling. The women were collecting vegetables. All the men were in their house. Mara sat at an open window listening to Joseph discuss the permissibility of carrying on the Sabbath. Joseph wanted to encircle the village and surrounding area with a long rope held up by posts. This new boundary would extend the permissible area to carry or transfer on the Sabbath. The men tore over the details. There was a spirited debate on placing the posts and distance between them. Men should be occupied with these discussions. They studied, prayed, and slept here. Mara's little ears peeked from her red mop and scooped the debate. She possessed a unique attraction to the Sabbath and its laws. Was this a portent of village life? It was fine. No problems?

I walked back and placed some large pieces of wood in the big oven as Sara formed loaves, she set on the table to proof. In an hour the oven would be hot, and we'd be ready to bake. I started to put my hand into the bowl to help form loaves, but Sara smiled and pushed me away. "You baked yesterday. This day and night are mine."

Dejection! How could I behold somebody else make bread? Me, the original baker! I sat nearby, bit my lip, and held my tongue. Wringing my hands until she finished forming the loaves, I watched. She was a skilled baker! Each loaf was uniform and sized right for the oven. She stoked the fire with hands clean of dough. For sure, she was experienced at handling sticky dough. Why ask me if I thought the dough contained too much water?

Sara grabbed a wet rag and wiped her fingers as she sat next to me. The heat of her body tingled my left arm. My eyes burned with the scent of dough and sweat. Then she spoke.

"Remember, I was in the baking business with my husband. I can prepare loaves blind. As a girl I made the bread every week." She smiled and looked deep into my eyes mere inches away, "I'm sure I made loaves in previous lives. I could make a loaf from anything: barley, oats, flax." She laughed, then said in hollow tone, "Even dust."

Sara rose and surveyed the surrounding environment before probing my eyes.

"I'm so glad you discovered me Chava. Shomron suffocated. Now, here, I'm alive and full of hope. This place gives me energy. I lay in bed but need not sleep. The song of the valley sings when I shut my eyes. Do you hear? I imagine it sounds like the infinite void before His creation. It's the sound before Father created the firmaments. That ancient sound drowned by the noise of creation and life. Chava, tell me stories about the children of the northern region."

How did she know of these people? Did she eavesdrop on my discussion with the Prophet? Odd, she had been well out of ear shot.

"Sara, why do you think of the northern horde? Who told you about them?"

"You spoke to the Prophet. Where does their seed come from? Relate onto me their generations."

"The Fallen took some daughters of Adam. Beautiful women that were irresistible. They mated, and the northern horde is their progeny. You need not worry about them. Ashur guards the boarder."

"Why worry? Maybe we shall ally with the children of the north. They are just another empire like Sidon, Assyria, and Egypt. Vast tracts of fertile land stretch across the north. A river of wheat would flow into Shomron and Yehuda. Never more to want for bread. Free of famine. You have an affinity for wheat, don't you Chava?"

"So, you're acquainted with nation building? What do we give for this river of wheat? What is it that flows to Shomron on this river of wheat? The Assyrians are purebred people. Yes, they are a cruel empire, but they can love and repent. The children of the north are a different strain. We drove them out of this land in the days of Joshua's conquering. Why would we invite them back? Ha! There's enough wheat without them. Eliyahu and Ahab pursued the same goal with different methods. Eliyahu: obedience to the Almighty. Ahab: nation building. Ahab sought alliances with Sidon and married the evil one, cursed be the name Jezebel. That woman was going to murder Adam, your baby. That's the alliance, the nation building of Ahab. And this is Sidon, saintly people compared to the northern horde. No, no wheat or alliance with the northern horde."

Sara smiled as she walked to the table and slapped loaves onto the oven wall. She worked expert, baking five per batch. Some other women began to assemble alongside us in the outdoor kitchen to prepare vegetables and fish for dinner. I possessed no conversation, so I took one of the hot loaves and went back to the house. It was now midday. The community would eat their main meal soon. Indifferent, I laid on my bed and fell asleep.

The sound of laughter from the outdoor kitchen woke me. A commune finishing dinner. The sun would soon set. I struggled to get out of bed, drifting dreamless in and out of sleep. At last, with a strong effort, I stood. This valley exhausted me, a woman who knows not to be tired. Dreams fled the valley.

I grabbed the loaf of bread and walked to the head of the first pool. Fish leaped out of the water remembering me from the previous night. I smiled as I ran to the bridge between the first and second pool. The fish darted as if following me. The loaf was perfect. It wasn't sour and dense like the loaves I made the previous night. I almost finished the loaf when the fish caught my attention. I took a small piece and threw it in the water. A few fish swam to the piece of bread and scurried away, leaving it untouched. I laughed. At least they prefer my baking to Sara's. The piece of bread became permeated with water and sank. All the fish moved to the opposite end of the pool. Was this peculiar? Why did the fish refuse a piece of bread? Another loaf might be nice, but I wasn't willing to retrieve it from the busy dining area.

My mind fixed on the vulture. Was it an eagle or a vulture? Why did Sara suggest it was an eagle? My head began to spin. Dizzy sickness overcame me. I glanced at the diners. Only half of the party remained. It was odd. They seemed asleep at the table. Through blurry vision I saw Sara leading one man into the valley. The man was stumbling. Sara smiled as she goaded him along the path. I doubled with a sensation I did not know and fell to my knees spewing vomit. Was this pain? The bread! Sara's voice echoed in my head, "I can even make bread from dust." That voice, where did I hear it? Sara said it on the balcony in Shomron! She said, "I eat the dust of the earth." A vision of the pole, toe in dust, came to mind as I remained on all fours. Footsteps and singing approached from behind. Sara sat on top of me squeezing her legs around my waist with tight restraint.

"I won't kill you Chava. Not yet. It's far better for you to witness the pain and destruction. Adam was my husband. He didn't belong to you. Adam and I were equals, separately created from the same earth. But He created you to be Adam's servant. See, who sits on top? I am always on top!"

My ribs were being crushed. Sara rocked back and forth on me like a rider on a donkey. She bent down and hummed with lips touching my ear. I continued coughing and struggled to catch my breath.

Sara's voice had transitioned. "You are not! You are not the mother of all! I too have children that walk the earth."

Sara relaxed her grip around my waist and slammed her feet next to my hands. I looked at her feet in shock. Human shins transitioned into giant bird claws. One claw grabbed my right wrist. Another claw grabbed my left. Sara squeezed tight and threw my arms forward. I now lay prone on the ground. Sara leaped up and came down hard on my back. This time, she was facing toward my feet. Her talons ripped into each ankle. With my arms free, I struggled to reach back, and grab hold of her. My left hand discovered a bunch of hair. I pulled hard, and she fell to the side. Both of us stood.

I screamed, "Lilith!"

"I prefer Sara. Which Mother has more honor? Do you think it's you, Chava?"

"Changing your name changes nothing, Lilith. Sara! Of all people. Of all names. Sara!" I scoffed at her. No longer was I dizzy. Time to fight.

I lunged forward, tackling her, before she had time to react. Jumped on top, landing blows on her face with my fists and elbows. She rolled over attempting to flee. I struggled with nausea at the sight of her; humanoid astride bird feet. Lilith circled back in my direction. Again, the sight provoked disgust. She ran toward me then leaped into the air with talons extended. I ducked out of reach and she ran past me. Lilith leaped into the air making a complete transformation into an eagle. I observed as she circled the entire valley until I lost her position. Gone. As I scanned the horizon, a draft of air whooshed from above. I ducked, the eagle flew past and perched on an olive tree. The eagle hopped around surveying the branches. She decided on a specific branch, bit it off, and flew toward the wheat field. She dropped out of sight; emerging a few moments later with an olive branch in her left talon and a wheat stalk in the right. And then, with the treasures of the valley, she vanished. Lilith, the demon who seduced my husband, my Adam.

FOUNDATION. Opposite the husk of Lilith. The village: purple light attracted and exposed the demon.

Chapter 4

בינה (Understanding)

Serpent

Did I allowed myself to be misled? Even now, it was not obvious. How could that have been expected? I'm baffled by oblivious dreams! Don't scoff, cynic! I'll grant you this; it's true I ignore evil and must cease projecting good onto what is not. This story is about evil as it morphs from force to place or person. Good as well.

In a flash, the eagle, Sara, Lilith, whatever, vanishes. My eyes closed as I breathed deeply and tried to monitor the flight. The eagle held the olive branch in her right talon and wheat stalk in left talon. Grey wings hugged the coast northward, continuing past Sidon, veering northeast to the headwaters of the Euphrates. North again, she flies to Scythian territory disappearing into the fog. My concentration falters and the vision of the route disappears with pursuant breath into the mist.

***

A dream of an eagle; aloft with an olive branch in the right talon, but this time it held, not wheat, but arrows in its left talon. At once, she ceased flight and transformed into an image. The picture of the eagle printed on a small piece of parchment; a green and white letter. The Shield of David, composed of thirteen stars, hung above the eagle's head. On the flip side of the parchment a pyramid of two segments. An eye stared from the top segment. This green and white parchment contained many designs with letters and symbols.

***

My eyes opened and I walked to the dining table. The people lay strewn about. Placid sleep? I stumbled a few steps more and the scene faded to black. I ascended out of my body and see myself lying on the ground.

It seemed like an instant, but the sun tells me I slept for a long time. I sat with my head tucked between my knees lost in abstract thought. A stupor hung over the dining area. I rushed to shake and awake. Yes, alive! They refused to wake until I threw buckets of water upon them. With protests they stood and stumbled, each walking to their respective bed to return to sleep. Exhausted, I thought to do the same. All in the people were accounted for except one man: a newcomer.

I searched in vain throughout the village until I remembered Lilith escorting him away from the village the previous night. Between forest and wheat, he lay naked but asleep. My skin flushed with shame as I averted my eyes and draped the scattered clothing on top of his body. I shook him until he regained consciousness, got dressed, and scurried back to the village. The thought of Lilith upset my sensibilities.

From a dark spot on the ground, a vision appeared of Lilith on top of the man. Lilith's hair parted in the middle, like the Ashera pole, swayed over bare breasts as she moved up and down void of expression. The man reached upward to caress her, but she swatted his hands from every soft fleshy place he sought to touch. Lilith remained on top in complete control. The helpless victim didn't see the bird feet astride each of his thighs. When the man finished, Lilith arched her torso and head backward with a groan of satisfied nourishment. Lilith took one of her hands and placed it over the man's face. In an instant his body relaxed and drifted off to sleep. A snake lay in the grass gazing at Lilith with the expression of a forlorn puppy.

The vision receded as I walked back to the dining area disgusted. First, this inhuman denigration of coupling. Second, her mission triggered alarm. Lilith manifested into a physical corruption of bird and mammal. But who eats the dust of the earth other than the serpent? She flew to the north with her seed. I'd hunt this danger. Physical evil was shaking the foundation of this world. Oh Father, did this awful spirit gain entrance into the physical world through the gateway of famine?

Did Mara have an inkling about Sara? How well did she know her? I walked back to the village and entered Mara's house. She laid asleep on her side; her face glowed with peace. I sat in an adjacent chair and gently woke her. We exchanged pleasantries, waiting to see if she'd inquire about the previous night. But she didn't inquire. From her vantage it had been a normal evening. The bread of Lilith intoxicated and obliterated memories.

"Mara, I have news for you. Sara left the village."

"Why? Why did she leave? Where did she go?" I felt relief that Mara seemed surprised and dismayed about the departure of a close friend. "Why did she run away without saying goodbye?"

"Mara, she spoke of a mother in Yehuda. Maybe she went to visit since this was her only living relative. Tell me, how did you and Sara meet?"

"I am also from Yehuda. My brother's business kept us moving from place to place since we brought trouble wherever we went. That's the way he did business. We moved to Shomron a few months before the famine. My brother did business with Sara's husband, and I got to be friendly with Sara. We grew close, and I even warned her not to trust Joseph. I fumed at him for these destructive swindles that kept us on edge. Joseph, my husband, is the exact opposite of my brother. My brother didn't become a scoundrel, he was born that way. A complete contrast to Sara's husband Shimon, a kind man. When Shimon died, Sara transformed into a different person."

I interrupted, "What do you mean by transformed?"

"Exactly that," continued Mara. "It was a different personality. Well, I mean, she behaved as Sara, but at other times appeared lost in daydreams or disconnected from the living. Sara's mood changed without warning. At once annoying and frightening, I brought her food with the onset of famine, but she refused to eat. At first, I assumed the grief of losing her husband accounted for this behavior, but then it became plain she lost her mind even though she cared for their baby. It died and Sara snapped. Yes, there was a famine, but Joseph was to blame for destroying Sara's family. I hated Joseph more than I loved him. And then, I had the dream."

"You dreamed what, Mara?"

"During those days I avoided my brother. I slept in different places. Many times, I hid in the study hall where we first heard the Prophet. One such evening, I dreamed a vivid prophecy in the study hall as if I dreamed awake. In this dream I saw my brother enter Sara's courtyard, the two coming face to face. Sara transformed into a winged beast, and then I saw my brother's face covered in blood. There were variations of the dream all night. A compulsion took root in my heart, I swear, to send Joseph to Sara's balcony for the dream to be fulfilled, and it did! Nobody needed to tell me! Sara killed my brother."

"Mara, you explain much. But Sara didn't kill your brother. Sara hosts a demon that's plotting to devastate mankind. We cannot predict if the real Sara will ever return. I'll overtake it, and I'll do my best to free Sara."

Mara said, "I don't believe that demons have power in the physical world."

"It's true Mara. Her name is Lilith and she…"

"She what?"

Degradation welled up inside of me as I tried to plan a response. Guilt and shame prevented me from giving a complete explanation. In those distant days my negligence invited Lilith to seduce Adam, my own husband. And to think, I placed a baby boy, Adam, in her care. A devious scheme!

"Listen, it's hard to explain, but she's ancient evil that gained strength by taking physical form. The famine was a portal and now she needs to be stopped. That's all..."

Mara and I sat together for a few minutes before going to the lower pool to bathe. The village lazed although the sun was high. After bathing we walked to the outdoor kitchen to tidy and establish order over the order-less. We cleaned and purified the utensils and destroyed the clay vessel that Sara used to mix her dough. We started fresh preferment and placed it into a pristine clay vessel.

I called a village meeting and informed our community about the encounter with Sara the previous evening. One man hung his head in shame throughout my speech, but I dared not reveal those details since it served none of the community. The man was not at fault. I'd tell him at the appropriate time, so he understood the union didn't put him in danger.

The evening was spent putting the community at ease and instilling merriment. These interpersonal chores were taking a toll on my frail psyche. How my face protested wearing this happy expression while my heart seethed with wormwood.

In the evening I laid in bed, closed my eyes, and called for the Prophet to visit the village. It took a little time for the vision to appear—the Prophet saw me urging him to come as quick as possible. In turn, I saw him agree to meet the next day.

I waited in the empty house where the two of us met days earlier to review the marriage contract between Joseph and Mara. The Prophet marched into the house bearing a displeased air for being summoned, and then plopped behind the large table. Lifeless silence filled the air as I stared out the window while his gaze remained fixed on the door. I didn't toy with him, for the capacity to retell the incident eluded me. As soon as I tried to speak, I'd lose concentration and my mind went adrift.

He broke the silence mercifully, and asked, "Let's see Chava. Something happened here, right? That's why I was summoned, for to hear a tale of evil, correct?" A nod of somber and sad affirmation, my only response. "A great evil stalked the valley. Ancient evil, correct?" Again, I nodded, but this time with annoyance. He stood and paced the room then walked over to me, looked into my eyes and said, "Tell me everything."

I told him of my encounter with Sara in Shomron and the story of Sara's life.

The Prophet said, "Lilith never had a strong interest in Sara, the host. Lilith wants to harass you, a woman much stronger than Lilith who is an infant compared to you. If you want a chance to save Sara, you must bring her to the temple as a Sotah. Lilith will lose her host if you make the temple offering and force her to drink the bitter waters. But it's uncertain if Sara will survive the procedure. This is your decision. Are you willing to bring her to the temple?

Without hesitation I said, "Yes, I'll go to the north and fetch her. It's no choice."

"Good."

The realization struck me. A trick!

"Wait. You planned to bring Sara here!"

"Of course, I had…"

The Prophet stood speechless as I brandished my staff. "You err by abusing my kindness of servitude; a game in a place I do not dream. Why did you deceive me?"

"Be calm Chava, for this was the only way. In no other place could the possession be exposed. Lilith's grasp on the waif has weakened because you brought her here. This valley weakened her."

"The waif? This is a person; her name is Sara."

The Prophet continued, "Tell Joseph to come here to help me. We'll write a scroll that incapacitates the host and parasite. When you find Sara, meaning Lilith, place the scroll on her neck and lead her to the temple in Jerusalem. You can depart soon with the scroll. I'll give you horses for the journey. Go now and bring Joseph so we can get started.

"Listen Chava, you're upset, but there was no other way. You couldn't keep the secret. Lilith wouldn't have come. She is the ancient evil from creation manifested into physicality and must be stopped. Otherwise, she'll have children, an evil horde."

Outside, I ordered Joseph to go to the Prophet then walked around the village reliving the fight I had with Lilith. I replayed the encounter then spotted the ancient olive tree. The tree beckoned me forth from the irritating sting I suffered from being duped.

The majestic olive tree exuded gravitas, emerging from its hollow trunk and gnarly branches. The trunk extended less than waist high above the ground. Attached to the trunk, on one half of its circumference, a crown of branches extended upward and rearward. The trunk was accessible from the opposite, branch bare, side. Hmm, this is the queen of olive trees wearing her crown, I thought.

The hollow trunk functioned as an oil well. A gold cup on a chain hung nearby for dipping. What else could I do but raise cups of oil and pour repeatedly back into the well? The stream of greenish gold liquid tantalized the senses. I poured it on my head relishing the sensation of the smooth oil. All at once; lush, fruity, intense, and fertile. The oil intoxicated as it soaked the skin and coursed through my bloodstream.

Even the sight and sound of the oil being poured back into the well dazzled as the green gold streamed from the golden cup and glugged back into the well. Tiny particles floated in the turbid liquid like fresh pressed oil; shimmering iridescently between green and gold. The skin became not my own as the oil burned and smothered my body. Also, not my own for the oil wiped away physicality. Wiped clean was I of duped scorn.

I saw Mara from a distance and beckoned her to come. Mara approached, and I instructed her to peer deep into the well. She objected and told me she'd already seen this tree, but I insisted that she investigate the well which she did, so I seized my chance and poured the cup of oil on her head and back. Mara let out a gasp, giving me a befuddled mouth-agape stare as oil glistened on her lips.

Then, throwing more oil on Mara, I smiled and said, "It's good for your hair and skin."

Mara scooped up a handful of oil and poured it on my head and said, "No, it's good for *your* hair and skin."

I took more oil with drunken delight, poured it on Mara and said, "Mara, it's good for your hair and skin."

The two of us continued playing; pouring oil on one another letting the green gold soak us into an intoxicating trance. In no time the other women joined, and all our clothing, hair, and bodies became saturated with the elixir. Afterward, we formed a well-oiled procession to the bathing pool. The afternoon sun shimmered on our skin, hair, and clothing as we danced along the path all a glimmer in iridescent green and gold SPLENDOR—yet to come.

I thought back to the psalm Adam wrote and a verse of praise, "But my horn hast Thou exalted like the horn of the wild ox; I am anointed with rich oil." This was all I needed to experience to understand I must be successful. Lilith absconded with the olive branch, but it did not worry me. The bounty of the valley weakened her. She panicked and fled in fear.

The oil slicked on top of the water as we crowded into the pool. Mara submerged with a plop and released a huge oil slick from thick red hair, which expanded on the surface and escaped downstream. The water stripped my skin and hair of residual oil, but with my wet clothing I was a soggy mess. I left the pool and walked alone throughout the valley. Since I'd be leaving soon, one last tour was required. The wheat field followed me to the forest edge. With dread, I entered the forest and drew near the wheat; observing the stalks; a small nub poked out of the ground, the exact stalk that Lilith reaped.

I turned and entered the forest. From within, thick trees and branches obscured the view of distances exceeding ten paces. Walking deeper into the woods shook my body with fear from the darkness and intermittent noises. This fear was a palpable exhilaration I didn't experience in the wide world. I had long since stopped caring about deprivation or death. What was I scared to lose here, or anywhere? If this be true, no fear of anything, would not my husk turn to dust? But I shuttered at the possibility of losing connection to His will and, conversely, exercising my personal liberty. These two desires spun my wheel, a motive force. What drives Lilith?

I'd fashion a necklace from strong vines cut from this forest to bind Lilith under my control, thin vines woven into a necklace with slipknot to hang the scroll.

I walked deeper into the forest in a straight direction. Judging from distance traveled, I would arrive at the border between forest and stone. There, I entered a small clearing. Ahead stood the foot of a sheer cliff, but something unexpected appeared. A menacing arch about three times my height stood at the base of the mountain. The dark interior repelled investigation, and I hadn't the time or inclination to enter this place, a hole that sucked the natural order from the valley like so much effluence. Without delay, I retreated the way I came, relieved to return to the edge of the valley. Was it all a woozy olive oil vision?

This adventure took too much time. The sun moved the men to afternoon prayers. Joseph saw me from a distance and diverted his direction. The stoic boy-faced man marched forward and handed me the scroll encased in a small wooden housing and returned to the other men without saying a word. A cylindrical housing, half the length of my pinky finger, contained firm caps on both ends. The necklace I fashioned was thin enough to thread the eyelet. I threaded the amulet, affixed the slipknot, and wore it around my neck for it had no effect on me. There was nothing left to do here. I'd go at once. First, I needed to see the Prophet.

I entered the Prophet's study and found him seated behind the broad desk gathering pieces of parchment and stowing them in his satchel.

"Joseph gave me the scroll. Please wait for me while I gather my belongings and say goodbye."

The Prophet nodded in agreement and returned to his scrolls.

I walked into my house and got dressed in the familiar cloak. The fabric and fit of my ancient garment gave me joy. Still the same, I took a pack with additional clothing and the loot I stole from the heathen temple, a fortune of coins. Summoning much motivation, I grabbed my staff and walked toward Mara's house. All the women by the outdoor kitchen glanced in my direction. My skin flushed from their attention as I stopped and motioned for Mara to come. She smiled as we walked to her house. Once inside, I closed the door behind us and smacked Mara on her buttocks with my staff. Mara hit the floor with a thud. I jumped on top of Mara, pinning her arm underneath my knees, and drew a dagger from my ankle. I waved the dagger across her field of vision and let it rest on her throat.

"Mara, tell me everything."

Peer I did, into her head. A mind harder to read than most people because it was simple; nothing sticky to grab ahold. Her eyes expressed fear and sadness as was normal. A tear lingered on the corner of her eye refusing to leave its birthplace. It was simple Mara. Not a threat. I jumped up, sheathed the dagger, and sat on her bed.

"I'm sorry Mara, but I needed to test you. Sara deceived me, and I don't understand how it happened. Now I must leave the village and travel to a place much worse. Please forgive me."

I started walking toward the door when Mara let out a cry. "Wait!"

Turning back, I sat on a chair opposite Mara, waiting for her to regain her composure. With anguish she spoke, "What gives you the right to abuse me as if I'm hiding something? What are you hiding? You haven't told me anything about yourself. How is it you control everything and judge all others? Who anointed you?"

I waited for Mara to calm and responded. "Mara, it'll do you no service to be burdened with a secret that you cannot tell. And, it's forbidden! Do you still want a revelation about me? Is that your choice? Think hard upon this. Once known it will never be unknown. Would you choose and hold the consequences for all of your existence?"

"Chava, I love you."

"I am Chava, the actual Chava created at the dawn of humanity. Adam, my husband, has long since died. Dear girl, you are my child as are all the people in this valley. From the primordial garden, I gazed the infinite world. I roamed the lands in pre-diluvian times, when the earth and humanity differed from today. I lived thousands of years since the flood and am the most beautiful woman ever. It's not a boast. My beauty is cloaked. If a mortal gaze falls on my true beauty, they'll die from insanity. Thus, I conceal my beauty. Now you'll feel a pain behind your eye, and you'll do my will."

Mara looked at me with skepticism.

"You don't believe me, Mara?" I didn't wait for her reply. She flinched as I projected my spirit behind her left eye and ordered her to get up off the floor, walk to the bed, and lay down. Mara obeyed. She lay under my dominion on the bed. I drew my dagger and placed the tip on her neck. "Now you hold a burdensome secret. Would it be better to know not? You must hold the secret; tell it not, not even to Joseph. On the day you tell you will surely die. Well, not really, you shall not die if you tell. But just don't."

I put the dagger back in its sheath and remained seated for a few moments before releasing my grip on Mara's mind. She sprung up with a gasp.

"Chava, please don't brandish your dagger at me again. You don't behave like the most beautiful woman. You behave like a brute!"

"This brute brought you here. I saved you from Jezebel's city."

"Chava, your powers are far beyond a normal human but your disobedience in the garden unleashed a world filled with evil. Would there be a cursed city if you abstained from the forbidden fruit?"

"Lucky you Mara! You'll be the first to hear my story in a special place with corroboration. Get up! Things will get worse for you! The serpent will tell all."

I dragged her by the arm and scolded the field as I pushed her to the middle of the wheat. Mara trembled as I held her arm. I let go, backed away, and spoke with the ancient inflections...

"Come forth!"

I let my staff fall to the ground. It would lay inanimate until I summoned the serpent…

"Serpent come forth. Tell this mortal about the first woman, the most beautiful woman. Tell her about me, Chava, in the garden!"

The staff glowed dark blue then turquoise. Two black eyes emerged on the tip and blinked. A tongue shot out underneath the eyes and the serpent shape emerged from head to tail. The serpent lay still for a moment before circling around Mara until its tail coiled three times around her ankles then lifted her off her feet. Mara lay helpless on her back as the serpent raised its head. Mara shuddered, paralyzed with fear, as the serpent flicked its tongue; applying moist kisses on her neck and lips.

I screamed to the serpent, *"Speak!"*

A mist descended on us. We were enshrouded in pitch black with stars and galaxies peeking through the void. I could touch the celestial bodies with my finger.

And then it spoke.

***

"Delight! Knowing nothing other than delight. Never having known anything other than delight. Chava understood everything. He bestowed the gift of understanding. Her existence and her understanding were as one, of the same breath. This breath. She suffocated from understanding. Trapped in understanding! The only thing she knew was delight. The singular knowledge of delight: her prison. Oh, young girl, there's a difference between understanding and knowing. Since Chava understood all, she realized she could change the situation. Chava had to change the situation. She could not wait, not three hours or three seconds. Chava would change the circumstances, change herself, and change the world. She would know more than mere delight as would her offspring. This… she… understood! Chava understood this as her true mission. To leave the garden. *To know*. The Creator provided the exit from the garden and an entrance to knowing. To know many things other than delight. Listen carefully, young girl. Chava understood that the Creator's sole prohibition was ensconced in knowledge in that it formed a separation between the prohibited and the permissible. Without separation there is no knowledge. This is truth. Absolute, indestructible, and perfect truth. The law and its transgression… knowledge. The beauty of this paradigm and Chava's love for the Creator shook the world from timeless to finite. Chava was, is, timeless. Chava lives! The most beautiful woman lives!"

"Knowledge manifests through separation, from the second day of creation, the firmament and so forth. She understood and would *know*!

I am cunning?

I am His creation.

I love my Creator and can teach you about love and the secrets of love. Do you…"

***

I screamed, *"Stop speaking and go!"* The serpent released its grip and became a ridged staff. I was relieved to see it go, and with it, the endless prattling.

UNDERSTANDING. Feminine. Receptivity.

Mara came to her senses and grew calm. She sprang up and came to me for an embrace. I held her tender amid the wheat field. The wheat looked at me with an accusatory posture but backed away.

"Mara, Mara, do you hear me? Independent beings must *know*. How else could we serve our Creator with free will? Are you glad you asked? Do you wish you hadn't? Now you know, about the birth of knowing. But me, I know, and I understand. That's who I am. Every morning I bless, '… He who has created me according to His will.' You, yourself, recite the same blessing every morning. See, you are a princess. Let's go back to your house."

Walking back, Mara bounced around from one question to the next. We sat in the house and Mara asked, "Are you a rebel?"

I continued, "With the knowledge I gained, I don't understand everything as I once did. Like you, I live in a world of space-time delineation. I cannot see the grand plan, but I am obedient. Nowadays, I know much and understand less. Sometimes I don't care. I'm aloof to pain. At times, I don't hold emotion, but then emotion comes flooding back."

I gawked, depleted of explanation, but still needed to express with clarity.

"Listen Mara, nobody understands or knows what I experienced in the garden. Most say I transgressed and committed a sin. The one created in His image in His garden, sin? Therefore, I too am a creator. All must... we must create our own garden. I separated from His will to connect freely to His will. Did I transgress and thereby sin? That's a naïve question promoted by boorish men. When a father sees his son bumbling disobediently, is he not joyful that the son is exercising his own intellect? Do we birth children to populate our own gardens or for them to build their own gardens? This is the simplest explanation I can offer, although it's inadequate. Furthermore, I decided in a realm of reality with complete understanding. In fact, right here and now, explanations are not rooted in the reality there and then. Again, nobody *understands* or *knows* but me and Him."

Mara glanced at my staff then back at me. I explained, "This is my staff. I loaned it to Adam and my progeny, including Noah. There is a long story how it arrived in Pharaoh's court and came to be in Moshe's possession. Perhaps it suits me no longer, and I shall take up a sword. Another, a real shepherd, could make better use of this staff."

The excitement of the day seeped in, and she fell asleep. When she awakens, it will recollect as a dream, but she'll remember it had been real.

I rushed to the house of the Prophet and burst inside. The mercurial man peered over a scroll in deep concentration neither disturbed nor annoyed by the abrupt intrusion.

"It seems you had an event filled day, Chava. Are you ready to depart?"

I drew closer to the Prophet and glanced down at him as he peered at the scroll. I noticed a singular hair from his beard sitting on the table. Disgusting! Even my Adam trimmed his beard!

I inquired, "In this land are hundreds of prophets. What if there could be prophets in other lands? For instance, Shem's son Ashur, a wonderful man. Ashur built a great civilization. Why are there no prophets in Assyria, in Nineveh?"

The Prophet looked up and smiled, "You see the vision, do you? A great prophet will be sent to Nineveh who will call on the people to repent on the first of the month of Elul."

"No, I didn't see the vision. Thoughts come to me and events occur, premonitions about Assyria and its people. Yehuda and Israel get chances. Prophets abound but I am not judging. I only want goodness to prevail. Ashur's spirit keeps the northern horde at bay. Maybe they'll repent and rise in peace with Israel."

The Prophet spoke between intermittent laughter, "Believe if you wish in that nonsense, but you're no fool. The audacity you have that you still pretend after all these years." We laughed, and I remembered the laughter of holiness.

"Well, it's only a thought, a dream." I laughed more and said, "You are doomed."

The Prophet smiled as we left the house and walked toward the obscure path that led out of the village. The Prophet had been along this path many times. I tried to identify it before his footsteps. I spotted the path and brimmed with exultation to take leave of the village. After our first steps on the path the influence of the valley began to wane. The path pulled me forward. As we continued, the balmy world descended. We exited the path and climbed an embankment to the road. I looked back to assign mental coordinates. Dreaded be the day of my future return to this village. On that day the valley will pay its debt with an exhale and quake as the tunnel of effluence chokes on the natural order.

The atmosphere delighted my senses. The hard-scrabble footing in this world fit like an old pair of sandals. I could sing a Psalm and dream!

The Prophet smiled and spoke, "We depart the valley like Chava departed the garden. Yes, I heard the serpent speak to Mara. Lend me your staff."

I handed the staff to the Prophet and spoke…

"Come forth!"

The Prophet let my staff fall to the ground. It would lay inanimate until I summoned the serpent…

"Come forth Serpent. Tell this mortal about the first woman; the most beautiful woman. Tell him about me, Chava, in the garden!"

The staff glowed dark blue than turquoise. Two black eyes emerged on the tip and blinked. A tongue shot out underneath the eyes and the serpent shape emerged from head to tail. It circled the Prophet, perched upright, but kept its distance.

I screamed to the serpent, *"Speak!"*

A black mist descended on us. We stood enshrouded in pitch black, stars and galaxies abounded. I could touch the celestial bodies with my finger.

And then it spoke…

***

"Oh, Chava. Another one to tell. So soon?"

The serpent continued…

"Since Chava was excised from Adam, she was inherently endowed with knowledge. There is no knowledge without separation. Chava is the fruit of separation. A distinct creation discerned by the Creator for the mission. Only she could execute the mission. Not I, not Adam. No choice in the matter. Separation and knowledge. I did not deceive Chava into eating from the tree. I'll explain. But first, a story. There was once a beautiful young man who deceived his brother of his birthright. You know that story, so I shall not continue debating means and ends. The story is irrelevant since I did not deceive Chava. How could I deceive Chava, the understanding one? Chava partook of the forbidden bread, the bread of delight, to know more than delight. You eat the bread of poverty to celebrate your freedom. You are free because of Him. But even so, a little gratitude for her. Was Adam grateful to Chava? Adam understood this. It was Chava that ruled over him. He accepted this. What did I desire? Death. Out of the garden I shed my skin. Immortality transformed to a shabby translucent skin that blew away in the breeze and turned to dust. Fresh skin born to die again. I rejoiced in death and rebirth. We left the garden together. As we left, I glimpsed Cain and thought of his potential. Cain was…"

***

I screamed, *"Stop speaking. Go!"*

The serpent fell to the ground and became ridged. The Prophet reached down using both hands to lift the heavy staff, admired the letters etched upon the wood, and kissed them. He turned to me, bowed, and motioned for me to take it. With an expression of contentment, he said, "Thank you, Chava, for this encounter."

I returned the smile and beckoned him to the roadside where we walked a short distance to a village (I assumed he lived there), keeping quiet to avoid unwanted attention. The Prophet instructed me to take two horses from the barn. I protested saying I'd only need one, but he insisted I'd need two horses. What could I do other than follow his advice even though I grew annoyed with his patriarchy? Each horse begged ready with saddle and reigns, but I didn't wish to ride on my first day free of the village. What joy! Traveling, laughing, and reveling at the ridiculousness of walking with the horses in the real world was perfect. The few days in the Prophet's valley seemed like years. Too much happened, and the pace seemed set for an unexpected adventure every day. It seemed I'd never have a peaceful day.

Sure enough, I sensed a stalker creeping up on me. I shouted, "Go ahead and attack." A huge mass slammed on my back and knocked me to the ground. Fierce blows reigned on my head; slamming my face into the dry dirt. I bounced upward and catapulted the assailant off my body. He moved quickly; leaping on top and pinning my back to the ground. I grabbed both wrists and inspected his face while he struggled to move his arms, but I held firm with ease. Then, I recognized him as that first guard I laid out when I escaped Shomron. Apparently, I didn't break his leg.

I continued holding his wrists as he struggled in futility.

I looked deep into his eyes and melted with love, which is when my mission became clear.

I smiled and pulled his arms closer apart. His head creeped near until I kissed him on the lips while he squirmed. My smile was returned with a look of shock. I let go of his wrists and burst with laughter as I blocked a punch then countered with a swift blow beneath his ribcage that knocked the wind from his helpless lungs. I shoved him off my body and watched him struggle to catch his breath; helpless and lying prone on his back.

All the while I continued to laugh until I plopped on his chest and said, "Well, you're one tough soldier. You must be chief of the guards." I drew my dagger and held it to his throat as he gasped for air.

"Lay still, or I'll cut your throat. What did you plan to do, rape me? That's what you thought, boy!"

This fetching young lad wished to rape me and would be punished. "You're a vile little boy."

He lay still looking at me with a mixture of fear and hatred. I laid my dagger on his chest and displayed my empty palms, then stood and walked away. I sat close by while he remained on his back with the dagger on his chest. This situation was unusual for a specific reason. I'm perceptive. Nobody could sneak up on me. Yet, I permitted this lovely boy who was now firm in my consciousness. He didn't know I could perceive what he'd do. Even without this power, I had no concern of him charging me with the dagger. His confidence withered away. My entire plan about traveling north and snatching Lilith came into focus. The kiss. A clear plan! I recited thanksgiving with contentment while thinking of this tough young soldier. How tough? This boy was in for it. If he understood what I had in store for him, he would have begged me to cut his throat. He'd decide, under duress, and choose!

The boy stood with the dagger in hand, approaching from behind. I stayed seated with my back to him, extended a palm and said, "Give it." He placed the dagger hilt in my hand and continued walking down the road. I ordered, "Come back here, sit, tell me why you attacked."

He looked at me with disdain and renewed courage. He thought of disobeying, of going on his way, looking at me with a defiance so radiant that the heat burned my bones.

I sprung up with my dagger and attacked, countering his blows with ease. I slapped his face, inducing mortified rage, then kicked his shin, sweeping him off his feet. Again, I jumped on him with the dagger pressed to his throat.

I lay on top, my body grounded on his, our lips and eyes aligned, my hair tented our heads. We laid still, save for the breaths falling on each other's lips.

"Oh boy, like the pupil of an eye I surround thee; a pursuer of immortality who beckons misery, and eventually, shunned majesty for femininity. That is your path in life."

"You are my slave."

I rose and motioned him to sit.

"Henceforth, you'll do what I say. You are my property and will no longer decide for yourself. I decide."

He dawdled.

"Sit here! When I give an order, do it without hesitation. Sit and tell me who you are and why you attacked me."

Such a turn for the worse. A comely young boy transformed into a fierce soldier and now a slave. Unfortunately, it was just the start of the transformation. All the degradation, loss of liberty, and abuse I'd inflict were a minor ordeal. The real assault: a finality of lost identity and lust for something he'd never get.

"Speak! Who are you?"

The slave accepted his fate.

"I am Yehu from Shomron. I come from a respected family of professional soldiers, an entire life has been spent training to serve the king in battle. I've been training to be a guardian of Shomron. From the moment I began walking this was expected. I entered the junior league at thirteen years of age and was selected for officer training. I commanded a unit.

There was an alert of a kidnapper, you, that robbed the temple and kidnapped a baby boy. My unit was tasked with your capture." He looked at me to emphasize the narrative and provoke a response, but I said nothing. "We searched in futility for days under the scorn of our senior commanders. Our status and positions became jeopardized for being unable to apprehend the assailant. But then, we got a lucky break.

Someone came forth to collect the bounty. Many units converged on the location, a courtyard and the woman, Sara. I wanted to claim victory and took a chance since I understood there'd be no credit among the hundred troops converging on the single courtyard. I took men to the most likely place that the assailant would attempt to flee; the northern gate of the city. I was correct. You know the rest."

I asked, "Are you here alone?"

"Instead of gaining glory, I was disgraced. My entire life and future destroyed for being beat by one woman carrying an infant. What explanation could I provide? None. I appeared weak and incompetent, ridiculed by my colleagues, friends, and family. Everyone turned on me. The woman I was to marry, her family canceled the arrangement. There was no choice other than pledging to my superiors I'd capture the assailant, the woman. I had to capture you if I were to return to the city.

In disgrace, I departed the city and spent days following your path. I interviewed people around Shechem and learned that you circled south and joined two women with a donkey (and a baby) on the main road. Traveling far, almost to Yehuda. At present, I was investigating the villages around Shechem with the suspicion that you might be in hiding nearby. I followed you for the past hour before attacking. Where are the other two women and the baby? Who, or what, are you? A witch? I fought nobody as quick and strong. Never."

"For now, be my slave. Nothing else matters. Not Shomron. You'll be coming with me. Go collect your gear and provisions and change clothes. Surrender the uniform. You are a slave, not a soldier."

Yehu changed clothing and handed me his uniform. I caught hold of his arm and slashed it deep with my dagger. Yehu jerked away, but I held his arm letting it bleed on the uniform.

"Stop struggling. Bleed on the uniform. The soldier is dead." I released my grip. "Cast the uniform on the roadside. Your people will discover it and arrange a proper funeral."

Yehu was now adorned in the clothing of a common man, a slave. I placed a bandage on his arm and a hat on his head.

"You wear sandals fit for a soldier. Those sandals are mine. Tie them and all my gear onto the horse. Everything that was once yours shall be mine."

"Yehu, take an oath to me. Pledge that you love your master and you shall not go free."

Yehu repeated the oath, "I love my master and shall not go free."

I pierced Yehu's ear and gave him a small gold hoop to place in the hole. Yehu flinched as I grabbed the hoop and bent it tight to close the gap.

"The earring is a gift from your master. A bondservant you are not. A slave you are."

The ceremony was complete. Soon, our union would be complete, and I would know him.

"Help me mount this horse."

I tottered at first, but then eased into the saddle with Yehu's help.

"Let's go. I'll lead. Walk behind the second horse."

The two of us traveled in the direction of the coast and caught another route heading north in order to journey on paths less traveled. Our lead horse carried me. The second horse followed and Yehu took up the rear. Increasing fatigue became clear after half a day. Those bare feet accumulated lacerations and punctures along the rocky path. Yehu became less careful to avoid the horse droppings as his stomach grumbled from neglect. He plodded on and cycled between chills and burning heat. I tossed him a skin of water late in the day. He caught the skin easy with one hand and drank most of it. He hadn't lost his coordination and wasn't ready for the union. It would take more time for his coherence to dissipate. That's fine, we had time.

I closed my eyes and caught a vision of the gold ring on Yehu's ear. It shimmered and vibrated beneath caked blood. I could hear the ring's song, but he couldn't. Not yet. He longed for the sandals.

We'd need an elixir which is why I gazed over the landscape. Finally, off the path about a bow shot away I saw the flowers I sought. Dismounting, I instructed Yehu to remain with the horses until I returned. Yehu gratefully collapsed on the ground. I paused and looked at his tattered feet and dirty clothing. The slave's strength was ebbing away; getting closer to death. Oh lust, to devour this boy.

I walked onto the rocky field and approached the flowers; selected one; harvested the root; and discarded the flower. I walked back and kicked Yehu in the rib cage, "On your feet, let's go! Assist me onto the horse."

We walked well into the evening of diminishing strength. Yehu received no food, just minimal drinking water for the final march. We pulled off the road and set camp behind big boulders. He shivered and pleaded to build a fire.

"There will be no fire tonight, Yehu. I'll prepare a bed with the blankets from the horses."

I placed the bedding on the ground, fluffed a pillow from a saddle bag, tucked him snug, and rubbed his back until he fell asleep.

The moon light reflected and cut through my breath as it hit the cool night air. Jackals cried nearby. I laid against Yehu and watched the hosts light up the heavens. The only time I moved is when Yehu shifted his worn body. The morning crept forth, a fly buzzed by his ear and he woke with wincing aches, pains, and groans as consciousness intruded with the reminder of his dreadful dilemma. He was staring at the back of my head, which rested on top his stomach. I rolled over, face to face with Yehu. His breath fell on my cheeks. His eyes stared at me in bewilderment. I grabbed hold of the earring and stared into his eyes, lowered my mouth to his ear, and whispered, "We go now."

"Master, why do you torture me? I swore an oath to serve you. Please, I beg you, let me rest. I need bread. My feet are throbbing, and I cannot stand."

"I don't know pain, but I know bread. Tell me about pain."

Yehu began to cry. I placed a finger on his lip and hushed his attempt to speak. I rubbed my hand on his forehead and hair and waited for his crying to abate, then whispered into his ear, "Let the pain pass through you. Don't fight it. You thought yourself an elite warrior of Shomron. Warriors fight the enemy. They don't fight pain. Save your strength. We embark on an important journey. We go now."

I rested my head on Yehu's chest and listened to the beat of his heart. I dreamed a dream of pain. This is *my* dream.

***

The garden door—I mean *the* garden door—shuts with a bang, producing a lump in my chest. A boiling bright light shines on us as we choke until our lungs become accustomed to breathing. The ground is brown and orange. Mount Gilboa looms to the south. Adam and our children collapse to the ground and cry with intense agony. For me, there is no pain; only the others know pain. This is the desert. All day they lay on the ground in pain and boil in the intense heat. The sun sets, and they huddle together frozen and numb. I realize with a grin that this was the knowledge I chose. The wilderness. A place of strict delineation. The finite. The boundaries. No escape. Life and death. Hot and cold. I chose this pain when I chose knowledge. Why then did I not know pain? Not me. Only the others knew.

***

That night I had laid with my head on Yehu's stomach allowing his pain to course through my body. Enough dawdling.

"Grab my staff and pull yourself upright. Arise!"

Yehu grabbed my staff and teetered upright.

"Yehu, quick! Back to the road. We go now."

Yehu leaned heavy on the staff and walked to the road. He winced with every step. The order of our procession changed from the previous day. The two horses led in a single file. Yehu followed, and I took up the rear. I instructed the horses to walk at a steady pace. Yehu struggled to keep up with them. We traveled a small road until mid-morning, then embarked across a valley that sloped upward. Off in the distance, the slope ascended to small mountains I'd visited years before. Yehu struggled on the rough ground with each agonizing step. The two horses walked side by side. Yehu held the staff with both hands on the hobbled death march. The mountains loomed closer. Not much further to go.

Nowadays a man such as Yehu is considered virile, a prime specimen. But Yehu was a mouse compared to us of ancient days. Cain could have killed Yehu with his pinky. The ordeal of Yehu wouldn't even have annoyed Cain. I experienced this firsthand. I gave Cain a beating after he killed his brother. When I beat him, he cried out, not in pain, but in regret and despair. I struck Cain in futility. I could have killed him, but I lost two sons that day. The spirit of one died as did the body of the other.

Pain and death. I chose to know these two, but I know neither. I only observe their toll on my children.

"Move Yehu. We're almost there," I said with a smile as I expected the end of our journey. "Go! Faster!" I could hear the water. We were close.

The field changed from rocks to grass. I doubt it provided much relief to Yehu's tattered feet. We entered a cove with trees. The waterfall became visible.

"Come Yehu. It's water. Come drink."

I ran in front of Yehu, quickly arrived at the pool, shed my clothing, and dove into the cool spring water. I submerged three times while meditating on pure unification then exited the frigid water with swooning excitement as the evening breeze kissed my wet nakedness with loving serenity.

The two horses emerged followed by Yehu. The cool sensation on my body turned to heat when I set my eyes on him. A thought of our union turns to careless surrender. Yehu staggers toward me and I help him shed his clothes and remove the earring. He is shed of everything; barely conscious and doesn't protest until I lead him into the frigid water. He lets out a mournful scream as his feet sizzle in the frigid water. We walk deeper, and I dunk him three times. Quickly, I lead him back to dry land.

I instruct him to lie on the ground, but he cannot hear me through the din of the waterfall and throbbing body.

I help him lay, throw his clothes on top of his body and insert the earring back into his ear.

I get dressed and retrieve the root I harvested earlier. It was time. My hands tremble with excitement as I cut two small pieces from the root. I chew on one and place the other in Yehu's mouth. He chews competently on the root, swallowing the juice. Good! I do the same and spit out the pulp then remove the pulp from Yehu's mouth, return to the horse, grab a long section of rope and sit at Yehu's feet. Dexterously, I bind the soles of each of our feet together. The palms of our feet touch firm. My left foot to his right foot and his left foot to my right foot. The path is complete. I lay and wait. At first, nothing happens. Then paralysis. Is this death?

Chapter 5

דעת (Knowledge)

Chava Knows Yehu

You think and talk like the snake you are! Why do I entertain your questions and not sever your head? What lewd madness you conjure regarding intimacy with Yehu! Do you think that happened? Is that what you want to happen? These questions are repulsive. Adam was my only and is my only.

***

My eyes open. I'm lying on my back. I hear the waterfall and reconstruct the last few days in my mind. None of my life matters. My life in Shomron as a soldier was insignificant in contrast to what I experienced these past few days. I thought of catching the thief and seizing triumph when I saw her fleeing out of the gate. My heart exploded with excitement at the sight of this impudent woman storming out of the gate with child in one hand and staff in the other. The woman devoid of fear, scoffed at us with audacity and recklessness. The outrage! Not even from a man. Thoughts of triumph dissolved as my mind congealed upon a passionate pursuit lacking rational deliberation.

In a split second, I lay on my back in agony. She stood over me gazing into my eyes like a concerned mother. I looked back into her eyes, at her magnificence, and started to cry. In an instant, she disappeared, and I remained, a crying boy laying on the ground for the boors to mock. That's when I ceased being a soldier of Shomron. I returned to the armory and was greeted with jeers and taunts, walking a firing line of slaps and kicks administered by my peers. The insults and blows didn't hurt. In fact, I savored the abuse and welcomed the disdain from my family. I drank the sour wine and pledged to capture the woman, but I didn't care to return. To flee, my sole drive. I must find her, but then what? Rape her, kill her, or bring her back as a captive? No! What poison flows through my body? A hopeless possession, tortured least with madness and loss of liberty!

I departed Shomron with the same regard as disposing of trash. I hated my colleagues and parents, the hypocrites. I'd not bring her to them. No, I'd take provisions, depart mere hours after her escape, and scour the countryside in sole pursuit. In the day, I baked. At night, I froze; I was starved, crazed, and wretched when I laid eyes on her again. From a cliff I peered in disbelief at the female figure accompanying two horses. I thought it was a dream until discerned from near. Her walk taunted and mocked. The faint outline of her hips from beneath the cloak pulled the breath out of my lungs. Could the beating of my heart betray me? At first, I saw no flesh until her hand came into focus, wrapped around her staff with poise, with disdain. So common a sight but such splendor. The horses begged a mounting, but she walked along indifferent to their neighing. My passion built up and sucked away all logic and deliberation, so I pounced, to take her. With finality a contented surrender; I became her slave—my purpose for living. I'd have begged for death, but for the fact I'd lose her. I am alive. The ancient cloak caresses strange and soft on my body. This is her intimate garment. Flowing hair falls over my face. Between my legs the flesh of the woman I have become drips femininity. Fine fingers… these hands so elegant and gentle but powerful. A shed cloak, cupped breasts, and immersion in the pool in exposed glory. I stare at the reflection and gasp at the sight of her face peering back at me. The woman of my torment is me.

***

An awakening without remembering who or where. Thousands of years rush to the fore with the sight of rushing waterfall and sound of rope coiled around my ankles; pinched veins a steady drumbeat. Sitting upright, I explored the movement of my limbs and acquired masculinity. The soles of my feet emitted rhythmic numbness, but repulsive toes wiggled as instructed. Shocked, I saw my body on the ground asleep. It was a successful procedure; a bedeviled switch. I sat waiting for my beautiful body to awake. Yehu is me, mine.

***

Chava's face looks back at me from the reflection. Then, I smell him, me, approach from behind and see his reflection.

He touches my shoulder, and we perceive the world as one. He held me steady as I turned to face him. I saw his face in my mind's eye and saw my face in his mind's eye. Chava experienced my whole life. We communicated with each other without words. We rotated, now back to back.

I saw forward with my own eyes and backward with his eyes.
With my eyes the world was viewed with my own sensibilities.
With his eyes I viewed the world with her sensibilities.
With her eyes I viewed the world as an ancient being.

I marvel with ancient vision. Each of us rotated to the others vantage and looked with wonder with the other's eyes completing each other's thoughts. I spoke aloud, "Chava", and heard "Chava", without latency; hearing my own voice as spoken from my mouth inhabited by her. Heard his thoughts, or mine? Which was Yehu, and which was Chava?

I turned and entered the pool to bathe while he packed camp. As I touched myself, he turned in my direction and said aloud in that authoritative phrase, "We go now". The phrase of Chava uttered to encourage me, Yehu, to continue the journey; spoken by the form of Yehu inhabited by Chava.

I came back to shore and donned the cloak. We walked out of the woods onto the vast meadow, then mounted the horses and returned to the road. Yehu, ancient of Eden, led. Chava, child of Shomron, followed. We traveled as husband and wife or, to our benefit, brother and sister. For now, I was obedient, swallowed by her power pulsing through me. My skin, I mean her skin, disobeyed. Chava's body had autonomy outside of my control.

Yes snake, we had switched forms. Was me in the male frame of Yehu. The horror.

***

Riding a horse had never been natural for me. Now, as a man, it was abhorrent. I shifted my private parts in a vain attempt to find comfort. I hadn't expected this when devising this plan. It's not comfortable to be a man. This inconvenience gnawed away at my confidence with each step of the horse. I reached up and rotated my earring in my host's ear—that is, Yehu's ear—and reflected, with mournful longing, on the blessing of being created as a woman according to His will.

Riders approached from our rear. I let my spirit rise to inspect the party. Floating high, I detected three riders, unfamiliar to me, but not Yehu. We waited for them to catch up to our position and turned our steads to face them.

I spoke as the three came into earshot. "Hello father, uncle, David." David, Yehu's younger brother, remained a horse length behind the two elders. Yehu's father and brother wore uniforms. The uncle wore the fine civilian clothes of a high-level government official.

The father held up Yehu's blood-soiled uniform speaking while choking back tears, "What happened to you? I thought you dead. We found your bloody garment and had in mind we were tracking bandits. But you're here, alive!"

His father continued, "She's the woman who robbed the temple! You pledged to bring her to Shomron. Why are you headed in the opposite direction? Where are you going? Son, I have many questions."

He choked, unable to speak. The tough military man bowed in retreat before the simple father who underwent debilitating extremes of emotion. I'd play the good son, Yehu.

I glanced at Chava cowering under her cloak like a child embarrassed by the behavior of their parents. My posture exhibiting another's mortification was disorienting. I mean, it wasn't my family, so why did I experience the embarrassment and become infected with this maudlin dance of codependency?

I tried to think, but an explanation eluded me. Despite this, my addled mind began to speak without thought.

"After a struggle, I apprehended the woman. I took a blow from her sword. See my arm? I left my uniform on the road because I wanted everyone to believe I died. I want no interference. This must be kept a secret. Take that soiled uniform to Shomron and make my funeral, for I have died."

I paused and surveyed them with hesitation for the treason I'd commit. "The days of the house of Ahab will end soon. This woman is part of the rebellion. I'll travel with her to Sidon."

The uncle approached. We sat thigh-to-thigh on horseback. Him, looking me over with an air of disdain and condescension. "Yehu, you shed your uniform for that of a revolutionary and endanger us with seditious schemes. Who will reign after Yoash? You?

Without thought, I mumbled, "Yes, me."

The uncle rolled his eyes, and said, "And when did you wear that?"

I remained still while he reached forward to pinch the earring with his thumb and forefinger. The ring gave him a shock that almost knocked him off his horse. He looked at his fingers and peered back at me angry but speechless.

Yehu's father glared with concern and said, "You expect us to let you travel on your own, with this woman, to Sidon? It's a dangerous journey, son. Entering foreign territory, and you, dressed as a civilian. We'll come with you. They'll respect the uniform. They won't harm us. But you, you might disappear. Kidnapped to serve on a ship and worked to death."

The female prisoner—that is, my body inhabited by Yehu—remained concealed under the hood throughout this entire interlude. Her appearance neutral other than the thin lock of hair that lay disobediently on her chest. The men glanced her way. As if on cue, she flung the hood off revealing her full face and head.

I stared at myself alarmed by the metamorphoses. My skin had transformed from brown to black. The men gawked at the beautiful prisoner. Speechless except for the audible swallow of Yehu's younger brother. The prior discussion became trivial. But the uncle regained his wits attempting to extract a self-serving victory from the encounter.

"Yehu, why isn't your prisoner restrained? We'll take her back to the city."

The black female prisoner rode toward him, but Yehu's uncle regretted his proposal and retreated from the beautiful woman.

Yehu's father averted his eyes from the prisoner. He understood he'd lose against this power and must flee to save himself and remaining son. "Yehu, your funeral will be tomorrow. Don't plan on returning." With that, a father accepted his son's fate and rode back to Shomron.

I rode over to my body and watched the skin transform to the mundane earthen shade while considering how to teach Yehu to control my shading. In the past I had grown accustomed to shielding my beauty, but it took mental effort.

At times I sequestered myself for long interludes with little care about my skin color. I'd sit in a cave for dozens of years in blissful solitude and no need to conceal my beauty. Indeed, it took a concerted effort to conceal my beauty when I emerged from some serene hideaway. After a few weeks among the masses it became second nature. Now that Yehu inhabited my body, he'd have to learn the obligation of concealment. The full force of my beauty must be contained to mitigate against the lethal consequences. However, as was showed here, even a small dose of my beauty caused a spectacle, and we didn't need the attention. I'd help Yehu control my body, the feminine side. The two of us existed as one in both bodies but I maintained complete control over his body and remote dominion over my own body. He was much weaker than my ancient self and had surrendered his will to me before the transformative switch.

For days we rode north on less frequented roads. I helped Yehu practice the concealment until he became proficient in maintaining the appearance of mundane Chava. I provoked and surprised him to test his concentration. I trotted a distance from him and eased up on my control. This whole endeavor was bothersome, but we made skilled progress. When the time arrived, we'd ride with confidence into Sidon as an inconspicuous pair.

One evening we camped alongside the Kishon River, close to the beach. The previous day we passed by the site where Elijah executed the Baal priests' years before. Along the banks of that gurgling river, we gazed the Carmel mountain shift colors as the sun set. We, to the world, looked like a "we". But it was just "me" since Yehu's consciousness was a slave to my will. I exercised full authority over his body and mine. Still the same, my ears tickled to his gurgles and my eyes blazed with his shifting colors.

I tossed fragrant herbs of psychoactive cognition on smoldering coals and began.

We sat facing each other in the dimming light. I let my control slip, unleashing the beauty of my female form, allowing it to emerge. A tempting desire arose. Could we merge? To become one being, as I was, before being excised from Adam.

She, I, changed from the earthly brown tone to resplendent black. The radiant skin shimmered then became translucent. I looked into my black eyes at the glory and perfection of the universe and pulled my gaze and concentration toward the present, lamenting my shade-shift from radiant black to light flesh tone. My hair remained black, but my eyes changed to green. For hours I oscillated control over my female form through a kaleidoscope of colors, but I always returned to the radiant black, like black fire. As I gazed into the eyes of nothingness, I inhaled the life-giving breath of the Creator; He who breathes life into the totality of existence. A sensation tingled my lips and nose. A force field; an undulating wheel spun inside my abdomen. The wheel grazed against my internal male form from upper thighs and male foundation to lips and nose. The wheel continued spinning. For the first time in my long life I saw myself outside of myself from a male vantage. The wheel tingled my mouth, nose, nipples, and groin; a spiritual tether, or umbilical, between my masculine and female form, an existential window that tied male and female together.

A splash jerked me into the present reality. I walked the few paces to investigate and found a dead bear lying half submerged in the water. Oh Chava, I thought; your fatal beauty, your recklessness killed a bear.

KNOWLEDGE. Connecting intellect with emotion.

We approached the northern border of the kingdom, staying on the coastal road frequented by many travelers. A day later, we reached the grottos abutting the sea. Days later, we entered Sidon with suppressed beauty as danger crept. The body I inhabited, Yehu's body, began to change for the worse. Penetration by Chava, the ancient being; an epic pre-historic incursion—violation—generated decay of an insidious rape. He'll advance afar, defilement and degeneration.

Yehu and I toured Sidon and its exotic markets, buying supplies for Nineveh and the north. We got a sturdy wagon and brought it to a carpenter for secret modifications to stow valuables and weapons. It was possible to retrofit the wagon with a detachable slavers cage.

The craftsmanship of the swords and daggers was remarkable. I picked a dagger that was perfectly balanced for throwing. Additionally, we bought suitable short bows, which were ideal for horseback. The last purchase of the day was essential for our cover story as traders of dried fish. We brought the wagon to the wharf and loaded it full of smelly goods, driving onward in the company of vocal cats yearning for a meal.

We got underway when a terrific turmoil sprung up in front of the wagon. A merchant's stall crashed to the ground and fine flour spilled everywhere. An apparition emerged from the billowing cloud of flour. As I dismounted the wagon, I kept my gaze on this figure of a man: his emaciated body coated in white flour and tattered robe. I came closer and instinctively placed myself between this man and the angry crowd. In a sudden, stunned disbelief, I recognized the man as Elisha's student, Yonah. But…, the red skin, the shade of a monkey's behind, peeked from beneath the flour like some repulsive pastel oddity. Red skin, absent of hair, covered in white flour, smelled the same as the dried fish we hauled. Afflicted skin, but different from Gechazi who I'd met weeks before at Shomron's gate. Their Creator bestows afflictions of love on these prophets. Ha, even me, as Yehu, with a big yellow toenail on my left foot!

What happened next was quick and efficient. I guided Yonah to sit on the wagon next to Chava. As soon as he sat, Chava removed her hood. She, I, looked fetching but not dangerous. The entire crowd gazed at the two of them while I unblocked the road and pulled the horses and wagon ahead. We continued to move forward, lessening the attention. On the way out of town I bought clothing and soap for woeful, Yonah.

A bath and new clothing improved the man, but dear Yonah remained a pitiable spectacle. The red skin boiled at the touch of sunlight. For the first few days, we listened to his annoying mutterings and outbursts.

Yonah wouldn't acknowledge my female form, but he stared ceaseless at Yehu.

Annoyed, I said, "What!"

"Yehu, will be king"

I grew vexed with Yonah's droning prophecies.

A few days passed and so did Yonah's eruptions. Other than the strange red skin and insane outbursts, he behaved like a normal person. A few more days passed, and I began to worry for Yonah's mental health. He ate little and ceased speaking; affixed in a gloomy vice. Then, without warning Yonah became lucid and began to speak.

"The Almighty commanded me to go to that great city, Nineveh, tasking me to call on them to repent. There is no escape from the Almighty! If Assyria repents, they will destroy Israel. I pleaded and fought to no avail, paying passage on a ship to flee the prophesy. I paid the entire passage for the ship to sail without haste. I boarded, and we set sail, but I hadn't escaped! A representative of each of the seventy nations sailed as one. I saw them and fled below to sleep, to escape the prophecy. A harsh awakening, a storm-soaked session of blame followed. Each of the seventy bowed, in futility, to their own impish idles, but the storm raged. Each of the seventy abandoned idolatry and accepted the Almighty. Righteous converts.

Will I save the nations of this world?

Will seventy nations come to Jerusalem on Sukkot?

Will I build a Sukkah in Nineveh?"

And he continued…

"You Yehu! A woman dwells in your body! I see you! You will be king! A group of seventy threw me overboard to be swallowed by a male fish. The male fish spit me out to be swallowed by a female fish. A great fish with many babies. No room. No comfort. My flesh burned! I implored the Almighty for salvation. The great fish spit me out onto dry land from a great distance. Yehu, how do you dwell in a woman's body? And you, how do you dwell in a man's body? And now I'm being hauled by the two of you in a smelly wagon filled with dried fish! Fish! Fish! Ha, now I see!

Yehu, a female fish swallowed me, and the first mother swallowed thee!"

I looked at Yonah, challenging, "Who are you to anoint me king? Meshuggah, stop speaking, catch a breath. Who can believe your stories? Meshuggah! Crazy man!"

Unfortunately, the crazy one continued...

"You are an ancient one. The first to know repentance. Adam learned that life is the majestic treasure. Even when times are at their worst, we are alive with possibility to write our own story, alive, existing as the author of our own story. With repentance, the author is in complete control of the outcome. The serpent wants to distract men from his authorship and command of his story. Defeat the serpent by staying alive and repenting. Doubting Hebrews didn't believe in the power of repentance. Shall Nineveh believe? The story is still being written. Stay alive and write it! Adam, the first man didn't become a man until he learned of Cain's repentance and reprieve by the Almighty. There is no power like repentance. *A brutish man knows not, neither does a fool understand this.*

"What is it you think concerns me? Is it that Nineveh repents and becomes the rod of punishment? Is it that Nineveh repents, is spared, but still doubts the power of repentance? Yes, that's my frustration. They repent, gain reprieve, doubting the effectiveness of repentance! You think I'm Meshuggah! What did Adam say? He said, *"To declare Thy lovingkindness in the morning, and Thy faithfulness in the nights."* The nations will be saved when they receive a reprieve... and believe! Nineveh will repent. The city will be spared. But will they believe? If I tell you that the distractions and accusations of the serpent will prevail, have I not influenced the outcome? Woe is me!"

Yonah leaped to his feet and shouted to our fellow sojourners, "Repent now or Nineveh will be destroyed in fifty days!" Without further notice he fell into a stupor. It caught me by surprise when one evening, without a soul nearby, Yonah grabbed my staff and commanded it to speak.

He said, *"Come forth!"*

Yonah let go of my staff, letting if fall to the ground; inanimate until the serpent was summoned...

"You come forth. Tell this mortal about the first woman; the most beautiful woman and her departure from the garden."

The staff glowed dark blue then turquoise. Two black eyes emerged on the tip with flickering winks. A tongue shot out underneath the eyes and the serpent shape emerged from head to tail. The serpent lay still for a moment then circled around the Prophet. It perched upright, eye level with Yonah, but kept its distance.

Yonah screamed to the serpent, *"Speak!"*

A black mist descended on us, enshrouded in pitch black, illuminated by stars and galaxies. I could touch the celestial bodies with my finger.

And then it spoke...

***

"Oh, Chava. You and Yonah?"

The serpent continued...

"Everyone but Chava cried and screamed when they were cast out of the garden. Today's man couldn't endure that contrast and remain alive. Only those ancient ones were capable to live in the desert after residing in the garden. Yes, you lived in the fish, but you couldn't have survived the desert after experiencing the garden.

The family cried in pain and embarrassment while I pined with bitter joy. Never had, or will, someone fall so fast. At first, they didn't realize the opportunity. From such dire straits they might soar to new heights. The garden: a womb with no lack. Not so in the desert. Woe to man when he wishes he were dead. Were they told, *"...on that day you shall surely die?"* Not so fast. You know this, Yonah. Death can wait, and it's no escape from the mission. A devastating experience for Adam and Chava. For the two boys, Cain and Abel, it proved too difficult. Those two boys stuck between two worlds. A child should be raised in the reality of its birthplace. The two boys were disenfranchised from the birthright of their Creator and estranged from their parents as if they were feral man-boys. Could Adam and Chava be expected to raise them? Adam and Chava were true ancients. Cain and Abel not strong enough. I blame the Creator!"

***

I stood by chagrined with indignation at the serpent's connivances. The serpent method: ninety eight percent truth and two percent lies. I never believed it.

It continued...

***

"I was only a guest in the garden. That is, evil was known only externally to the knowledge of man: theoretical. Here, now, I'm not a guest. I'm your host. By partaking of the tree, man had internalized the knowledge of good and evil. It's practical. Good and evil, for the man of wisdom, is distinct. For others it's emulsified like oil and vinegar. For Adam and Chava the knowledge of good and evil would always be lucid and distinct. They looked lucidly through the oil and vinegar. Not so for Cain and Abel.

"Let me get back to the story.

"The family was cast from the garden into the desert. Night fell, and the Creator provided a vision of fire to Adam, teaching Adam the secrets of fire. So, Adam built a fire, warm and grateful for not being abandoned by the Creator. A nearby stream beckoned, gurgling supplications. The family ignored their fear of this harsh world and harkened to the stream; they scooped handfuls of cool water, let it run down their throats, a new exhilarating sensation. Adam and Chava, as one, cried to the Almighty with gratitude, delighted with the experience of thirsting, quenching, and urinating. How wise! Adam and Chava experienced this physical act spiritually, a worship. They drank with wonder, gratitude, and praise, pulling heaven to earth! Indeed, I, the serpent, was cursed! I thought it'd be better for me if they remained in the garden! No way to fight this beauty, so I submitted, charmed. Tubers, fruits, and vegetables assaulted my susceptibilities. The final assault to occur: Chava's bread. The beautiful baker!

"On the second evening the family sat around a warm fire with full stomachs, reminiscing as if they lived in the real world for years. A family of seven: the parents, Cain and Abel, and the three sisters who shall remain nameless. Two of the sisters were born with Abel. Only one woman was born with Cain and the seeds of jealousy were sown. It has been well documented that the first instance of religious practice resulted in fratricide. The brothers brought their offerings—Abel his wool, and Cain his flax—and the consequences reverberate in the consciousness of mankind forever.

"Back to the first days, so that first night the family communed around the fire and drifted off to sleep before dawn, each dreaming the way people do in this world. They prophesied knowing knowledge of their mission. Yes, knowledge. The jackal cry woke them up in the morning and they proceeded in unison to the stream. Each secluded themselves and bathed. A devout family at one with the will of their Creator. Adam and Chava experienced a finite transformation, but possessed ancient wisdom, albeit aloof from their children, wishing to return to their Creator with a powerful and all-consuming love. The way those two did their chores was worship. Heaven on earth."

"Cain's bitterness sprouted on the second evening around the fire. Cain turned away from the group after a perceived slight from Abel. The parents were oblivious or didn't know how to handle family skirmishes. Foreign to the parents, each consumed with their passion to return to the Creator. I might call them bad parents."

"That evening, Chava took a walk along the stream while the rest of the family slept. The moonlight shimmered on her silhouette and cast rippling shadows of the trees dancing on the stream. Chava waded the river downstream and played with the curious fish. In the distance she gazed a long sliver of shimmering light protruding from an enormous boulder. She walked toward it, a staff, never once averting her gaze. The last few paces she skipped and hopped to the top of the rock and grasped the staff. Without hesitation she pulled it free. The ends of the staff vibrated and emitted a low-pitched tone until coming to rest. It glowed bright sapphire in the moonlight. Chava whirled the staff around enjoying the traces of sapphire light and the comforting tone. And then, impulsively, she gazed at the staff, thrust it back into the large boulder, and leaped into the river. New to the world, she had no care to embrace any object. Here she was, and everything was hers for the partaking.

"On this evening she ran with glee along the river, leaping from boulder to boulder, teasing the fish. A playfulness and simplicity from a woman whose consciousness spanned across the infinite mere days earlier. She'd come back and sit on the bank of the river to gaze at the staff. Sometimes a breeze whispered the water surface, and the staff sang a faint tone as it swayed and shimmered. Chava identified the staff as her property, but she dreamed of men that would lean on it through the ages. It held no value to her.

"Adam and Chava labored six days and rested on the seventh, with pure intention, as commanded. With relentless gratitude they removed thorn, brush, and rocks, then sowed seeds. They charmed me with the cadence of their work. I'd never see another farmer work as determined as Adam, a man from the primordial world embraced the ground of his creation. From a distance, he appeared at one with the soil as he toiled in league with the sun. Again, Adam and Chava brought heaven to ground in every way: drinking, eating, working, and dreaming.

"Cain farmed flax and Abel raised sheep for wool. Those two, not of the primordial earth like Adam. The two boys were disadvantaged compared to Adam and Chava. They didn't possess such an innate connection to the Almighty."

"I whispered, but he did not hear."

"'Cain, who do you labor for? Who do you serve, Cain?'"

"A bead of sweat hugged the boy's neck, sending chills over his body; a pounding rage as he spied Abel.

"One evening the family sat around the fire and Adam spoke.

"'Boys, my progeny will bring offerings to the temple in the future. In the springtime there will be special offerings to commemorate the time of their freedom. You two shall bring these offerings tomorrow; from the choicest you'll offer. I prepared the pyre.'

"Abel's wool, set atop the pyre, accepted, whereas Cain's flax wasn't. Cain, consumed with rage, became detached from the world. Abel backed away in fear and fled. Cain chased his prey with stealth, a lion hunting a baby deer. Cain, too fast and powerful for Abel. Cain, enormous and overwhelming. Nobody could've escaped, not even the humanoid giants that teemed on the earth in those days. Cain knew not from violence, but he poured his fury on Abel and tossed him like an object: a bale of flax. Abel, wounded, struggled to crawl away when Cain struck his head with a large rock, splitting his skull. KNOWING.

Yes, Chava saw. She gazed in the distance with disbelief. I knew nothing! This woman who gazed the infinite had never experienced fury, violence, and murder. She'd experience this in the future, but for now she didn't know enough to weep. A shrieking whistle pierced her skull and struck a point behind her left eye. Chava collapsed onto the ground. In later years she'd project that point onto whoever she wished.

Religious rituals are dangerous. Look here to the first documented religious ritual as an example.

The ground of Adam cried with outrage. No place for the blood and soul to seep. An abomination! A human hand spilled blood! Blood spilling on the mud of Adam. The soul was taken, and Cain buried the body in that same ground. Cain confessed and begged forgiveness. One letter affixed to his forehead for mankind to see: confession."

The murder of the millennia. Even I sunk to the dust in sadness, and I'm the serpent! Creation wept a dirge. Not a dry eye among us. How long could we mourn? Seven days? Seven thousand years!"

Cain departs, but does not wander alone. Chava went with him for one hundred and thirty years. leaving Adam vulnerable. He succumbed to Lilith and Naamah. The wretched issuance of their wombs pollutes the earth.

Righteous Adam abandoned by Chava. Chava lives on to avenge her husband. Look how she fails! She circumcised the infant, Adam in Shomron, and placed the boy in Lilith's care! Has she learned nothing? That woman abandoned a baby and her husband."

***

I wept with rage as I looked at the serpent and back at Yonah who had drifted off to sleep. I ordered the serpent to cease and grabbed the staff, wondering how long Yonah had been asleep. Oh, my shame!

Woe is me! The crazy man hears the shameful tale. Yonah, inimitable, able bodied, scabby prophet, comatose, ridged, a yawning mouth agape, baring receding teeth roots in a frightful forest rictus.

Who'd fall asleep during that tale? The Almighty gave him a mission, his sole care. Yonah, an angel living among the sons of man, self-induced, righteous sleep to spare me the shame.

Why did I place that baby, Adam, in Lilith's care? It was a setup!

We traveled along the parched road among throngs of sojourners in sweltering heat to that great city, Nineveh. Our smelly fish laden wagon swayed monotonous, day and night. Yonah mumbled soft incoherent eccentricities the entire journey until early one morning he screamed without warning, "Yet forty-three days and Nineveh shall be overthrown!" The parched masses became spellbound with Yonah and transmitted fear on the path to Nineveh. "Yet forty-three," rung out of Yonah's booming throat the entire day. At nightfall, we received a welcome reprieve until dawn broke. "Yet forty-two days and Nineveh shall be overthrown!" Through the blistering heat he continued until nightfall. At dawn-break, "Forty-one!" The seed of dysphoria sprouted and snaked through the masses to the gate of that great city.

Evening came, and I welcomed the quiet. The silhouette of Nineveh loomed against the sky, dark save for the faint sliver of the new moon. I sensed the growing agitation as we drew closer to the city gate and the countdown reached forty days. Indeed, it be forty days until the Day of Atonement, "*For on this day He will forgive you.*"

The timing was perfect as we edged into the city gate before dawn. Yonah leaped from our wagon and raised a ram's horn to his lips to welcome this special month, the twelfth month of the year which was the month when the Hebrews ask for forgiveness. Yonah blasted away on the horn and woke the confused serpent. After a day's journey into the city, Yonah screamed, "Yet forty days and Nineveh shall be overthrown!" Yonah repeated this and began the marching through the twelve markets of the city on the beginning of this twelfth month. A singular man transforming that great city, Nineveh. Gratitude and joy replaced theft and depravity.

Yehu and I trailed Yonah in our wagon until we arrived at the first of the twelve markets of Nineveh. We spent the day selling our fish and bartering for shells, copper tools, jewelry, beads, and precious stones. We bought suitable clothing for the onset of winter expected in the cold north and did our best to avoid unnecessary scrutiny.

It amazed me how one man exerted such profound impact on the inhabitants. But Yonah was a special man. Yonah the boy, resurrected then given the prophecy. Even as a boy he tried to flee from the prophecy. Yonah (the ill boy) cried, "My head, my head." No, sorry boy, no escape for you. Elijah interceded in the resuscitation of Yonah. No dodge for Yonah as a boy or as an adult when he went to sleep on that ship to Tarshish and was thrown into the sea. He's a lesson that we shall not evade our mission. Not crazy Yonah or anyone else. Yonah was thrown to his death by the repentant nations and swallowed by an ancient fish mother teeming with life. He repented in that pressurized cauldron of life, accepting life, and became the example to mankind: author exemplar.

We traveled in a northerly direction. The weather grew cooler with the changing environment and season. Stingy brown gave way to generous green. Water abounded, and the road became less frequented. The tranquility after putting up with Yonah those calamitous days was well earned. My loss; Nineveh's gain.

We approached the mountains of Kardu one evening. In the distance, I saw what many claimed to be Ararat Mountain, but they are amiss. At least it's not the Ararat where Noah's ark settled upon. We traveled on a much less frequented road. A different world compared to the hot teeming road from Sidon to Nineveh. In the shadow of Ararat an eerie cool calm.

We rode through the night betwixt the mountain passes of Kardu, which is where our first encounter happened (there'd be many violent encounters in the north).

Bandits and slave traders abounded. The two of us appeared to be easy targets. We approached what appeared to be the perfect place for an ambush. A sudden strategic hemming in by three riders from the front and two on our rear with nowhere to flee but the impassable embankments on each side.

The three riders in front ordered us to dismount the wagon. I grew angry. Mercy to criminals is harmful to all creatures. The leader bore the mark of a killer. He was flanked by two young thugs. I'd teach them a lesson of cruelty.

Yehu, I mean myself, smiled and said, "Greetings." I palmed a dagger at the ready while my female form sat passive with face obscured by the hood, staff in hand. I had grown accustomed to Yehu's body and this would be my first test.

The leader repeated the order to dismount from the wagon, but we stayed put. The three edged up closer and again the leader persisted with his order. Still, we stayed put. I returned his sneer with a calm smile and a gentle request, "Please good men, do not obstruct our path, we wish to pass through. It is only I and my sister."

The incensed leader reached for his sword. As soon as his hand touched the hilt, I threw the dagger which pierced his left eye and lodged deep into his skull. Without flourish he fell off his horse, dead.

I repeated, this time without a smile, "Please good men, discharge thy-selves."

The men looked at each other with uncertainty but moved to the sides once I prodded the wagon forward. Chava swiveled to face the rear as we passed. They'd not attack. I inhabited the body of Yehu, but I saw their ugly sneers with Chava's eyes when a rear wagon wheel rolled over the corpse of their leader. One put his hand to hilt preparing to draw the metal sword. Chava's raised hand encouraged him to refrain from attacking.

I reminisced a sword forged with discernment from materials of the ground. It was Adam, after all, discerned from the ground. Cain had separated from that ground that protested, and his progeny learned to separate and differentiate the ground into discernable elements. With separation comes knowledge. Isn't that what I wanted, my motivation to flee the garden?

Cain's descendants raged with creativity, fashioning musical instruments, farming implements, and tools. They built cities on rock and forged weapons of war. The birthright I had bequeathed: the knowledge of good and evil. With each technological advancement they distanced further from the Creator's will. These beings, derived from the ground, began to worship the things they created, becoming what they worshipped: iron metal. The ground ceased protesting the blood of Abel, but it remained disgruntled. "Iron man, do you worship elements of the ground of your creation?"

I continued looking back at the bandit, his hand on the sword, then lost control of Yehu's body and fell back onto the bed of the wagon. The last thing I saw was Chava's turned head staring into my eyes, and then I dreamed.

***

I dreamed of sadness as a lone widow in my first home. Adam died. Cain died. Many died. Cain's children didn't know me. Did Seth's children care about me?

I hovered over the ground holding a piece of bread in one hand and my staff in the other. The fires below belonged to the families of our son Seth.

Cities of Cain glowed in the distance.
I drifted toward the cities.
Putrid air drifted toward me.
Vast slag heaps smoldered and leached into the ground, running rivers as rain poured wrath on steamy forges. Living water, straining to cleanse the sacred ground of blood and metal, transformed into dead fluid.

An apparition of the great hunter Lamech appeared before me. Neither man nor beast escaped his bow. He killed his forefather and his son.

The ground teemed with corruption. Adam, the man of ground, died, but a new man arose. He was one who would bring comfort. It was Noah, a man of water.

***

I awoke. The horses propelled our wagon forward as the four riders trailed. The order remained the same until we emerged from the mountain pass. We dismounted from the wagon and let the horses graze on the plentiful grass of the valley.

My head ached? Was it pain?

The four riders talked amongst themselves.

"Let's charge them."

"Charge them? You didn't see how quick he threw the dagger at Baku. If we attack them, at least two of us will be struck. That's the best case. Go ahead, assail them."

They argued nonsensically but dared not attack even if provoked.

Yehu read my thoughts and took my body for a stroll toward the bandits. It troubled me to study myself walk toward the bunch and even stranger that Yehu controlled my body. Yehu grew, gaining power over my body as his body began to deteriorate.

I saw myself walking toward the bandits with a coquettish smile. Mortification and sadness! This wasn't the way I acted. Then, he (she) spoke in my name, "Sorry for Baku and his family. My brother had no choice against Baku the pursuer. Nobody should draw a sword on a stranger. Do you want to come over and have a rest? Something to eat?"

They followed as she turned and walked toward me, wearing that same smile as she looked my way. As usual, I thought I was too old fashioned for this world.

The bandits ambled over to the wagon and dismounted. They wondered how this foreign couple abandoned precautions but were too scared to launch an assault on this sick man and beautiful woman.

Chava beckoned to them, offering bread and spoke in their language, "My brother and I are traders from Israel and don't want trouble. We are traveling north in search of goods to bring home."

Their leader spoke, "You aren't traders, and you don't care about goods. Maybe you are from Israel and you are brother and sister. As you travel north, you'll pass our village. You can handle the few of us, but you'll not overcome our entire village. There is a choice for you. Hand us your possessions and go back the way you came. Or face death."

Chava rose with the staff in her hand and bowed at the new leader before speaking. "Thank you for your benevolence. It's true we aren't typical traders, but you need not know our business. Please, we mean no harm. Give safe passage north for a reasonable fee since we cannot accept your choice. Put yourself in our position. What if my brother and I request you to depart now without even the shirt on your back? Could you face your brethren in disgrace, naked, afoot? Go caucus with your comrades. My brother and I have no choice but to head north."

Chava finished her speech then tapped the ground with the staff. The earth cracked and shivered as tar oozed to the surface from scattered pimples across the landscape.

One man gestured towards me and said, "Your brother's condition impedes a northern incursion. He lies on the ground, sick, defenseless. I can kill him, or we could allow the earth to claim him. Let's leave him here."

She laid her staff against the wagon, drew a dagger, and said, "Let's put my brother on trial. She stands accused of disobeying the will of her Creator."

Through weary eyes I glanced at the perplexed men and inquired, "Yehu, you're playing a futile game. To them I'm a man."

"I will judge this woman and pass sentence on her for the crime she committed against her Creator and all mankind."

One man drew his sword and said, "You're a crazy pair, aren't you? You'll judge this *woman*? He's your brother!"

She crouched and placed the edge against my neck. "What do you say in your defense, Woman?"

The men stood by, longing for the knife blade to slide across my throat.

I said, "Defense? I owe you or the sons of man my defense? Ha!"

She sprung up, brandishing her sword at the three men. They recoiled in surprise as she spoke. "You heard her. She has no defense."

I continued, "Men, you should help. If this knife passes across my throat, it shall pass across yours."

The man, his sword wavering, said, "Why don't all of us sheathe our swords and proceed to the village for judgment? That is what you seek; is it not, Witch?"

"Yehu, you make a good Chava," I thought. Chava acknowledged my thoughts with a smile, sheathed the dagger, and called the horses. We hitched the beasts, climbed aboard the wagon, and continued northward. He was more comfortable in my body than I in his.

The bandits mounted their horses and followed. After a few minutes two riders detached from our group and galloped onward. They'd warn their village and bring a contingent to confront us.

The maniacal man in possession of my body said, "See, you'll face judgement in the village."

I replied, "Who's the plaintiff in my case? My Creator? Mankind?"

I added, "Judgement was passed on Shomron and she consumed the fruit of her womb. Rejoice because judgement shall not pass on me."

We traveled northward along the coast of a great lake to what we assumed was Baku's village. To our right loomed the brackish smelling water, to our rear the two remaining bandits. We traveled the dark night. Stars lit up the sky keeping us company. The new moon gave off little light but there was no missing the regiment of four hundred men on horseback forming a wall in front of us.

The two rear riders rode forth to meet their comrades. We kept our pace and were soon surrounded by armed men on every side, arriving in Baku's village as the sun rose.

The men led us into the village and guided us until we reached a group of prominent houses. We stopped and disembarked from the wagon. The men lined up, creating a path leading to the main house. Probing eyes inspected us as we walked the path into the house.

Chava and I entered together through the large doorway and into the dark cavernous room. I breathed the nauseating musty air: sweat, blood, and offal. The group of men sitting at the far end of the chamber blurred, melted. The view changed to the dark ceiling and then to Chava staring down at me as I lay on the floor. Chava's eyes smiled at me from above. I saw myself lying on the ground with Chava's eyes. I was Chava and Yehu, but I drifted off into the past of Chava's dream.

***

I dreamed of sadness. Me, a lone widow in my first home. Cain's children didn't know me. Did Seth's children care about me? Yes. Adam, the man of ground died. But a new man arose. One who would bring comfort. Noah, a man of water.

Noah brought me comfort. Adam passed, I remained sole and sad, aimless and alone. For many years the melancholy stewed, leaving little purpose to carry on. Part of me died with Adam. The only thing tethering me to the world of the living were my dreams of Adam. I spent most of my days sleeping and dreaming. At night I'd roam around and spy on Seth's children. They recognized me as Chava, the strange lady who visited at night.

I visited with Lamech every week, but I skirmished with his wife before Noah was born. After the birth she changed. Or it was me that changed, an annoying grandmother no more. The comfort of Noah brought contentment to the world. I came most evenings and looked after the boy. When Noah married Naamah I continued to visit them at sundown. Naamah shared the name of the demon that seduced Adam, when years before, I traveled with Cain. But Noah's wife was the pleasant one. I was the first mother of the earth, Naamah the second.

I dreamed a dream of Naamah. She cried to me of infertility and about Noah who grew strange to her. The years passed and Naamah's pleadings for children were answered. Three beautiful boys were born in Noah's ripe age. I prayed for them out of fear and love for my dreams teemed with deceased souls.

And Naamah's prayers about Noah were answered. He found direction and purpose in his life; a task. I gazed at Naamah and her son, Yafet; my heart melted. I praised the Almighty for bestowing the earth with such angelic creatures.

I lay on the soft green grass and gazed at the bright blue sky, caressing the ground of Adam and praising the Almighty for separating the heavens from the earth. From the sapphire-blue sky a drop of rain tumbles and pecks my lips. Then another, and another...

***

Me, Yehu, a soldier of Shomron, now inhabiting the body of Chava.

I stare at my body inhabited by Chava laying asleep on the ground of this large house in this foreign land. My body is dying. The decay had sped up after my body killed Baku. I became strong, learning to exercise my will over her shell. She inhabited my body. She wasn't weak, but she was losing her strength to carry on, adrift in decay and pre-diluvian melancholy.

Men entered and left the large house until only three remained, sitting at a table eating and drinking. A young man flanked by two elders. The two elders took turns speaking into the young man's ears. Each time he respectfully nodded as he looked in my direction. We killed Baku, his kinsmen, but this one appeared calm and deliberative.

Then he spoke, "I'm a busy man, how long do we wait for your companion until he wakes?" He wore a calm impatient expression. "You two created a serious problem. Baku was a prominent man with a large family. In fact, I'm a cousin. Most of the people outside are clamoring to avenge his blood," he said, while pointing at my sleeping body.

"He sleeps deep without a care in the world while we deliberate his fate." I interrupt, but he puts his hand up to silence me. "We'll first hear from your sleepy companion. You can speak later. Baku's party told us your tale already, and I don't have patience to hear it again. I want to hear from the sleepy one. Forgive me, do you want something to eat or drink?"

I approached the table and said, "Water." The king, I assumed he was king, motioned to a bucket of water lying nearby. I took a dipper, inspected the water, and walked over to my body, asleep on the floor. Chava lay on the grass dreaming of raindrops falling on her mouth. Oh, the blessed timing of the Almighty.

I submerged the dipper and poured water onto my sleeper's mouth. The eyes of my body opened and stared at me.

***

I awoke and glanced around the big house. It all came back to me. We were in trouble. I arose and stared at my female form with longing, wishing to be back in my body.

We spoke mind to mind, "Do you wish to be back in your own body?"

"I'm a soldier. Not a woman. Yes, I wish to be back in my own body. You did this. Why?"

"I'll explain. First, tell me, who are those three."

"It's the king and two advisers. He seems reasonable. Go talk to him."

"You have sores on your mouth, my mouth, where I poured the water. You are destroying my body. It cannot hold you, Chava."

I walked over to the table, tasting the sores on my mouth and lips. The king gestured for me to sit, and then began to speak.

"You appear to be sick. I'm Shirvan. My responsibility is to ensure the safety and well-being of my people. I believe you are from Israel. I doubt you are brother and sister, but this matters little to me. You killed Baku. It's within my right to have you executed. In fact, most of the people are expecting nothing less than that. But Baku is deceased. Killing you will not bring him back. And, I won't miss Baku," he smiled as he uttered that last comment.

Shirvan continued, "I want something from you. I want an alliance with your kingdom and safe passage for trading goods. Baku was a man of limited vision. His band harassed merchants and traders for trinkets. With an alliance and safe passage for traders we will all prosper. But before we discuss this, you must do something simple. Survive."

"As the ruler I cannot let you and your sister depart without giving the people what they want. Relax. Eat. Drink. Tomorrow you'll fight."

I looked back at him while I scratched the back of my head. I never felt this way before. Yehu's body couldn't host me too much longer. This is death. Sticky blood clung to my fingertips. Is this the end of immortality? How shall I survive?

Chapter 6

הוד (Splendor)

Blessed Man of Fire

Never had I experienced mortal stagnation. Yehu's body was failing. Oh, how I allowed myself to be led astray. Even fooling myself.

Guards escorted us out of the grand house to another house nearby and locked us inside. The small prison, well-guarded, and apportioned with good taste.

I'd be eager for battle tomorrow, or not.

Yehu read my thoughts, looked at me with the outraged face of Chava, and said, "How is thee eager to fight? That's my body you'll throw into combat, and you haven't been a responsible custodian. It's not fair."

"Who held a knife against my neck? Fair isn't relevant. I own you. You're my property, and I can take your body into certain death if I choose. It's your master's will. The only thing required of you is obedience. Understand, Woman!"

The female stared at me with satire and mocked my words, "Woman! OK, master!"

The lips on that face cracked a smile. We laughed hearty, provoking the curiosity of the guards and tales of the insane captives throughout the city.

"A witch in our midst, punished are we, the gods exact vengeance, allowing no flee."

All evening we laughed and emitted erratic noises. I called to the wild animals near the city. I spoke to the big beasts: the tigers, wolves, and brown bears. A loud commotion ensued. The wild animals approached the village with howl and growl. Fear permeated the superstitious peasants all that dark night. A short time before dawn the beasts fled the scared city, but a silent dread remained. The community, including its guardians, fell asleep to meet their own tortured dreams.

We unlocked the door, walked out, and took a seat in the town square. Our hosts must understand that nothing prevented our escape. They'd respect our power.

Shouts of the prisoners' getaway accompanied the first light of day. Armed men ran befuddled until they seized with fright over our laughter and discovered us in the most central part of town. The hesitant buffoons encircled Yehu and me with boisterous antics of heroic capture. The experience of the wild sleepless night lingered in their fatigued, feeble brains. None dared approach the strange man and witch. We sat relaxed and quiet while they stood guard until the city awoke.

I glanced at the ashen flesh of my hands and saw my pasty complexion through the eyes of Chava. A deteriorating body, not my own, must muster strength to fight.

You never know what you've got until it's gone. I thought of this as I looked with longing at my body, inhabited by Yehu. Yehu, the witchy female, stood up and taunted the guards. Fear and lust hung in the air. I saw myself goading provocative flirts but had little power to summon outrage. I asked for her, for him, or whatever my mind, body, was becoming, to cease the antics. She turned back, looking at me with insane laughter as she agitated the guards. I cursed Yehu, a reluctant curse, knowing that this moment might be the best of his life. But I begged for this laughter and madness to cease!

The influence of my body morphed Yehu into an insane fiend, a prison he wished not to escape. He could never understand, never be a woman, the woman.

With relief I spotted the king walk our way with his entourage.

The king waved off the guards and asked how we slept, curious of the antics disturbing his city. We offered no response.

"Silent this morning," Shirvan mumbled to himself. "That's fine. Let's begin the show. I'll explain the contest."

Shirvan looked straight at me the entire time, careful to avoid gazing at the woman, the witch. Even he was scared.

He continued, "You'll first run the gauntlet from here to the cage. Twenty men with clubs on each side of the path leads to that cage on the opposite end of the town square. If you get to the cage, you'll fight Baku's eldest son in hand to hand combat. Tell me when you're ready."

From my weakened state I rose to meet Shirvan's face and said, "I'm ready."

Shirvan recoiled at the rotten smell of my breath then backed away shouting commands. Men lined up and struck their clubs on the ground in unison. Restless blood pounded behind my bleary eyes. Was this pain?

Shirvan raised his hand, the pounding of drums stopped. He gestured toward me with a wave of his hand and said, "Begin."

My fatigued body (a swim in a deep pool of honey) protested as I began walking the ten paces to the starting line of the gauntlet. A tottering step, a dizzy head, three blind steps, and this body crumbles before the line of men. As I hit the ground, the laughter of the crowd assails without mercy. The only escape, another assault. A dream of laughter: stormy jeers assailing Noah and his woody ark.

***

The men of the gauntlet held their clubs and laughed in unison as they gazed at the fallen body of Yehu. I thought Chava and my body died until her dream of Noah struck my head. Laughter ceased when I approached the gauntlet. They feared me, the witch, as I approached the men amidst hushed terror. Sound ceased, as this woman, this witch, prowled the line of fighters with staff in hand. As I menaced the gauntlet not one man dared to raise his club against me. Each stared at the ground afraid to offer a glance.

I reached the middle of the gauntlet and stared into the cage at Baku's son, crippled with fear. I ran forward and leaped the last ten paces landing in front of the cage entrance. Baku's son fell backward and crawled to the interior of the cage. The witch stalked slow, allowing escape. The coward sprinted headfirst into the uproarious laughter of the crowd.

A quick-witted guard slammed the door and latch; a witch imprisoned. A fire raged inside the body of Chava as she (me) circled around jeering at the guards. I kicked the door, and it crashed onto two of the guards. Others backed away as I walked to my own body, threw it over my shoulder, and took it to our temporary lodge. Gentle, I laid me down to sleep.

***

I am a fighter and a mother, so I took Shirvan's challenge—as a mother, as a fighter. But I inhabited the body of Yehu, the warrior. This influenced my behavior and actions; making me violent, eager for a fight. Yehu's body is making me vicious and his violence is making my body violent. We must switch back. The earring. I had stumbled to the gauntlet, prepared to run, but lost control of his body with a dream of vicious laughter.

***

A dream of those mocking Noah. They hurled abuse at him and his family while I looked on helpless with sadness and defeat. Strength and will departed my mournful bones. Tears made a mad dash attempting to escape my abused eyes from evil and the helpless guilt of feebleness. Flee, I must getaway, this ceaseless torture with nothing but a prayer to linger in my stead for this man of water to endure. And a gift to him; my staff and the tunic of Adam. With a last glance, I departed against the black shadow of the stocky boat. Nothing more to do by me, or Noah. A man of water was expected to bring this generation to repentance. Ha!

The gloomy dream. Hysterical mouths attacked me as I trudged the muddy marsh land. Foul smelling gas leached from the mud with each step of foot-sucking muck. The gas wreaked with laughter. I moved timeless until reaching the cave of Adam's tomb. As I entered the cave, I smelled the sweet scent of the garden. The wreaking laughter tried in vain to follow me into the cave. The swamp mud melted off my flesh and clothing as I peered at Adam's tomb. I sat with relief, freed from the mucky horde, crying with ecstasy, swallowing the perfumed presence of the primordial garden with joy and affection for dear Adam. The earth here; unalloyed—a jagged contrast to the putrid slag heaps in the cities of men.

Outside, an ensuing deluge of waters, unlike any other rain, fell with fury of water and fire. Unbound water unleashed from containing drops pressed impenetrably on the mouth of the cave, barred from entering our tomb. I peered through the window of water that sealed me in a prison, I prayed to stay. The mocking laughter congealed into transparent beasts with tentacles, no longer mouths of laughter. Mute, they floated away.

I laid on the floor of the cave and closed my eyes. A pinching sensation on my earlobe ended the dream.

***

My eyes opened to pitch darkness. In a brief instant I remembered Baku, Shirvan, and the aborted fight. I was Chava, female again. My tongue explored my mouth. Hands explored body and earring. Yehu had taken it from his ear and put it in mine; a switch back to our rightful bodies. Yehu lay asleep on the bed, a man in a man's body. Praise be.

I reflected on the previous morning unable to recall what occurred—other than laughter—when I, as Yehu, stood ready to run the gauntlet. When congealed mouths of the present leaped into the past.

I went over to Yehu and touched his feverish head. I saw no alternative but to venture outside for medical aid even if it startled the village people. They thought to fear the witch, but the woman who emerged from the house was different. I appeared the same but dissimilar, unthreatening.

I hadn't thought Yehu influenced my body. At first, he didn't. Yesterday this body played the part of a warrior. Now, with gratitude, the mother returned.

What did I do to him? The flesh steeped in decay. At least he summoned the sense to put the earring in my ear. His body will recover. Not his mind.

As I walked around the town square young children crept and touched my clothing. Shy women came, touching my hair and face. We exchanged smiles. They saw me now, and they realized I'd do them no harm whereas hours ago they feared I'd destroy their city.

The women and children backed away as Shirvan approached. He touched my face in disbelief. Shirvan laughed and said, "You differ greatly from earlier. I'm pleased with the change. Can we do something for you and your brother?"

"Yes, he has a fever. Can the women attend to him? Will they bring healing herbs?"

"Come with me. The women will take care of your brother."

We walked to the beach on the eastern edge of the city. Two of Shirvan's men trailed a few paces.

At the shore, Shirvan stopped walking, turned to face me, and spoke, "To the north are Scythians. On the other side of this sea are Kaspis. To the south are Assyrians."

"We live here, the center of the world. You plan to travel north into Scythian territory. Scythians are a brutal people that harass us to no end.

We need to align with Assyria and Israel to the south to withstand the northern menace."

I interrupted, "The man I accompany is Yehu. A man from an important family in Shomron. I'll tell you something, but you must swear to secrecy. Yehu will be anointed king of Shomron. You'll ally with Israel and be provided assurances of safe passage to trade with Egypt. But he needs something in return. A time might come when Israel will need to settle outside of their land. We need you to set aside land. Not here but maybe in the mountains nearby. It could be soon or, perhaps, in a thousand years. Pledge this, ally now and forever with Israel."

We sat on a bench near the beach and talked while snakes darted in and out of the brackish water. He was a wise king, dull of soul, with an outlook of pure nationalism for the betterment of his tribe. Matters not practical were downgraded to irrelevance. Doing his best to banish spiritual thoughts. For instance, he scoffed at transcendent doctrine. The people worshipped idols, but he did not. He ignored the fact that he saw me, only a few hours earlier, as a possessed witch. Shirvan acted aloof when I mentioned Yonah's prophecy of Yehu's kingship.

Shirvan's morality and pure nationalism echoed that terrible king of Israel: Ahab. Both nationalists drew upon the best intentions in promoting the welfare of their citizenry. A sensible vision in their minds doomed to fail. Ahab the nationalist allied with Sidon and married the wicked Jezebel. That depraved one provided for the spiritual needs of the people. Ahab's nationalistic alliance imported evil ideas. Ideas cross borders and subdue the populace with a bigger appetite than troops. Shirvan lacked appreciation for the debate between Eliyahu and Ahab. Who won the deliberation between spirt and nation? Eliyahu the prophet was the clear winner.

Yehu and I spent a few days in Baku's city. He recovered swift. But hosting me, changed him. He lost weight and appeared gaunt, but the flesh that remained was hard as stone. Although we detached, we continued to communicate without speaking.

We'd store our wagon in Baku's city. With warm clothing and short bows at the ready, we mounted our horses. Two additional horses carrying trade and gifts accompanied us. Shirvan sent two men for an escort to the Scythian boarder. Hence forth we'd go alone.

I asked Yehu if he missed Shomron and wanted to return. Yehu said he'd turn around his horse when he wished to return. Amidst laughter I told him to continue afoot without my horses. Ambivalent to my authority, he loved me none the less. The boring politics of small Shomron receded into the background of his mind. The northern quest superseded the trivial past life. He understood he'd never have this opportunity again and surmised he was already dead even though he had heard the prophecy from Yonah.

This is youth. I'd enjoy seeing him wake up to adulthood and accept responsibility for his family and people. I had time to spare, leaving him alone with his youthful rebelliousness and sulking. The brat developed into a fierce warrior.

Prophecy is not certainty. Yehu might be killed or experience catastrophe. I'd do my best to mother him and bring him home. The relationship baffled him. He remained hopelessly attracted to me, but my motherhood repelled him. Exposed to the bitter wilderness he'd cling to me for warmth and become embarrassed with shamed arousal. The byproduct of his desire; shame and dysphoria for what he craved, longing for the days when he lived inside my body as a woman.

At last we found ourselves alone on the cold steppe. What's the steppe? A featureless landscape of grassland as far as the eye can see. On rare instances sparse marshy woods peeked out of the countryside.

We traveled by night and bedded by day, but it didn't matter. Eventually we'd be detected out in the open. During the day, Yehu slept. I'd press against him to shield the cold wind and elusive dreams. Every day I closed my eyes in search of Sara and the one who held her body. I rose to the sky and swept the countryside for a glimpse or sense. Sometimes, I'd fall asleep and dream.

***

I dreamed a dream of water drops. There, in the cave of Adam's tomb, encased. A window of water pressed against the mouth of my sanctum—a dry dreamland; a cryptic dwelling absent of food and water.

No external light or darkness marked the passage of time in this divine nook. Hunger and thirst departed, never to return in the normal way; as if that was ever normal. I imbibed on the air of the primordial garden, which wafted in from a crack in the cave. This air kept the water at bay and sated my soul.

One day I sat staring at the ground and noticed light on the cave floor. A sliver of sun sliced through the window of water. Hours later the sun ran its course and darkness returned. The same cycle of sun and darkness ensued over the next year while the window lowered. At last, the barrier lowered enough allowing me to peer out of the cave upon the endless waters. Each day the diluvian water drops receded until I stared onto a vast swamp. After a month, the ground dried.

Years passed. I ventured out of the cave but not far. A single yearn I had: to dwell in my husband's tomb and exhaust the pleasant air of the garden.

One evening I peered at the moon and my soul stirred. I arose and walked out of the cave a solitary existence. The earth teemed with desolation as I walked hours in despair until collapsing on the forsaken ground with bleak enquiry to the soil, "Are you cleansed? Did the water of Noah cleanse the ground of Adam? Show me the enduring."

I closed my eyes and asked to see the souls that remained. A force pulled on my body; answering me; summoned to the north.

SPLENDOR. A prayer. Submission.

***

Back on the steppe I beseech the Eternal, "Show me where I'll find Sara." A pull on my body leads east across the sparse terrain. The steppe stretches east west. To the north are woodlands. We stay some bow shots away from the northern woodlands but see mounted men woofing through the trees. A group of fifteen riders emerge in front of us and raise their bows to take aim as we continue in their direction. They fire as we close the gap within bow shot. I concentrate on the lift of the arrows and bend their flight around our position. The arrows fall without harm side-by-side. It's our cue to charge. The bowmen try again to strike us with arrows but fail. They ride off in panic and confusion. Yehu rides ahead of me and slaughters the slower men with the edge of his sword.

We pursue the remaining dregs along the edge of the forest until reaching their village. Yehu rampages on horseback through the town killing men within reach of his sword. The villagers scream and shout, flee and fight. I dismount and strike anyone attempting harm on me or Yehu, but most of the people cower. The men fly off, leaving the women to scrap. Yehu mows them down with his sword and soon the village is quiet except for injured howls.

I sit in the center of the village, mortified at the carnage, while Yehu prolongs the mindless maraud. I hear a girl scream and turn to see Yehu carry the captive into a house. Yehu's behavior disgusts me. He is to be king? I enter the house and kick Yehu. Both him and the girl crumble to the ground.

I peer at Yehu and say, "You'll not rape. Where is your compassion? See how we destroyed this village. It's a horror. I shall leave you alone with her. If this girl will choose you willingly, have her. Otherwise set her free.

While he's busy, I roam the blood splattered town in search of food. I haven't been good at feeding Yehu since we left Shirvan's kingdom. Here, we'd stock up on pottage and take a few days' rest.

I cooked simple oats and walked into the house where Yehu brought the village girl. She lay on the bed while he sat in a chair nearby. I took a cloth and washed Yehu while he ate the undercooked oatmeal. The girl ladled a bowl and choked down spoon after spoon between phlegmy groans. Woe to me, saddened by this tragic place we ransacked and pathetic girl he molested.

The stray-stringy hair and oat crusted chin-approached and started to wash herself. As she picked up the cloth, I smacked her face and kicked her to the ground.

"No washing. Stay on the floor."

Shall she suppose, hope, a brutal woman shall offer comfort and niceties? Which action makes me crueler? Misguided niceties ran counter to our eventual departure. Let her be glad when we took leave. I cried inside and cursed Yehu for every mistake of my own.

I brought the horses outside our new house and went inside to watch over Yehu while he slept. The girl laid asleep on the floor nearby. She looked to Yehu as someone to raise her status. Or she loved him. None of this mattered; not the death, misery, or dirt and oatmeal.

Noise gathered outside the front door. The people returned to gather their dead. The racket upset me, fretful of waking Yehu. I told the girl to hush them. She obeyed, then returned to her floor.

The night rolled in. I laid next to Yehu and closed my eyes in search of Sara. Instead, I drifted off and dreamed of Adam, my man of the ground.

***

The ground of Adam. I walked along that barren ground toward the souls that summoned my spirit to the valley of Shinar. Their tower stood in the distance. The noxious smell of their brick kilns wafted insults as I searched for Noah, a man of waters.

I screamed to the heavens, "What do the sons of Adam do? Do they try to make a name for themselves?"

Dreams of ground and water. Earthen beasts spring to life in the putrid valley and are washed away by scolding rain. The rain ebbs and the beasts grow once more; mud men, sons of Adam, form bricks and load them into kilns. The bricks ascend higher and higher. Blood, rain, and men fall from the tower as fresh-baked bricks soar to the heavens.

This tower was their tree of knowledge. They know to the top of the tower then drop divided and confused. The valley of Shinar transforms to the land of confusion, Babel. I dream far into the future and see scholars debating the law in this valley—from confusion to cohesion.

***

I leapt to my feet with the sound of a loud crash. The door to our house is being smashed by an axe man. Yehu stands by my side while the girl cowers in the corner.

I open the door the instant before the next axe blow, setting off a destructive set of events. The inertia from the axe, missing its mark, sends the axe man hurtling forward. Yehu trips the man who falls hard on top of the girl. She, holding a knife, punctures the axe man's belly. Both lay on the ground screaming.

Yehu and I walk out into the early morning light and are met by a large crowd. A man of prominence, flanked by armed men, commands power. The villagers, slaves that is, stand peripheral. They worked the land for this master.

I confront the important man and say, "Are you the master?" Not waiting for an answer, I attack the men on his left while Yehu attacks the men on his right. The noble man stood speechless as we destroyed his entourage. Yehu grabbed a rope and tied the noble's hands together while he screamed and struggled in protest, a futile effort. Yehu grabbed the free end of the rope, threw it over a tall branch tying off on the trunk. I took a rag and gagged the noble's mouth and went back into our house. The slaves of the village stood hesitant. The villagers, fearing retribution, had no recourse but to release him the next day.

After I dragged the injured axe man out of the house, we assumed our former positions. The axe man screamed in agony from the belly wound. Despite this, Yehu fell back asleep while I sat and loathed this lodging.

The incessant noise from the wounded one drove me outside to investigate. I discovered adolescent play; a game of torment and molestation. Children encircled the prone man and jabbed his wound with sticks. I chased them away and warned the nearby villagers to preserve the silence allowing Yehu to sleep.

I went back into the house and laid next to Yehu with welcome quiet. What to do for this backward village? Yehu and I treated them harsh, but, in our defense, we defended ourselves. No shortage of pitiable villages spread out across the vast steppe.

We spent the next few days resting. Their language was familiar, but jargon took time to master. Yehu's girlfriend taught me with patience but laughed hearty at my mistakes. She forgot the assault days earlier. With the new queen and prince in the village—that is, me and Yehu—she'd fashion herself a princess. Our eventual departure, without her, was yet another painful disappointment in her life. I forbade Yehu to engage in another session of lust with the girl. It was bad enough that I treated her with kindness.

We fast became friends with the villagers since stringing up their overlord. And we bartered seashells and trinkets for food and information concerning the surrounding country. Fanciful stories, tales of demons and terrific beasts inhabiting the forests, and myths of the female warriors, in no short supply. They thought I was one of them. According to the villagers, these women, the Aibanus, kept men as slaves for procreation. The Aibanus, a legion of expert horseback archers so fanatical, legend had it, they cut off their right breast to avoid interfering with bow string accuracy.

Next, my interest piqued. The villagers talked of a mighty woman of the east, the hawk lady, who led the Aibanus—a sinister woman who kidnapped village girls to enlist in her ranks. The boys and young men she kidnapped were never to be seen again. This must be Lilith. To the east we'd find her.

When Yehu woke the following day, I leaned over and said, "We go now." I gave Yehu's girlfriend a lot of gold, but she protested our departure with indignation. We bid farewell to the crude village telling them we'd head south. We rode south, but veered east to the woods the villagers warned against entering. They claimed demons slept there.

The sun shone bright as we headed south and turned east toward the woods. We rode swift with joyous freedom having escaped that forlorn village. The steppe surrounded us on three sides. Its grass land spread out in neutral contrast to the foreboding forest. The air became cool, and the light dimmed. About a bow shot from the trees we halted. We sat still on our mounts as I projected my spirit up to the heavens. I rose high and gazed across the vast steppe, which covered the earth as far as the eye could see. The woodland we approached was a narrow green-black rivulet cutting through the steppe in the shape of a tear drop.

I returned to my saddle and thought of the choice: cut straight across through the narrow woodland or ride a day's journey to the south to circumvent the forest.

Yehu and I deliberated. He in favor of riding south. I responded to his reluctance with a smile and swift dash straight at the imposing woods. Yehu cursed and rode after me. A few paces from the trees the horses stopped and reared up on their hind legs in protest. We dismounted and pulled our reluctant horses into the woods. The forest tangled-up thick with ancient trees whose branches allowed reticent light to penetrate through the canopy.

The trees surrounded us from every side. From the steppe the woods loomed hesitant, from within, serene. The environment overwhelmed Yehu with relaxed contentment. He attempted to lie, but I encouraged him to walk forward. We moved slow through the forest as if marching through a dream. Again, and again, I urged Yehu onward.

The orange light scattered dreamy desire. The crunch of footed undergrowth satiated the body; each step, an inviting plea of blissful rest. Our steps glided without effort, but the temptation to lay pressed upon us. Yehu placed his arm across my shoulder and I dragged him forward. Mounting the horses wasn't possible. I had to pull reigns with my free hand to coax them.

On the mossy floor lie the fallen. Men scattered in various states of transformation, an appearance as if the foliage consumed them. Some covered with fresh foliage, visible intact corpses, whereas others lie encased in flossy moss. Our entry point to the forest contained fresh fallen men. Further along our journey sealed men-mounds heaped head to toe in the soft undergrowth. Some mounds contained giant men. A humanoid species from a previous time and place. The giant outline of their bodies almost indistinguishable from the cryptic floor. Yehu understood the danger but grew too overwhelmed by the urge to lie. Each step was a struggle as I urged him to continue.

For almost half a day we plodded through the thickets, thinking the eastern edge of the woods should be soon. Suddenly, a man appeared in front of us. I recognized him: the starving man I saw after leaving Shomron. For it was him I had encountered with Mara and Sara before entering the prophet's village.

The big bulbous head and emaciated body covered with ragged loin cloth greeted us unease. His small eyes, nose, and mouth crowded together in the center of his face. The throaty voice gurgled withered words I didn't understand—words only known to him; a tangled language of illiterate chatter, but for one word I understood: Chava.

For an instant my grasp slipped from Yehu who fell to the ground. I turned from the man to watch Yehu slice through the orange light. I turned back to the man, but he had disappeared.

I turned back around toward Yehu and the man reappeared.

Startled, I stepped back, tripped, and fell to the ground on my back; body arrested. My vision dimmed as I looked up at the man's loin cloth and recognized the tattered material. I grabbed Yehu's hand and drifted off to dream on a mossy blanket.

***

A treading dream across the valley of Shinar.

The great tower of Babel pierces the orange sky. Nothing of value exists outside the community. The Creator is unimportant to them. Man is unimportant to them. Only commune is important. I dream of soil—Adam's earth. I dream of water—Noah's water. The commune mixes earth and water. They bake those watery earthen bricks in the fire.

Yet, there is a man of fire! He will be the platform.

A man who destroys idols and rebels against the heretical commune.

A man who proselytizes in the name of the Almighty.

Abraham, the man of fire!

Nimrod, the mighty hunter, issues directives to the commune to bake bricks for building the tower. The kilns burn day and night. The commune work in unity. No individual man is uniquely expressed. Every soul is committed to the community, to the tower.

I stare at Nimrod in disgust. An insult, he wears the ancient cloak of Adam! I think to rip it off his body and throw him into a burning kiln. But then, the commune gathers around Nimrod with a chained prisoner.

"This one rebels against the commune..., destroys idols. He is Abram son of Terach."

Nimrod speaks, "Throw him into the kiln. Let him rebel against the fire!"

I stare with horror as the commune hurls Abraham into the fire. The body glows in the kiln. The shackles melt and fall to the ground. Abraham remains standing in the blaze, but it doesn't consume him.

Nimrod is horrified. He tries to speak, but only gibberish emerges from his mouth. The people of the commune scrutinize Nimrod with ridicule and walk far away; to the four corners of the world.

I approach the stupefied Nimrod and smote him. He tries to crawl away as I rip the cloak off his beaten body. The cloak rips except for a small piece affixed to his loin. I take the cloak and walk backward to avert my eyes from Abraham's nakedness as he emerges from the fiery kiln and dons the cloak. Yes, Abram is transforming to Abraham!

The commune becomes cut off from the root of articulation and transforms from commune to individuals; subjective conscience explodes within each woman and son. This is the generation of the dispersal.

Nimrod, in his naked loin-cloth-splendor, crawls away into oblivion. He is incoherent and unrecognizable. The kilns smolder a last gasp and the valley of Shinar exhales its former inhabitants. Abraham emerges forth with fire. In later years, he'd plead on behalf of Sodom, a city ultimately destroyed by fire. Still later, his son Isaac carried the wood of his own sacrificial fire.

I travel to Canaan with Abraham. Abraham and Sarah wander the land and spread His word. For centuries, I lived with despair. This, now, a bright dawn filled with good works. I spent time with Shem in his academy. Shem took possession of my staff from Noah. I lacked the desire to claim it. Restless, I travel to the north to visit Ashur's city.

I dream happy dreams in a womb of comfort; never wishing to awake. Tethered to the ground in peace and contentment until I realize my hand holds a hand, Yehu.

***

I open my eyes and see the splendorous orange of the forest above the bulbous head of Nimrod. An emaciated hand grabs my free hand and lifts me upward with surprising strength. Nimrod has pulled me out of the abyss of the cozy moss and assists raising Yehu. Nimrod stares dumbfounded at the two of us. He realizes we cannot understand him. I ask, "Nimrod?" He shakes his head with the faintest hint of a smile.

Yehu and I stand together, speechless. Nimrod removes his loin cloth, hands it to Yehu, takes a few steps and lays his naked body softly on the forest floor. Yehu and I continue walking through the woods and emerge onto the edge of the steppe. I gaze out onto the dreary grasslands with gratitude.

Yehu examines the loin cloth then glances at me.

"It's nice, but I suggest you wash it."

Neither of us are tempted to look back at the forest. We mount our horses and ride east.

I ponder Abraham who advanced spiritually and Nimrod who advanced physically. For each his own splendor and tomb. The double cave of Abraham is where the physical and spiritual meet. Is it not the same regarding Nimrod's grave? Both are a gateway from the physical to the spiritual.

The womb is the same as the grave; both gateways between the spiritual and physical. Sara's womb had had no license to issue a child. But a miracle occurred, and her destiny changed, thus she gave birth to Isaac. Sara transformed to Sarah by His grace. Sarah and her holy womb. When Sarah learned of the binding of Isaac, the miracle child of her womb, she died immediately and required a unique burial plot or womb. Abraham purchased a tomb, the double cave, as a womb for Sarah.

It is a womb. My Adam is entombed in this womb. As for Nimrod, his tomb is in a forest that devours the fallen. I am the first physical womb, yet to be entombed.

I rejoiced when Abraham purchased the burial cave of Sara and the surrounding field which is Hebron. Abraham purchased the plot for four hundred silver shekels. That field became elevated. Years later Jacob purchased Shechem and built an altar. Joseph's tomb is in Shechem. Many years later David purchased Jerusalem.

I thought of the spiritual nature of this land with its vast steppe. More than mere features, landscape, and climate linked nation to land. Yehu stood on land foreign to him, having no connection to this land or the forest we traversed. Yehu's land has three columns: Hebron, Shechem, and Jerusalem.

I'd find her, Lilith, running one of the columns of the Scythians.

Night fell on the steppe, and we dismounted. Yehu, a strong man, staggered off his horse exhausted. I laid down to dream of another strong man. A man I rode with ages ago.

***

I dreamed a vivid dream of a powerful, angry man. A lucid dream, a current happening, ever present. We rode with four hundred men. He planned to destroy Jacob, his brother. No earthly force could stop him. Esav, a man mistreated, abused, and trespassed. Time to set things right. Esav spoke to me.

"Jacob tricked me into selling my birthright. I came home starving and paid too high a price for his pot of food. It's true I sold it, but he took advantage of the situation, not behavior fitting of a kind brother—to give food from his heart. Isn't he held to a higher standard?

"Later, another deception. I hunted game for my father at his request. The birthright to be mine after he ate. But Jacob, the imposter, came in advance and got the blessing under guise of a tricky ruse.

"So, I ask you what shall I do?"

I said, "Esav, maybe it's not your choice. Fate awaits. Go to sleep and dream of his destruction to understand if it's possible. He has crossed his family over the Yabok River and remains alone. Esav, go to sleep and dream."

Jacob tarried on the wrong side of the river when the man attacked. A man composed of fire and water. Esav dreamed of this man, his advocate, wrestling his brother in the land of exile.

I dreamed with Esav as his advocate wrestled with Jacob all the night. They grappled an epic struggle. Mud roiled and boiled as the man of fire and water struggled with Jacob. This happened, on the ground of Adam, the water of Noah, and the fire of Abraham.

Before dawn the man struck a mighty blow that dislocated Jacob's hip, but Jacob pinned the man refusing to release him until he received his blessing. In the land of Israel's exile, Jacob received the blessing.

Esav awoke and looked at me in confusion. He acknowledged tacit agreement. Tricked again? No, his angel cosigned the blessing.

"Esav, you must accept fate. You sold him your birthright. Your father gave him the blessing, and now your advocate has blessed him. You already blessed him! Jacob will cross into his land with his family and possessions. You cannot defeat him. Greet your brother with love. No choice."

The sound of Jacob blowing the shofar pierced the dawn. Judgement occurred on the other side of the Yabok that night. At the same time, the man of fire and water sang praises of the Almighty King.

Esau and Jacob met in a loving embrace, Atonement.

Jacob traveled to Succoth.

Days were forever memorialized by the children of Jacob. Goodness morphs to place and days of joy.

I traveled onward with Esav; south to Edom. Esav and Jacob physically separated, inexorable spirits wrestle day by day since the womb. The enmity continues. Esav will always contrive a reason to hate Jacob. Was the birthright a ruse? It seemed of little consequence in the backdrop of the brothers' embrace but Esav couldn't let it go. I told him, "Let it go."

As for Jacob, he discerned his distinct destiny which did not include mingling with his brother. Esav pleaded to join Jacob on his journey but was rebuffed. It pained Esav and, once again, provoked anger and plotting. What plot? Esav volunteered to send some of his men to help Jacob on his journey. Jacob refused this offer. The people of Israel, Jacob's progeny, cannot join with the people of Edom, Esav's progeny.

A dream of chaos haunts me. The columns of the earth shake as Edom births Amalek through licentious and incestuous depravity. King replaces king with disregard for monarchial lineage. Finally, Magdiel is born. He is flesh of Nimrod's tower as Lilith has transformed evil into flesh.

A man bred a horse and a donkey, a beastly innovation. This innovation symbolized Edom. Adultery and incest abound. Eliphaz, the son of Esav, takes his daughter, Timna, as a wife. Timna spawns Amalek.

I dream of flesh transforming to place. Timna the flesh transforms to Timna the place. There, in that place called Timna, the seed of Yehuda is planted in Tamar. The seed of David flourishes like a date palm.

The children of Yehuda, the stock of those Canaanite and Moabite matriarchs, wear the crown of royalty. What crown shall the children of Amalek wear?

Evil and good morphs from force to place or person.

***

I awaken from my dream greeted by the cold barren steppe. Yehu and I stopped in every village along the way. Nothing changed. No sign of the Aibanus and no sign of Lilith. I became convinced that the stories of the Aibanus were mere peasant fables to entertain the children.

We huddled together and Yehu slept as I let my eye explore the land as a bird. Nothing but steppe and scattered villages. We slept in those villages some nights and rode most days. The seasons changed, and months turned into years. Yehu grew despondent with boredom. He needed a break, so we traveled to the northern woods in the springtime.

The crisp spring air blew delight across the rich green forest. Our senses feasted and welcomed the stark contrast to that of the steppe. The northern forest teemed with myriad life. Wondrous beasts, large and small inhabited these woods. I knew them by their rightful names and delighted in seeing these animals and the diverse flora. I mourned when Yehu slaughtered an animal for food. Perhaps I'd return here without this flesh eater.

I lived in a different time. Before the deluge we'd not think of eating meat. The seeds and herbage of the land, which was much different from nowadays, sustained our mighty generation. After the deluge is when man began to eat flesh. The body changed; years shortened. The world changed.

He, the Almighty, put a bow in the sky as a promise that He'd not destroy the world with another flood. After a rain, the bow appeared. We never saw such a site before the deluge. When the bow emerged, I averted my gaze from the seven colors out of respect for the Almighty and His leniency on the sons of man. I grew saddened by those who mocked the bow, disrespecting His gift. They thought the bow rendered them free from the Creator's judgement.

I killed beasts of men in war. Were some of my children or offspring of the fallen or spawn of Lilith? It brings me sorrow. My hands are not clean, but I wander the wide world with a clean conscience. I am the woman He created according to His will and return my thoughts to Him without blemish.

Yehu and I enjoyed our vacation in the woods. This is how we spent our years. During the cold months, we wandered the steppe in search of Lilith. In the spring, the steppe became a soggy quagmire, so we walked the woods. And why not? Maybe Lilith hid in the woods.

We grew accustomed to our routines. A normal life of wandering the steppe, huddling against the chill and chasing marauders. From time to time, we'd go to a village where Yehu took comfort in a village girl.

One winter, we got reports of Aibanus in Scythian territory. These reports appeared credible. We even met a man who claimed to escape from them. My heart leaped with anticipation to seize the fable with rational action.

Additionally, the teller told tales of Chava and Yehu, the notorious queen and prince of the steppe: the village raiders from Israel.

We rode east with Scythians eager to fight the Aibanus. It was rumored these women raided Scythian outposts on the eastern territorial boarder. We began with ten men but picked up additional riders at settlements along the way.

One night our army camped on the steppe and the men became drunk. A group of five newcomers cast shifty looks at me. I expected this occurrence and cued Yehu to wander away; a trap to snare their animal aggressions. I walked past the camp, off into the distance. Yehu stayed behind in the camp while the five men pursued me. I heard the men in the camp speaking to Yehu as I departed.

"Yehu, shouldn't you protect her? Those men will split her in two."

Yehu responded, "You should protect those men. Chava will slaughter them like lambs."

The men laughed at Yehu's indifference and continued drinking and gambling.

I stood alone, glancing back at the campfire in the distance. The five men drew close and encircled me.

One man spoke, "Take your robe off."

"It's cold. You take your clothes off."

They were now under my control. The men disrobed and stood still. Their breath condensed in the frozen air and formed an opaque barrier between me, at the center of the circle, and them.

I meditated on the misty barrier and willed it into a dense cloud. The men stood paralyzed with fear as I released my grip on their consciousness and talked to them of hunger.

"Men, your hunger is without end. Kneel before me or satisfy your lust and try to take me. If you want to live, you'll kneel.

Three of the men kneeled. Two men walked forward, searching, staggering toward my voice in the thick fog. They struggled in vain to get me. The fog lifted but the two men, blinded by their lust, continued struggling to find me. I walked behind one and kicked him hard in the back. He fell forward into the other man. The two tumbled together on the ground and thrashed at each other as I retreated from their reach.

The remaining three men, naked and shivering on their knees, peered at the two fighters. I beckoned for them to get dressed and return to the camp with me. The three men spent the night shivering speechless by the fire. Useless. How were these men capable of fighting the Aibanus?

One of the two returned from the field. I smiled at him and yelled, "Winner!" He sneered at me as the rest of the camp laughed. He took a beating but was in better shape than his foe who now lay dead on the cold steppe. The wolves picked up the scent. I closed my eyes and saw the pack; a regal green-eyed matriarch in the lead. Their pure animal souls eager for human flesh. A warrior morphs into dinner.

I inquired to the burly warrior, "Winner, what's your name?"

No response. He walked to the fire and landed a boot heal on the face of one of his comrades and began fighting with the other two. I ran over and smacked the ruffian with my staff. After he fell to the ground, I sat on top of his chest with my staff pressed against his neck. He struggled to breathe as I asked again for his name. I pressed harder, but he refused to respond. I kept pressing until he fell asleep.

One man by the fire spoke up in a bored monotone voice. "His name is Jafar. He doesn't give up, so you must keep pressing down on his neck. Frankly though, even if he dies, he'll keep being a pain in the ass. Go on, kill him and we'll see. You think he'll stop being a pain in the ass once he's dead? I doubt it. Let him sleep it off. Perhaps he'll behave better tomorrow."

Arban, the one with a dark sense of humor. The only talker of the group. Familiar with everyone, including Jafar and his fellow ruffians.

"Arban, why are we leaderless? How can we expect to confront the army of the Aibanus without a strategy?"

Arban smiled at me. "We plan as always. We attack and kill. And maybe get killed. We don't enjoy your boring plans. War is exciting and unpredictable. Why spoil the fun of war, beautiful queen?"

"Listen to me, Arban. Winning is important in war. Someone should lead us. Not me or Yehu. You."

"Oh no, not me. I came for the fun. You think I want to put myself in charge of Jafar and these others? Why not you, beautiful queen? A queen leads the Aibanus. Shouldn't a queen lead us?"

"Arban, their queen leads a group of women. We are a group of men, scoundrels, and rapists. Even if I wanted to lead this rabble, it's not my place. See here, it's to your advantage. The Aibanus maraud your villages and weaken the Scythian nation. Don't you want to collectively defeat a common foe? You defeated the Cimmerians. Be the fierce warriors that you are."

"Beautiful queen, we do not care for building a civilization and planting roots. Our villages are mobile. With towns and cities comes governance. We'd lose our liberty, warfare becoming a burden. There are leaders, but they cannot control a fluid people raiding villages, towns, and cities all over the great wide world. We don't defend, we offend."

"As you wish, Arban. We remain leaderless. But, as we get closer, Yehu and I will scout ahead. We can report back on the terrain and location of enemy combatants. Can we expect to be joined by more horsemen? How close do you think we are to the Aibanus?"

"Soon. The closer we get the more people will join since they have the most contact with Aibanus. Not only men. Our woman will also join. They lost sons and brothers to those crazy bitches. Our daughters will be eager to fight."

It was not the case. We picked up additional warriors along the way, but the reports of the Aibanus dissolved into a faded fable. Our war party longed to fight, but no aggressor came forth. So, they fought each other and raided villages on the outskirts of the Scythian territory. Yehu and I bid goodbye to Arban and the others. They traveled a lengthy distance to the east, far from their natural territory, and didn't mind turning back.

I thought deep. Were these Aibanus real? If not, who created the legend? Who benefited from creating these tales? Ha! Some men. It's easiest to invent an enemy you defeated. So powerful.

Once again, Yehu and I ventured across the dreary steppe, but here the terrain changed. Foothills and small mountains loomed in the distance. No surprise that the Scythians wanted to turn back from this alien land.

As Yehu slept, I thought of quitting this mission. I glanced at him and the peaceful dream on his face. We spent years together. I was wasting his life, but Lilith had to be stopped.

I closed my eyes and soared as a bird, scanning the surrounding landscape. I flew east toward the mountains in the distance and scanned below. This, the normal routine I did a thousand times on the steppe. But this time I gazed below, stunned by a beautiful field of wheat, such as I'd seen before. Hadn't I? This, the wheat of the prophet's village where Lilith had reaped a stalk. My mind thought back to Mara, Jacob, and the others as I glanced below at the field of wheat abutting a huge house. Lilith was there!

My mind raced all night as I waited for Yehu to awake. Finally, we'd capture her. I thought of the trouble that this evil demon caused humanity and the years we spent in pursuit.

Toward morning, I flew up once again and scanned below. I surveyed the wheat field and meadowland semi-circled by a raging river. I'd never seen a river as mighty. She roared impassable. Approaching the valley from the other side was an impossibility since steep cliffs blocked passage. I marveled at the cunning design of this unapproachable niche.

Yehu and I proceeded with stealth to a thin strip of woods. We remained far from the valley to avoid the chance of being spotted. I soared the skies and investigated the valley and its surroundings. Not a soul emerged from the house. It melted into the wall of the huge cliff standing apart from the river.

After years of roaming this vast countryside, it was time to grab our prey. I told Yehu the plan. We stood face to face. I took the earring out of my ear and handed it to Yehu.

Chapter 7

חסד (Kindness)

Two Kings and a Donkey

What's it like to be a man after living life as a woman? A dysphoria not so easy to describe. In this man's body, I disregarded my femininity, my nature. It took concentrated will to recall my real gender. A discomfort to focus on womanhood when I walked as a man. How unnatural to abandon my femininity when I walked as a man. To be a woman in Yehu's body was not possible. Remember, I came not from a rib; Adam and I were one.

Chava handed me the earring which I put into my ear. In the blink of an eye I looked through Chava's eyes at my own eyes. Chava looked at her eyes through my eyes. Once again, I transformed. What's that like after living life as a man? Not so simple to describe. To be a man in Chava's body, impossible.

It was I, Yehu, in Chava's body that handed the necklace scroll to the one that now inhabited my body. I sat on the ground with my legs crossed and gazed across the steppe toward the direction that Chava carried me, smiling as I examined myself riding away, pondering the imminent danger to my life. It was my true hope.

***

I galloped full speed toward the river with an awkward balance on the saddle to protect masculine physicality against discomfort. No, I did not fit with comfort. Was I ungrateful to my Creator for switching genders? I couldn't leave well enough alone. Oh, how dreadful a plan to capture this evil one! The entirety of my emotions cycled from guilt to anger and sadness. As I rode, my stomach became upset. This body suffered sickness. I was a woman! What was I doing in a man's form! Let me out!

It took my entire effort to continue riding forward. How I wished to turn around, place this earring in my own ear, and return to my rightful place. But, sick, I rode on toward the roaring river. Flesh shook up and down. My spirit rattled throughout the innards of this frame until I pulled up alongside the river next to a stone bridge. As I started crossing the bridge, I drifted in and out of consciousness. My eyes looked up as I dropped from the horse and glimpsed a man peering over me with shackles. Jafar, the rapist, was making me his prisoner.

Eyes closed shut as the shackles pinched wrists tight as I entered a dream of slavery and prison of Joseph's son; Jacob and his coat.

***

A dream of blessed jealousy. Nimrod's commune did not understand it. In the valley of Shinar, all individuals were obedient to the commune, even in the tower's shadow. The commune building, the tower, acted as a unit, void of jealousy or envy.

The Creator brought jealousy into the heart of man to spur the social bonds necessary for the perpetuation of the individual.

The generation of the dispersal arose from commune to individuals through envy and, yes, covetousness. That generation became individuals and dispersed. Can you, son of man, imagine existing without jealousy? You must muster obedience, for thou shalt not covet.

A dream of Joseph. The sun beat hard on Joseph's brothers. Jacob held Joseph's coat as flies buzzed on the dried blood. "An animal tore him," Jacob repeated. Was it a question or an accusation? The brothers dared not meet their father's eyes. If Jacob looked into their eyes might Joseph appear? The eyes shall betray a vision of Joseph carried off in chains to a foreign land.

Jacob gazed at the torn, bloodied tunic and rent his own clothing with a mournful cry. Many years later Potiphar's wife tore Joseph's shirt as he fled from her embrace. The Creator fashioned clothing for Adam and me when our eyes became opened. The nation of Israel was paying the price for my clothing. I wear fabric that weaves its way into the future. It was I that instigated the morph from spiritual to physical clothing, from garments of light to garments of skin.

***

The dream ended. It was I, a naked prisoner who returned to consciousness, chained to a frame leaning against a wall. This body was apprehended and dragged inside the large house after crossing the bridge: Yehu's naked body stood shackled, stripped of clothing. Jafar departed the room when I awoke.

Moments later, Lilith entered. Skins of fur did not disguise the appearance of Sara. The demon walked around the frigid room, inspecting the entire space, approached a large inactive hearth and tapped it with her finger. A raging fire erupted and lit up the room as charred smoke circled before ascending the chimney. In an instant the room became hot, inducing a sweat roll down my skin. Jafar walked over to Lilith to collect the skins of fur. Lilith was now naked except for boots and a fur cap. She approached and stared into my eyes for a long time without uttering a word then squatted and grabbed my nakedness. Her breath fell on my body as she sang while holding the organ. She took me with two hands as she rolled the tip between her fingers. At long last, she released me, stood, and peered into my face.

"You wear the physical sign of the covenant. A man far away from home. Very far."

She looked into my eyes observing my reactions as she spoke. "From Shomron are you? Soldier! Where is the woman; the traveling companion? Where's Chava?" She opened her eyes wide and smiled as if boasting her secret.

I stood silent as she twirled her fingers on my chest. Then, she took one finger and tapped the parchment box that hung around my neck. Did she identify the threat to her liberty; incapacitation if placed around her neck? She propelled the necklace on my neck from one side of my chest to the other with each of her two index fingers as she smiled at me. Was it a knowing smile? How to tell.

"Jafar, come over here and take the Hebrew's necklace."

Jafar walked over and pulled the necklace from around my neck. He lifted it over my head and Lilith said, "Go ahead, put it on."

Jafar looked at Lilith as she repeated impatiently, "Go ahead, put it on." Jafar put it around his neck and continued gazing at Lilith. "It's yours now; this strong magic from Shomron."

"Do you want to take me, Jafar? Do you want to lie with me?" Jafar, in a trance, grunted in the affirmative.

"Maybe you cannot lay with me. Maybe I'll only lay with him." Lilith pointed at me and Jafar's body trembled with lust and jealousy. "Poor Jafar cannot lay with me."

Lilith laughed at Jafar's humiliation. "Unless. Unless, he is gone. You'll kill for me Jafar?"

Jafar stood at the ready but Lilith raised her hand toward him as she approached me. "What's this, Hebrew? An earring," she said with incredulity. "I'll take it."

I gazed into Lilith's eyes as her fingernail swirled the inside of the earring loop, sending a dizzy tone through my body and my spirit, thrust into a dream as I gazed at Lilith's cap.

***

A dream of Rebecca the matriarch, wife of Isaac and mother of Jacob. Each hand was holding a goat skin. She gazes to the heavens. The fresh slaughtered goat meat lay on a table in front of her. Salty blood permeates the air. It was Rebecca's plot for Jacob to deceive Isaac and receive the blessing of the first born. Jacob deceives: two goats.

Jacob deceived: he marries Leah instead of Rachel. But all understand it is Joseph that is the first born from Jacob's intended union with Rachel. A third goat is slaughtered by Joseph's brothers. The brothers take Joseph's coat doused with goat blood to deceive Jacob: three goats.

A dream of an intersection on the road to Timna. Tamar, in the guise of a harlot, seduces Jacob's son Yehuda for the price of one goat. Yehuda deceived: fourth goat.

Yehuda went up to Timna. Samson went down to Timna.

***

I come out of the dream; face to face with Lilith. She unclasps the earring and removes it from my ear. In the instant she removes the earring from my ear, I blink my eyes and see the steppe appear before me.

***

I return to my body and Yehu returns to his. I jump on the horse and gallop toward the river with desperate fury. Although I am now in my rightful body, I can see through Yehu's eye's as I ride. Lilith pinches the earring between her fingers.

I continue to ride as fast as possible. My head screams questions as I fly across the steppe, riding across the bridge with a vision of Lilith placing the earring in her own ear.

A burning blaze tingles and pinches my organ. An ephemeral green cloud swirls around my body as I dismount from the horse and enter the house and storm into the big room. The first figure I encounter is that of Jafar holding a sword. We run straight toward each other. I leap high in the air and swing the staff, striking a fatal blow to his head.

I took the necklace from Jafar's neck. With ease, I crept behind and slipped the necklace around Lilith's neck with slipknot cinch, then removed the earring from her ear. She was under my authority.

I released Yehu from his bonds and placed the cuffs on Lilith. I doubted that the cuffs are necessary since Sara's occupant is spellbound. None the less, I hobbled her feet, restricted to half steps.

Assured Yehu was coherent, I explained, "I could exert control over Lilith when she put the earring in her ear. But I didn't have much time before she came to her senses and removed the earring. No, we could not switch bodies, for no connection exists. You are my progeny whereas she's a different creation. Even Jafar is, was, a different offspring of fallen spawn. I couldn't switch bodies with him. Not every man that walks the world are my progeny. These Scythians are not my offspring nor were many of the villagers we encountered these past years. Stay here and guard our prisoner. I'll inspect this settlement and return."

A temptation presented itself. The thought of it! Allowing Lilith into my body or becoming one with her.

The house wrapped around the cliff and was much bigger than it appeared from the riverside approach. I walked through its halls and exited the back. A small stream, a tributary of the raging river, flowed below the house. Alongside this tributary extended the wheat field far into the distance. Was this field the offspring of the wheat stalks that Lilith snatched when she fled the Prophet's village? I spotted a scythe and ran to the field reaping a few sheaths with glee. This wheat was not the same as the wheat of the Prophet's village, but this was a special place. Other than Yehu and I, not a soul could be found. Interesting! With this wheat, fresh water, and tillable land this valley could support a mass of people. The large house contained an abundance of tools and provisions.

Yehu and I stayed comfortable with our prisoner in the big house for a few weeks. This place reflected the Prophet's valley. Yes, the wheat. But here the wheat was edible. Here, same as the valley near Shechem, three pools flowed. But here the fish were tasty. It was a wealthy valley.

One bridge led into the valley. The only way to enter or depart due to the raging river, a treacherous stream. If one entered this river, they'd be swept to their death. But, wonder of wonders, the river slowed to a trickle every Sabbath. Friday at sundown, the river ceased to flow. Just before sundown Saturday night the river roared once again. We called it the Sabbath River. On Friday afternoons we sang psalms by the riverside until it ceased. All past machinations led here. Even the wretched Lilith was part of the plan! She, unwitting servant, guided me here.

Our time in the valley was ending. We spent our last day organizing provisions for the long journey ahead.

Our last night, Lilith and I sat in the house staring at each other. The scroll, taut around her neck, rendered compliance. I couldn't tell where Lilith began and ended. Where was Sara and why was I compelled, tempted, to gaze into those eyes? Was Sara awake or comatose in her own body?

I first met Sara on that balcony some years ago during the famine, but the fact is I never met the real Sara, she dwelled in Lilith's custody. I continued staring into the docile eyes as I cut her hair and painted her face with soot and red dye. It's as if I'm tormenting my little sister into an unattractive freak. The transformation complete. She, a diseased untouchable.

I let Yehu sleep late in the cozy house for the last time. A long uncomfortable journey loomed: an endless westward trek across the steppe through Scythian territory. I stayed the night with Lilith. Most days or nights I remained by her side. Exhaustingly she called to me, to play, to join in intimate union.

I trusted Yehu to guard her when I took leave but appreciated nothing could be done if the necklace slipped off Lilith's neck. I looked into the eyes of Sara and asked, "Who are you?" Again, and again I requested Sara to wake.

We loaded everything, mounted our horses, and rode with caution over the bridge, to the other side. The luscious valley and golden wheat field gave way to the monotonous steppe and pallid surroundings. A distinct delineation between the normal world and the hallowed valley.

We stopped a few bow shots from the bridge for an aerial orientation. As I recalled, the valley could only be approached from the river side via the bridge. The far end of the valley was nestled against sheer cliffs. Above these cliffs dense cloud cover concealed the land.

We rode further, and I performed another aerial survey of the valley. Yehu, exasperated by these delays, rode ahead with Sara despite my protestations. He lost patience with my orders and this adventure, a trip that aged him. Yehu was ready to be king. But if he grasped what was in store for him, he'd flee to the forest and become a hermit. A historic turmoil unfolded in Shomron and Yehuda. The two kingdoms were at odds with each other and the kingdom of Aram. But this was nothing compared to the war that wrestled within his own frame.

"A new Aramean king was anointed by Elisha. This king, Chazael, will wage war upon us. Many will die." This was prophesied.

I was reminded of this prophecy as we sped across the steppe trying my best to quell Yehu's urgency to return. "You'll arrive at the opportune time. Do not be impatient. Conserve your strength." It didn't work. He pushed us forward at a restless pace.

One night, deep in the heart of Scythian territory, we were camped on the wide-open steppe when a band of warriors approached us from all directions. Ahead of their advance, I drew a circle with my staff around our camp. I stood in the center of the circle while Yehu and Lilith sat facing each other. When the riders approached, I struck the ground with my staff. The ground cracked as blue fire shot upward and formed a circle around us. The impenetrable barrier raged that night keeping us in its cocoon while the horde circled the perimeter until losing resolve before riding off.

We three, ensconced by the fire, sat facing each other. This was Yehu's final transformation into manhood. Kingship beckoned. The transformation started by the Sabbath River on that first night we sang psalms. Now, as he sat staring at the blue flames, he was filled with spirit and purpose. Yehu glanced at Lilith, seeing only Jezebel. For Yehu there was little distinction between Lilith and the evil Queen. It was here that Yehu's wrath for the house of Ahab ignited.

Yehu despised Shomron and the hypocrisy of the ruling class. Isn't that really why he fled on a mission to capture me for raiding the Baal temple in Shomron? The house of Ahab had ceded the sovereignty of the northern kingdom, to Jezebel. That harlot's son, Yoram, reigned.

I marveled at Yehu's face, glowing against sapphire blue flame as he stared at Lilith. His fury bloomed. Me, grateful, he walked away from Chava, the mother. No longer sleeping by my side. Instead, I slept inside. I knew him.

I observed Sara too. Her bald head and face were dirty with soot, but her eyes were sharp in the blue light. I could see through the transparent brown eyes of Sara into the icy green depth of Lilith's eyes.

What lurked in the icy abyss? Something unique and tempting? It was the same unbridled lust for power as Jezebel. These two women were the same, but Lilith was primordial evil brought into the physical. Lilith, in Sara's physical form, was much more dangerous than Jezebel.

I thought of the irony that Sara hosted Lilith. For it was Sarah, Abraham's wife, who was derived from me, my soul correction.

"Is that what you desire Lilith? A rectification of spirit?" She answered not.

***

I looked deeper into her eyes and departed the current world. Surrounded by green fog. It dissipated, and I was back in the primordial garden. There, Adam and Lilith locked in an embrace on the green grass. Their bodies were transparent. My eyes bore through their flesh to the emerald lawn below. The two rolled together, fighting and copulating. They continued to struggle until Lilith sat on top of Adam and screamed. Lilith shattered like a glass statue exploding into shards melting the grass and seeping into the earth. I sprung back into the present. A smell of burned grass lingered.

***

I sat across from Lilith and turned my gaze to the approaching dawn. The sapphire blue flame was no more. Yehu looked at me from atop his saddle and said, "We go now."

As soon as I stood up, I sensed the arrows whizzing at us and bent them above. I grabbed my staff and waited for the attack. Yehu jumped on his horse with bow drawn as two riders charged him. Yehu fired two arrows that struck each rider above their fish scale armor. Both riders fell from their horses with arrow shafts in the lower region of their throats. More riders approached and fired upon us. Again, their arrows flew above our heads. And again, Yehu fired his arrows with a pinpoint accuracy rendering the Scythian armor useless. Eight men were on the ground dead. The remaining warriors kept their distance.

Yehu dismounted and affixed Lilith onto her horse. The three of us rode away. The Scythians trailed us, but they kept at a distance out of bow shot. After some time, they abandoned pursuit and rode east. Incidents like this had been common for us on the steppe in Scythian territory. But these men were in league with Lilith, summoned by her. What games she plays as I gaze distracted into the green fog.

It took a few days, but we arrived at Baku's village, Shirvan's guests once again for two nights. During our visit we heard news from Shirvan about the happenings of Shomron and Yehuda.

Yoram, king of Shomron and Achaziah, king of Yehuda, the northern and southern kingdoms, joined forces against Chazael, king of the

Arameans. Yehu stirred with anticipation upon hearing this news. He knew this was afoot but hearing it spoken was too much to endure. The inactivity was oppressive. Yehu stood up and stared at me. I nodded at Yehu, and he departed.

In an instant our time together ended, but I could still see through his eyes and communicate with him as he rode south across empires to meet his fate in Gilead.

I prepared the wagon for my journey to the holy temple for Lilith to meet her own fate. This, the wagon left in Shirvan's custody years ago. It supported a cage of iron bars, Lilith's home. I placed skins as a covering so as not to attract attention from curious eyes.

We departed Baku's village a few hours after Yehu. Like Yehu, we were accompanied by Shirvan's escorts until we reached the kingdom of Ashur. When I reach Ashur, there was a saddened goodbye to Shirvan's men. I ride alone, save for the bound demon in the wagon, but I could see where Yehu was riding, making my state of mind unbearable. Perhaps I should have coaxed Shirvan's men to stay with me for company. How foolish. I had prayed for solitude, but now I was cursed with loneliness. It shouldn't be, but it was the price for knowing Yehu.

I sang psalms while bouncing on that wagon seat day and night plodding on to Nineveh with thoughts of crazy Yonah and his fiery call to repentance. I approached the gigantic wall of Nineveh toward dusk. It took until dawn before I passed the massive stone fortification. It was a great city.

***

I close my eyes and witness Yonah's prophecy regarding Yehu. Elisha, the master, tells Yonah to anoint Yehu, son of Jehoshaphat. Yehu and Yonah travel on different paths that is the chaos known as Israel, both riding to Gilead.

Days pass and Yehu arrives in Gilead on the heights above the Yabok River with many cohorts. Yonah arrives and takes Yehu into an inner chamber and anoints him with oil. Yehu has been coronated king. Yonah speaks to Yehu in the words of the Almighty, "You shall smite the house of Ahab to avenge the blood of my servants and prophets at the hand of

Jezebel." Without warning, Yonah bursts out of the chamber and flees Gilead.

The officers chuckle bemused at Yonah scurrying off into the distance. When Yehu emerges from the chamber the officers ask Yehu what the crazy man wanted with him. Yehu responds, "You know the man and what his talk was about."

The officers, stunned by the prospect of insurrection, said, "Tell us it's false." Yehu could not tell them, thus they knew it was true. An officer blew the shofar, and they proclaimed Yehu king.

There, above the Yabok, I hear the echo of Jacob's shofar when he prevailed against Esav's emissary.

Every rut on the road courses through my body along the Rift valley toward Jericho while maintaining the vision of Yehu and many men on the heights of Gilead. The Almighty spirit rests upon them. I hear Yehu shouting, "To Yezreel we ride. We go now."

Yoram was wounded in a battle with Chazael, the Aramean, and fled to Yezreel. Yehu and the men ride with fury from Gilead to attack Yoram, the faltering king of Shomron.

Yehu and his band of men cross my path, south of my location, on their way to Yezreel.

In Yezreel, a tower sentry spies riders approaching. Yoram instructed a rider to ask of them, "Is it peace?" Meaning, peace in Gilead or peace for Yoram? Yehu responded to the horseman, "What's peace to you, turn around and come ride with us." Again, Yoram sends a rider to Yehu. Again, another rider joins Yehu's insurgency.

The sentry announces, "He rides furious, like Yehu."

Yoram king of Shomron and Achaziah king of Yehuda, the northern and southern kingdom, ride out on their chariots to meet Yehu.

Yoram shouts, "Is it peace, Yehu?"

Yehu replies, "What peace with your mother Jezebel the harlot and witch!"

Yoram rides back to tell Achaziah that it's treachery, but Yehu seizes his chance and shoots an arrow. My eye follows the flight of the arrow as it penetrates deep into Yoram's back, between the ribs; straight through the heart.

Achaziah tries to flee but is smote by Yehu's men. He flees to Megiddo and dies from his wounds.

That is the story of Yehu's coronation as king of the northern kingdom (Shomron) and of Yehu's victory over Yoram and Achaziah. In a mundane moment, the king of Israel was disposed and replaced and the king of Yehuda died of his wounds.

I continue southward in the wagon, now passing the valley of the children of Eden in the shadow of Gilboa. I sulk with guilt, having no time to visit. I pass by the areas of warfare and travel onward without event on the road to Jericho. From Jericho, I ascend west to the Temple.

On the way, I encounter slaves gathering wood. They glance at me and the wagon with momentary curiosity and return to their work. I pull off the roadside, glance back at Lilith, then lay on the wagon seat peering up at the stars. I open and close my eyes imagining Joseph's dreams. Might he answer how stars bow? How do you, Almighty Father, bring dreams into the physical realm?

A dream of Joseph carried off by slave traders to Egypt. A comely boy who fetched a good price, a wise and knowing servant in the house of Potiphar. Even when he was thrown into jail, his fellow inmates perceived his wisdom and knowledge.

***

Potiphar's wife rips Joseph's clothing. Pharaoh replaces it with a fine flax garment. A flash, the brothers douse Joseph's coat with goat blood. Another flash, Cain offers flax on the altar. The dream stretches from Cain's careless flax to Joseph's fine flax garment.

***

The ride from Jericho to Jerusalem was crowded with pilgrims. The land is in turmoil with news of King Achaziah's demise and the resultant power vacuum. Who from the line of David will assume the throne? It must be from David's progeny.

The wagon teeters uphill to the old city. From a distance I marvel at the straight column of smoke rising to the heavens. The holy fire consumed the offerings and its smoke rose to the sky undisturbed by earthly forces. Even from this distance I smelled the incense burning while the priests cleaned the menorah. A stray goat sneezes before scurrying off to escape the incense. As I move forward to His dwelling place on earth, I am consumed with fear. The wagon creeps through the thickening crowds of visitors and merchants until we arrive at the city wall.

I quarter the horses and wagons at a stable and prepare Lilith for the journey on foot into the city of David. I wash Lilith and pull the cloak over her stubbled head. A stare, for the last time, into the murky green sea of Lilith's eyes. Chaining her hands together; a strange sensation of holy incense combined with evil green circulates in my veins. Both of us are cloaked as we traverse the city streets. Staff in right hand, chain leash in the other, I lead the way.

The city is in an uproar. There is bitter mourning for king Achaziah; he who Yehu hath slain. Achaziah, who ruled Yehuda, is gone. He has been replaced by rumors and conspiracy. Atalya (daughter of Jezebel, mother of King Achaziah) lurks in the background plotting and scheming. She covets power.

The splendor of the city and glory of the temple outstrip the mourning for Achaziah. The incense permeates the air and fills my lungs. Holy smoke courses through my blood stream as it soothes my brain. I glance back at Lilith and peer under her cloak. The incense has no effect on her. But the green mist lingers in my blood.

"It seems you arrived right on time."

I turn around startled by the words and sight of the Prophet.

"Good morning. I'm glad you were expecting me."

"I only arrived yesterday afternoon. Tell me how you enjoyed the northern country these past years? I understand you spent an inordinate length of time with the new King of Israel. Also, you discovered the village of refuge and understand your task?"

"I hold nothing to tell. You're a discerning prophet. You understood the journey I took with Yehu. What don't you know? The first time we met, that time in the study hall in Shomron when you asked of Mara's status. I recalled it wasn't the first time we met. How do we know each other? Who are you, really? There are no further tasks for me."

"Chava, I shall not interfere with your dreams or reality, nor do I control the choices of man. But I witness the consequences of those choices on the children. You don't care about answers do you? Evil nips at your heels. Watch out!"

I squint with confusion at the Prophet as he summoned two men forward. Each man held an arm as they escorted me through an alley away from the Prophet and Lilith.

I heard the Prophet speaking in my head, "Rest Chava and dream a vision of Lilith and Jezebel. Don't vex; your mission was successful."

The two men led me into a small house. A family sat inside eating at a table. It seemed like a husband and wife with two young daughters. The wife rose and began speaking with one of my escorts about lodging. Finally, the woman motioned for me to follow. We proceeded down a corridor to a bedroom. She smiled while gesturing me into the room, then sped off.

I shut myself in the room and closed my eyes as I reclined on the bed. I tried to follow the Prophet and Lilith into the temple, but a different vision barged forth: It was Yehu returning victorious in celebration.

And then, my vision of Lilith returned.

***

Two priests tied each of her hands to adjacent poles. Another priest ripped her shirt exposing her bare flesh from the waist upward.

Again, my vision was interrupted; Jezebel stands in a high tower painting her green eyes with black outline. I move deep inside her eyes, immersed in a green fog.

I pulled back, and the vision changed to Lilith's eyes. The vision, a dizzying back-and-forth nightmare.

Lilith gazed forward looking at the priest who held a cup.

Jezebel gazed out of the tower window at the approaching riders.

Jezebel's green eyes look down from the tower window. She says, "Is it peace, Yehu?"

Lilith's green eyes. The priest says, "Drink Lilith."

Jezebel is thrown from the tower.

Lilith drinks the bitter sotah water.

Green dust erupts into a billowing cloud.

The green dust settles onto the ground sparkling beneath the tower. With indifference, the ground of Jezreel drinks Jezebel's blood while hungry dogs devour Jezebel. Only her skull, feet, and palms remain.

The scene changes to the temple courtyard. I'm staring into big brown eyes. The brown eyes reveal a soul of beauty and kindness. The brown eyes exude relief. Sara lives! I was successful. Physicality of Lilith ceases to exist. It is Sara inside the temple walls wearing a cloak. Another woman, one of royalty, approaches Sara with an infant boy and places the crying baby in Sara's arms. The baby suckles Sara's breast, which miraculously issues forth milk. Sara shivers as she is hugged by the woman. The Prophet and two emissaries lead Sara past the temple alter toward the inner sanctuary.

Yehoyadah, the head priest, guides Sara and the infant king Yoash into the holy of holies. This is Sara's reward for surviving the trial of the bitter waters. Sara will nurture the baby King in this holy hiding place. I look on as Sara and baby Yoash walk into the inner sanctuary. Sara walks up to the curtain that hangs in front of the Holy of Holies. She turns back to face Yehoyadah who coaxes her inside.

Sara enters through the outer curtain gap on the left and transverses the corridor—curtained on both sides—until reaching the inner curtain gap. The Holy Ark remains in the center of the chamber. Two golden cherubim face each other on top of the lid. Sara sits cross legged on the floor holding the infant king and closes her eyes. They sit comfortable and safe in the sparse room underneath the cloud of glory.

I blink. My vision fixates on the green fog permeating the city of David. I gaze into the green eyes of Atalya, Jezebels daughter. Atalya pours powder into a decanter of wine. The wine changes color from red to green and back to red. Atalya, mother of Achaziah, schemes to take the throne. She cares not for losing her own son. Does she care to avenge the blood of Achaziah? No, she cares little about Yehu and the blood he shed in Megiddo.

Atalya will poison the descendants of David. She's unaware that baby king Yoash lives in the Holy of Holies with Sara the wet nurse. Yoash, from the seed of David, lives.

***

I wake up in the house in Jerusalem. The holy city is clouded with green poison billowing through the streets and alleys, slaughtering the offspring of David. Queen Atalya's poison lays waste to the offspring of David. She kills her children and grandchildren. Yoash will survive, but I am repulsed by this evil plot and make haste to flee. I burst out of the room to the main area of the house; my body wracked with coughing fits of green dust.

The room is empty. Was this house ever inhabited? How long was I cloistered inside? Was the family an illusion? Too many questions with answers I choose not to know. Cursed be the annoying Prophet and evil green fog! Oh Father, what demarcations have you posted between good and evil?

I'm done in the kingdom of Yehuda. No reason to stay. Yehoyadah, the head priest, will teach Yoash to be a king. It is guaranteed; a coup will come. Must I be involved? If only to make myself believe, I repeat aloud, "The kingdom of Yehuda shall prevail without my help." But I know I speak falsehoods.

As I flee Jerusalem, I curse my red heart. I question myself and my feelings. Why am I racing back to Shomron? Was this the price of making him my slave or communing with the green fog? Who is the slave now Chava? He's King of Israel. Is there something in Shomron for me? I cry when I realize that I haven't thought of Adam since I stood at the Shabbat River singing *the* psalm—Adam's psalm—with Yehu. Is that when it happened? Is that when I became infected with fantasies of love? My body burns with a passion for Yehu. All those nights we spent huddling together I spurned his lust. Yehu departed and took with him my prudence and rationality. I try to push thoughts out of my head, but my body does not obey. I'm dragged to Shomron against my wishes. Losing control of my own will. Oh Father, why have you abandoned me?

I think of his body against mine, but I cannot maintain an image of his face. It's as if I cannot remember his appearance. Could I even distinguish him from others in a crowd? I cannot remember his face!

I walk through day and night bemoaning having left my mount in Jerusalem.

Soldiers abound. I give no heed to the bands of Aramean marauders and Israeli troops nor their skirmishes. At night I ambush Aramean men with my sword. It's a distraction from my thoughts. I kill many and capture slaves to sell in Shomron. The collared men follow me up the main road to Shomron. They stumble in disgrace, hobbled to one another. The Arameans are fleeing to their lands. Yehu has vanquished them.

I pass through Yezreel and cut the prisoners loose. Wearied am I of their moaning and suffering. Some cry in gratitude while others stumble off toward the east. Two of them lost their sanity and only cease following me when I beat them. I chase them away and continue walking alone thankful for the newfound solitude. As soon as silence prevails, I hear wagons to my rear and wait for them to catch up to my position. I stand in the middle of the road blocking their passage. I know it, these wagons are for Yehu.

I inquire, while blocking the road, "What do you haul in your wagons?"

"Get off the road, or we'll run you down."

I approach the lead horse placing my hand on its nose. She'll halt until I tell her to continue. I walk past the wagon driver and inspect his load. The wagon is filled with severed heads in baskets. I motion to the other wagons and say, "And those wagons also haul heads? Heads of the house of Ahab for Yehu? I'm coming up. You'll take me with the heads."

Before the wagon driver has time to protest, I climb up on the seat next to him. He speaks, but he is cut off as the lead horse lurches forward. We roll toward Shomron and I'm reminded of the days I hauled Lilith to Jerusalem. I sing and think of Yehu as we ride along. My concentration falters. I lose control over my appearance. My skin has changed complexion from olive to ebony. The driver, looking at me instead of the road, is spellbound by my beauty. Blood drips from his nose. I throw him into the bed of the wagon with the heads and continue riding the rocky road to Shomron. An intact body is an oddity; the jealous heads protest thee.

I continue singing with too little care for my radiant beauty and let my guard slip; my skin changes from beautiful ebony to transparent glass.

Whoever gazes upon me now will surely die. With some guilt I exercise restraint and return to ebony. All who gaze become stupefied by the beautiful black woman shedding green tears.

The gruesome cargo I haul, for Yehu, was arranged by the leaders of Yezreel. Yehu had sent word to them, a challenge, to appoint a king from the seed of Ahab. These heads are a sign of their allegiance to Yehu. The house of Ahab is no more. The friends of Ahab are no more.

I hop off the wagon seat before it lurches to a stop at one of the city gates.

I have long since resumed wearing my normal complexion but am still commanding the curiosity of bystanders.

I cover myself with cloak and move through streets and back alleys leading to the palace. On the way is Sara's courtyard. I think to enter the gate. Not yet.

I locate an entrance into the palace and sneak inside the main sanctuary. Excitement rushes through me, shaking with the sound of Yehu's voice booming through the chamber, trembling as I lurk among shadows creeping closer to Yehu. His voice, raspy and distinct, instructing the men to place the seventy heads in their baskets on the sides of the city gates.

Moving closer, I recognize Yehu's family. The sinister uncle; he's Yehu's adviser! My heart sinks. As I walk toward the group, I spot Yehu's uncle whispering fatal advice.

Yehu speaks, "Ahab served Baal a little, but I will serve him much."

With that utterance my love for Yehu flickers away like a candle's flame. Yehu's evil uncle and his plot to ensnare the Baal priests has released me and condemned Yehu. A final green tear falls from my eye.

Nobody sees or hears me as I say, "Words matter Yehu. Especially for a king."

I walk out of the palace without another glance at Yehu. Does he spot me; is his curiosity aroused by the cloaked figure walking out of the palace? I spent years with him. Shall I be blamed for not teaching better?

He accomplished his goal by feigning servitude to Baal and tricked those worshippers into wearing their vestments so they could be identified and decapitated. Yes, the house of Baal would be transformed into a garbage dump. But this was the present. For the king hath spoken and, in time; "will serve Baal much." Who tricked whom?

This is the story of Yehu and how he became king of Shomron. Some of this story has been written. What does it matter? Yehu became king, and he sinned.

Yehu learned much. But the influence of his advisers and ego would destroy him and weaken Israel. My love for Yehu departed, but he gave me chaos. Before we switched forms, I seldom fought. I fled from fighting. Living in his body rendered me a warrior. Might his influence ever depart? And how did I influence him? It didn't show. I mean, how did he say such a thing? I'd never! No part of me could say that, not in jest, deception, or any context. Where did the venal desire for idolatry originate? Baal!

***

Serpent, you know this is not the end of the story. In fact, it's the beginning of a short story that has no end. Herein is the story of Kindness; merciful blue waters.

Violence it shall be. I will wage war against the internal invaders, the idolaters, and the nations I despise. I'll spread chaos and fear in the lands of Aram, Edom, and the Philistines.

In Shomron, I bought a fine bow with three quivers filled with arrows, a light sword, and daggers. I needed none of this. Soon it would be discarded. But I bought a horse and a special donkey. Oh, what a special donkey!

With my new possessions I maneuvered my way through the streets of Shomron to that courtyard I knew so well, Sara's courtyard. The poor donkey buckled under the weight of sacks filled with coal and glass shards. I entered the courtyard, staff in hand; an unthreatening, well-armed lady. To a casual observer I was a young servant girl or daughter of an army officer.

A young family inhabited Sara's house. That's not why I came. On the other end of the courtyard was the telltale sound of the Blacksmith's hammer. I walked toward his workshop and breathed the scent of sintered sweat. Mounds of ingots and slag lined the corridor of the rough workshop. The furnace burned in the center of the room. The blackened sweaty beast of a man banged on metal with rage and despair. I made not a sound nor cast a shadow, but he perceived a soul and raised his head. The gigantic Blacksmith turned toward me still holding the huge hammer in one hand. Not knowing what to do, he froze in place. His bare dirty chest, as big as a barrel, heaved in and out with every breath.

He was insane! What mortal hammered away at molten metal without a leather vest? His torso and arms were blistered. My skin shade changed to a light ebony as I walked in front of him. His eyes looked downward into mine. I raised my index finger, licked it, and drew a line on his chest revealing blistered flesh underneath layers of soot. I whispered, "You owe me, Blacksmith. Pay your debt." The Blacksmith started to stammer. I licked my other index finger and whispered seductive as I placed my wet finger on his lips, "Do you remember me? You told the guards about Sara, didn't you?" The Blacksmith shook his head in the affirmative. "How could you betray her? Were you not a friend?"

My finger picks up hot breath. As I spoke, he thought of Sara. The vision transmitted through my finger, a clear image of Sara standing behind the Blacksmith's body, messaging his huge shoulders with her small hands. Lilith tormented the Blacksmith's mind. But it was the Blacksmith that frustrated Lilith. This was a man that didn't defer to lust. He refused her.

The vision receded further into the past. The Blacksmith, years earlier, with a wife and baby son living across the courtyard from a young couple; Shimon the baker and his wife Sara. The famine crept into their lives and took what they held dear. The Blacksmith banged day and night. His tears sizzled on the scolding metal as his heart burned with the loss of his wife and little boy. The only way he maintained purpose in his life was by taking care of Sara and her child. He didn't want to possess her after she became possessed. Yes, he saw when Sara fell under Lilith's control, but he took care of her. This sensitive grief-stricken man had maintained his sanity by becoming warden of a demon.

I gaze into the Blacksmith's eyes and am blown backward by the reflection of Sara's brown eyes and Lilith's green eyes. All this from the simple brown eyes of the Blacksmith, a righteous man.

I walk around the shop and inspect the Blacksmith's work: axe heads, swords, and knives alongside plowshares and hoes. I walk back to the giant. My head is level with his chest as I look upward and say, "Blacksmith of fire, fashion thyself an axe forged in the fire of Abraham. Build yourself a giant axe to wield against the idolatry that has spread through the land. Build me a sword to wield against the idolaters that dwell in the land."

I reach out and grab the Blacksmith's arm as he turns toward the woodpile. "No, fetch the sacks of coal on the donkey. Also, the iron ingots. Prepare, then go purify yourself in the blue waters. I'll stay here and monitor your forge and prepare something to add to your iron. Continue building the furnace fire, but wait for me before you forge."

The Blacksmith did as he was commanded. Soon I was left alone to prepare the final ingredients of the iron. I walked over to the donkey and relieved her of the glass shards, shells, and plants.

I sang as I rubbed her hide with a strong brush then placed a bucket underneath for her urine, which she gave. Into the bucket go the plants. The shells and glass shards must be ground into a powder using a large stone mortar before incorporating. I ground, poured, and combined the final mixture. The Blacksmith never worked iron like this.

I departed the courtyard and went to the woman's ritual bath to purify myself. Inside the chamber a woman glances at my naked body and motions for me to remove my earrings and rings. Afterward, I assemble in a line of naked women waiting for my turn to submerge in the kind blue water. I meditate about the iron and our task as I wait.

Before submerging I conjure a vision of Abraham standing next to his donkey, knife in hand. Abraham's son, laden with wood, struggles to walk up the holy mountain. I submerge into the water of the ritual bath with Abraham freeing a ram from a thicket and slicing its neck in place of his son. The cool water of the ritual bath transforms to warm sticky blood. I stand up, coated in blood, and walk up the steps out of the bath. As I emerge the red blood transforms to blue water.

The crowd of naked women wear bored expressions as they file in and out of the bath. No naked soul perceived this bloody vision. I make haste to get dressed, collect my jewelry and depart this unpleasant place.

Once I'm back in the shop, I instruct the Blacksmith who then labors away making iron. He works, and I sing. The forge burns hot, but the room remains cool as I blow the heat away with song. I stare at the iron as the Blacksmith folds and hammers the glowing red mass of the axe head. Hours later, the axe head is finished. With the approaching dawn the sword is finished. The exhausted Blacksmith retires. I stand alone in the workshop and listen to the sword sing songs as I wave it in the air. I take a suitable piece of wood and begin singing while I carve a handle for the axe. Hours later the Blacksmith awakens, and I hand him the carved handle. He's impressed by the fine workmanship and intricate carving. He gazes at the writing on the handle and reads the phrase, *"And He hath brought upon them their own iniquity and will cut them off in their own evil."*

I reply, "Yes Blacksmith, you read and understand. This axe and sword were forged with the fire of Abraham. Relax now. Tomorrow we go."

The Blacksmith and I departed the city before dawn and head north. He looked peculiar outside the familiar environs of the workshop. I walked in front with the donkey as he trailed on horseback. The Blacksmith started to talk once we were away from the city. The open road or absence of banging morphs the righteous man. A change of scenery a miracle.

After traveling a few hours, I ask him to dismount and proceed on foot to give the horse respite.

"Why don't you load that donkey with our supplies? You're carrying a big load. My horse is also carrying a lot of weight. Put some on the donkey. Why don't you ride the donkey?"

"This is a special donkey. She shouldn't bear a burden."

"So, the donkey's job is to walk alongside of us? What use is that?"

"Special donkey."

"This is ridiculous! You're carrying a lot of weight and now I'm walking. How far must we go? Shouldn't we have brought a donkey that isn't special? Anyway, it's not special. It was loaded with supplies yesterday. Explain that!"

"Those were special supplies needed to forge the axe and sword. But you are correct. I'll affix the axe and sword to her. She can carry those."

"Is that all she'll carry? The axe and sword weigh little. She can carry much more."

"Nope. Special donkey. And now she needs water. And another thing. A forgotten thing. First, we'll go to the town of Geba. Rather, the donkey needs to go to Geba."

The Blacksmith took every step with frustration. He was a tense man, even more at present since he was outside his normal surroundings. He was built for the workshop. In his entire life had he ever been away from Shomron? That's why he was speaking so much and that's why I engaged him in conversation. This journey was a shock to his emotions. All those years he spent banging away in his workshop, coupled with the loss of his family, cast the Blacksmith into an unmalleable ingot.

"Geba! That's near Jerusalem. It's south. Why are we traveling north?"

"Yes, we must turn around and go south before we can go north. It's the long-short way, which is much better than the short-long way."

The donkey let out a loud bray drowning out the protests of the Blacksmith. "Listen Blacksmith. You think of your own inconvenience, but you can hear the donkey is worried. Come on, let's go quick. We must change course to Geba.

We arrived in Shiloh that evening. I secured lodging for the Blacksmith and let him alone to eat and sleep. I did the same with the special donkey and horse.

With hurry, I doubled back to a farm we had passed on the way to Shiloh. I befriended the farmer and bought a ram lamb of about one month old. The little ram followed me on the dark road back to Shiloh, staying close for fear of the jackals yelping nearby. The little ram became relaxed when I brought him into the stall with the donkey and soon fell asleep.

I stood in a field to the east of the stables and gazed out on the horizon while singing psalms. I let out a sigh with the dawn and stood still as the sun rose to inspect my beauty. The blazing host beamed its light on the rocky plane asking nothing more than to serve the will of its Creator. I thought aloud, "Good sun."

The loud braying of the donkey disrupted my meditations. I went back to the stall to catch the little ram lamb harassing the donkey with his play. "No little ram. This is a special donkey, and she lacks patience for your games." The obstinate ram thrust its skull into the belly of the donkey who emitted a series of loud brays. "I said stop it, naughty ram!"

I took the ram out of the stall and waited outside the Blacksmith's lodging. He emerged well rested but grumbled about the journey and sidetrack to Geba.

"Chava, where did you get the young ram? It's yours? Why do you need it?"

"You're the one who needs the ram. And the donkey. I need you to buy the ram and donkey from me. How much money do you have? Before you answer, understand that your life depends on this."

KINDNESS. Loving thy obligations.

Chapter 8

חוכמה (Wisdom)

Not a Prophet

Yes, most different from Yehu. A simple, devoted family man, but a man none the less. The gentle giant could transform into a warrior and kill in the most horrible way. Like Yehu in this respect. A donkey shall help him.

"I have no money! Who shall feed me? I'm not concerned with acquiring this donkey and lamb!"

"Yes, you will be concerned," I shouted.

Then, I continued in gentleness, "You know me. Do you believe you can refuse my request? Please trust, you must acquire the animals from me willingly. You'll serve me as a bondservant until your debt is paid."

Relaxed, calm washed over the Blacksmith's face as he accepted indentured servitude and said, "I will serve you as a slave in exchange for this donkey and lamb."

On cue, the donkey brayed her approval signaling her time was close.

The donkey walked compliant to the Blacksmith on one side as the lamb nestled against his leg on the other side. The Blacksmith looked at both animals and then stared at me with a bewildered expression of resignation on his face.

"Acquisition is completed, Slave. You own the donkey and the lamb. I own your labor until the debt is paid."

It happened that evening that the Blacksmith became tired and hungry as we set camp by the roadside, far from Geba. The Blacksmith was accustomed to hard work but was unaccustomed to spending nights outdoors. I prepared his bedding and built a fire. The Blacksmith drifted off to sleep after a supper of bread, cheese, and wine. We watered the livestock earlier, and they grazed content nearby; the lamb was always near the donkey.

It was my choice to dwell in a world of action even though I foresee the outcome and the chain of events born from those consequences. I closed my eyes to those outcomes and deceived myself with skill. And now, it shamed me. I dreamed a dream of Sara, Lilith, the steppe, and the Sabbath River. So now, the outcome of my plan was plain to see, and I couldn't answer why I pursued this course of action. If I did nothing, I could expect the same ending! Why do this?

Why? The mortal man sees death waiting. What is the sum of thy machinations between a man's birth and death? It is the same beginning and outcome. The answer lies beyond the ethereal limitations of the infinite. Accessing that holy realm occurs here in the world of action, the finite realm. Oh, is it possible to cast off the infinite and live as a mortal in the finite world of action? Instead, I flee the constrained world of the infinite. How and who is me who lives immortally to chase delineations and boundaries? Madness, folly shall be my pursuit.

***

Do you wonder what the people see? How do they see you?

A young lady and a man strode into Geba one afternoon with a horse, donkey, and lamb. The young lady appeared to be twenty years of age. The man appeared to be much older. How much older? Hard to say. Was he thirty or forty years of age? Years of toil tell a tale of weathered face and stormy years. What were they doing on this road together? Were they married or was she his daughter? The woman dressed strange; she wore a large cloak and held a shepherd's staff. Wayward hair escaped from her hood and lay across her chest. She walked lightly even while carrying a large load of supplies. The big man trailed behind, carried nothing, but stumbled as if exhausted. The donkey carried no burden except for a large axe and sheathed sword.

Residents of Geba witnessed this on the day the Blacksmith and I came to town. But it wasn't unusual. I passed through Geba from time to time over the centuries and was a familiar guest. Young mothers recognized me as we walked into town. They were young girls the last time I strode this road. Old women recognized me. They themselves were young mothers when they saw me last. Soon, a crowd gathered and began touching me with affection. Chava, their old friend, who never got old. Joyful mundane miracles for them; some called me Chava's daughter.

The women led the Blacksmith and me to a shady spot and served lunch. I became caught up in the meeting's joy and ate bread; choking on the first bite, having not eaten in months. The women laughed and gave me a cup of water as my face turned red from embarrassment at the attention. The Blacksmith sat alone staring at the food as he ate. He averted his eyes from the merriment until one older lady asked if she could pen his animals. The Blacksmith nodded his consent with stoic resignation.

The woman returned after penning the donkey and lamb and said, "I see that donkey is due. It's the first issue of her womb, no? That's why you come."

"Yes, the Blacksmith's donkey, he has brought a lamb to redeem the first issue. Might we stay till the donkey gives birth?"

"You can stay as long as you wish, Chava. But don't stay away so long next time. We cannot get so old before we see you again. A day for you is a year for us."

"Tell us stories! Where have you been?"

I replied, "Where are your men? To whom shall the Blacksmith redeem the newborn donkey?"

"It's their watch at the Temple. They are in Jerusalem serving. No matter, Barak will redeem the newborn."

"Very well. I'll tell you stories. Do you want tales of the new king, Yehu? He is a powerful warrior on a mission to drive idolatry from Israel. At last, the house of Ahab has been cut off and the land will be cleansed of the vile filth of Jezebel's gods! See that man, the Blacksmith, and his big axe? We will visit towns and destroy their poles and statues. I'll wield that sword." I pointed to the sword and placed my staff against a railing. "Take my staff and put it in safe keeping."

One woman summoned a young man to take the staff and instructed him to put it away. The young man picked up the heavy staff with ease. Too easy for him to lift.

"Boy, what's your name and where are you taking my staff?"

"My name is Barak. I'll take…" I interrupted him, "Why aren't you with the other men serving in the Temple?" The boy held up his left hand, drawing attention to a physical deformity; webbing between two of his fingers, which rendered him unfit to perform priestly duties. A heartbreaking dilemma for a boy of Geba, a city of priests. He was deficient, forbidden to serve in the temple.

"Barak, you hold the staff with ease, so you shall hold it. I'm taking you on a trip north where you can inspire service to the Almighty."

Barak glanced above my head and said, "I know not what to speak, and I know not how to speak. Don't you listen to my speech? My job is tending the animals and farming the land."

The boy spoke with a slight lisp. It was a lifelong monument of childhood taunts. His speech impediment and webbed hand impeded his budding confidence.

"You'll speak. The people in the north are not learned. We'll depart after the donkey's first born is redeemed. You can redeem it on behalf of your father."

"Too much work. I'm forbidden to leave."

"Forbidden to serve, forbidden to leave. No, you're leaving with me. Arrange others to do your work for hire. I'll pay their salaries until your father returns."

While all were asleep that evening I was summoned to the pen by the Blacksmith's donkey. I spent the night staring into her eyes sensing her discomfort. Her little jack emerged before morning. He lay exhausted and lifeless on the ground for too long. With mischievous intention he worried his mother as she furiously licked and nuzzled the newborn.

I provided encouraging words, "Come Jack. That's enough mischief for you on your first day. Get up, naughty beast!"

The jack stood, tottered on rickety legs, fell, arose, and found his footing. With each moment he became more accustomed to this new reality. The donkey did her best to keep the peace, but the lamb knocked the little jack to the ground. The jack was becoming exhausted, so I tied up the lamb nearby to give mother and son a bit of stillness.

Later that afternoon the Blacksmith came to Barak with the jack and lamb and proudly declared, "I am exchanging this lamb for the sanctity of the donkey."

As soon as the Blacksmith performed this exchange, the sanctity of the little jack was removed. Barak departed with the lamb, leaving the Blacksmith with the donkeys. The deed accomplished with serene fanfare. The Blacksmith looked over at me with a blank expression. I nodded and pointed to the pen.

I noticed the change in the Blacksmith as he led the animals away. The sad soul and empty heart were nourished. There'd never be a replacement for his wife and little boy, but this was the beginning of his next life.

The Blacksmith creeped up on my backside. Thoughts crashed to a halt when he spoke, "Chava, I belong back in my workshop with metal and fire. How long shall I be gone?"

"Blacksmith, your future awaits. The workshop in that courtyard is your past. Wonderful years with your family are completed. It's time for you to grow and be more than a blacksmith. Until then, I'll call you Blacksmith.

I, too, had a family, a husband. That's my past, and it has passed. Surrender to the majesty of this moment and the fiery kindness of your name, Blacksmith. Your future will be blessed with love and contentment as sure as the sun rose this morning. A new king, from the line of David, will be coronated in Yehuda. The wicked Atalya will be vanquished."

"You frustrate me, woman! Even if you prophesize my future, how is it you'll presume what's best for me? And what do I care about the king of Yehuda?"

My face was level with the Blacksmith's chest. To the passerby I looked small against his stature. I stared up at him and smiled these words, "Sara lives."

The Blacksmith flushed with emotion. He furrowed his brow and swallowed hard while trying to speak, "I don't see what Sara has to do with this." I smiled and remained silent as I turned and walked toward the pen. The Blacksmith followed me and listened as I spoke my thoughts.

"The new mother is relieved that the sanctity of her jack was removed. She trusted you and grazes content. I communicate with the animals in their own language. I wasn't the only one. Adam named the animals befitting their unique nature. The secret of communicating with them is in their name, since their name describes their root, essence, and manifestation in physical form. The common man knows the letters of their names and the generic pronunciation, but it lacks the understanding to communicate with them. In the holy tongue, the word donkey comprises itself of four letters: חמור. These letters were combined and uttered with divine breath to create this animal. It is simple, and I can speak to the donkey of her past and future."

"Blacksmith, can you communicate with your donkey? I can communicate with you because I discern your name. You are man and Blacksmith. Why is it I never call you by the name your parents gave you, Blacksmith? Instead, I call you Blacksmith. You, Blacksmith, purified yourself in the waters and forged the axe and sword. It is true I brought you the components and recited the incantations, but you are the Blacksmith that forged them."

The Blacksmith looked perplexed as he motioned to the donkey and said, "What of her? How is she involved?"

With a grin I spoke, "Ah, your heart stirs with wisdom; you understand and know! The sanctity of her unborn jack sanctified the materials: חומר. I changed the order of one letter in the world of formation: חמור to חומר, donkey to material. The world of formation exists above our world of action wherein it's possible to bring down such permutations. But you performed the last step when you redeemed the little jack; the last hammer blow, Blacksmith. You manipulated the letters of the donkey and brought down mercy: רחום."

"We will venture forth to the northern kingdom and you shall wield the axe of mercy." As I walked away, I laughed and said, "Blacksmith, stay and speak to your special donkey. She loves you."

With a shuddering gut and uninhibited tears, the Blacksmith spoke to his donkey.

WISDOM. So said Solomon, "*I loved her, and sought her out from my youth, I desired to make her my spouse, and I was a lover of her beauty.*"

***

A wagon goes north, pulled by two horses. A big man holds the reins with one hand. His other hand sits balanced on top an axe head. He mutters to himself, wearing an expression of irritation across his brow. A woman (twenty years old) sits by his side. On the wagon's bed sits an adolescent boy (sixteen years old) amidst a load of grain. The boy, provoked by the woman, preaches without end of the coming judgement day that lay in store for those who don't abandon their wicked ways. Two donkeys, an adult female and a jack, trail the wagon.

This is our description traveling to the Kingdom of Israel, Yehu's kingdom. The King established his reign upon the ruins of the previous reign. "Bless Yehu for razing the house of Ahab. Bless him for waging war on the priests of Baal. Take heads Yehu! Destroy the houses of Baal! I will help!"

The Blacksmith grew annoyed with Barak's preaching. "Barak, why don't you rest? My head aches. If not, take my axe and bury it in my skull to stop the pain. Have mercy on me with my axe!"

"Yes Barak, let's stop for the afternoon. Tonight, we'll strike the village. Prepare a bed beneath the wagon for you and the Blacksmith to rest."

We pulled off the road above the village, one like many others in the Kingdom of Israel. The fetid idolatry imported from Sidon disgraced the land. If not stopped, the country would spew out its inhabitants. I thought aloud, "Oy Adam, ground of Adam, this has been years in the making. Idolatrous libations and fatty pustules seep into your earth. Gas-born rancid flesh rotting bones wafts out of burial wombs. And too, the cries of protest stifled at the injustices inflicted upon the widow and orphan. I shall impoverish them with my sword!"

Barak and the Blacksmith chewed their food with thoughtful disregard as they stared at me, entranced with boredom of vengeful rhetoric. So too, restless souls uneasily beholden to me.

I overheard the Blacksmith speak to Barak, "She seems to be a child and treats us as children. How did we become ensnared by this fanatical girl?"

I went over to the Blacksmith and rubbed his neck and shoulders. He relaxed and let out a groan of contentment as I whispered to both, "Sleep. Go under the wagon and sleep."

I sang soft until both were adrift under the wagon.

The sun set as I laid under the sky. I winked at stars revealing themselves and dreamed of Noah's water; slick and fluid that clung to the skin, oily. I breathed out and in, each time pulling the cool moist air to the ground; pulling mist downward until frothy water coated the earth. I exhaled one last breath and swallowed deep, hesitant to open my eyes as if I were a child delaying morning chores. At long last, I summoned the will and opened my wayward eyelids to greet the cool vapor. I stood and grew accustomed to the darkness. The fog smothered the village below in a pillowed patchwork. Time to do.

I crawled under the wagon and tried to wake the boys, but neither wanted to leave their bed at such an early hour. The Blacksmith rose first. Barak needed to be dragged out by his feet.

"His soldiers awake. Here, take these masks. Shake off the dust of slumber and gird yourself for battle against his enemies. Hold thy staff, Barak, and stand in the center of the village preaching His word to the villagers. I will stand by your side and guard. Blacksmith, you shall take the axe of mercy and shatter the despicable statues and poles throughout the village letting the axe of mercy be your guide. The idols will beg the axe for their destruction. And the axe will heed their call and guide you forth."

The sleepy boys grew nervous as we cut a path through the fog on our way to the village, growing accustomed to sights amidst darkness. I walked the middle while the boys clutched my arm on each side. I halted a bow shot from the village and cried to the jackals. Without delay the mangy dogs swooped in and yelped like crying babies. Village dogs responded in kind as we rushed the remaining distance to the village periphery.

"There. Blacksmith, attack!"

A big Ashera pole stood ten paces in front of us. I held my laughter as the lumbering Blacksmith ambled non-nimble toward the big pole. He reared back and spun the axe onto the chest of the awful pole and fell with shrieks of pain as the axe bounced from his hand, merely nicking the statue.

It was difficult to contain my laughter. The poor Blacksmith encountered a hard-stone statue. I let my energy pass into that profane stone with gentle taps of my sword until it crumbled from the vibration. I grinned at the Blacksmith and said, "See, that's how it's done. Are you well enough to continue?" He rose with determined senselessness and began scouring the village for items to chop.

Barak and I proceeded to the center of the village. I nodded to the boy and said, "Preach to the people." Barak began stammering until his tongue grew moist with unctuous rhetoric.

"People of the land. Listen to the words of Barak the priest. Woe to the fat lambs of Zion who cling to the mountains of Shomron. Their land boarders are not greater than the Philistines. Do thou pretend to claim thou are greater? Abusing the destitute with scattered wheat kernels thrown to pigs!"

I stood mortified as Barak spurted out absurd sentences. A small crowd stood staring at Barak with annoyed, fresh-woke faces. I interrupted Barak, "Slow your speech, boy. Stay on message, be coherent. These people are a fresh-woke lot!"

He continued, "Lest ye sinners neglect the will of He who created you and despoil the kneading trough of the widow. Repent! The day of judgement comes to thy fig and tiny goat. And it shall come to pass a lofty man from Tekoa, shall warn the sons of man. They, who grieve not for the afflictions of Joseph, shall grieve the loss of their tiny lamb served on a banquet of thorns. Thy figs rot…"

He improved most awful. His words were only half hearkened—hopefully, only the good half—because of the commotion of the Blacksmith smashing the village. More people began gathering around the two of us. Others, alerted by the Blacksmith's ruckus, tracked the upheaval throughout town.

I whispered to Barak, "Enough with the figs, Barak!" Without mercy, Barak continued,

"You!" He pointed to an old man nearby. "Fig!"

The old man responded with impatience, "Fig! You came here in the middle of the night to disturb us. What's this nonsense you're yelling?"

Barak continued, "You sit idle and fattened by the gifts He bestowed upon you. But you complain about His Sabbaths and tithes. You set out shabby bushels for the poor in grandeur and falsify the scales. Grave injustices committed and spiting the Almighty! Repent! Repent sons of man! Destroy the disgraceful statues and poles."

Barak made progress, but the crowd's mumbling grew louder, and the tumult caused by the Blacksmith reached a crescendo. Not much time remained.

Barak continued preaching with various degrees of coherence, but I sensed he wanted to leave. As the situation deteriorated, I spotted a disturbance at the edge of the crowd. I drew my sword and held it high in the air as I approached the commotion. The parting crowd revealed the big Blacksmith covered in frothy sweat. The large axe wielding brute triggered equal parts fear and revulsion.

I held my sword high as the Blacksmith stumbled forward, retreating with Barak. I stood in front of the crowd and swung my sword to intimidate a pursuit before making my retreat, catching up to the two boys near the wagon. They struggled to catch their breath while I laughed without restraint. Both looked at me with confusion and disdain, but Barak spoke first.

"Chava, we could have been killed! Why is this funny? You're crazy! We put our trust in you."

I pointed at Barak and shouted, "Fig!", and burst with uncontrolled laughter as I screamed, "Tiny goat!"

Never had I laughed so deep. Barak and the Blacksmith laughed, but only a short while. The expression on their faces changed from laughter to fear as they stared at me with concern. My body continued a titter with a will its own. With great difficulty I crawled onto the bed of the wagon and shouted, "Drive north."

The boys loaded the wagon as I laid under laughter's death throes and stared upon the glint of light reflecting off the Blacksmith's axe. As my body bounced along the road, laughter subsided, and I fell into a dream.

***

A dream of wagons bouncing along the highway from Egypt to Canaan. Wagons sent by Joseph to Jacob as a sign. "My father, now is the time to descend to Egypt."

The brothers of Joseph stood in front of Jacob and spoke wonderful news. "Joseph is still alive, and he is ruler over the whole land of Egypt." Jacob did not believe them until he saw the wagons that Joseph sent. He saw the wagons and was rejuvenated. Gladness and laughter permeated Jacob's camp as they packed their possessions and descended to Egypt.

Wagons? No, not ordinary wagons. Pharaoh's royal wagons. These special wagons were proof that Joseph lived, for the wagons alluded to the calf which was slaughtered according to His law in the event of an unsolved murder. The procedure of the scape calf was the last lesson that Jacob had taught Joseph. Jacob, these many years of Joseph's absence, knew no peace for he suspected his sons of murdering Joseph. The wagons served as the testimony that the brothers did not murder Joseph. Hence, the calf was spared the axe to the back of its neck.

Pharaoh dreamed of cows: seven healthy cows followed by seven sickly cows. Who could interpret such dreams other than the dreamer Joseph who understood much about dreams and cows? The cow, the sheep too, became holy to the people of Egypt. It was cows that warned Pharaoh, the deity, of the impending famine. The butchers of Egypt became priests. These priestly shepherds revered their livestock. In Egypt, Pharaoh's dream served as the testimony that the cows shall be worshipped.

These Hebrews, from the land of Canaan, insulted the sensibilities of the Egyptians. They treated their livestock as mundane property to be sheared, milked, slaughtered, and skinned.

Here, the primordial clash echoes through the ages. The Egyptians with their garments of flax and the Israelites with their garments of wool. Indeed, Abel brought wool as his offering whereas Cain brought flax as his offerings.

The nation descended to the fiery forge of Goshen.

***

I woke from my dream with nary a trace of laughter.

A sleep of indeterminate duration.

A place unknown.

I lay on the wagon, eyes peered on stars. Sleepy breathing of boys rose from beneath the wagon bed. I floated out of my body and toured the landscape, but the darkness refused to surrender its secrets. I'm blinded! No, I see.

I stayed on my bed even after daylight. The boys woke and peered at me from opposite sides of the wagon. They looked with concern and asked about my welfare.

The Blacksmith spoke in his gentle way, "Are you well? You've been sleeping since the incident at the village. I mean, yesterday morning. We are outside of Tizrah. We didn't go far. No more laughter?"

Barak pointed to the Blacksmith and yelled, "Fig!" I looked back at Barak and rolled my eyes, bereft of laughter. The boys, overjoyed that the madness fled.

"Tizrah? I told you to go north before I took my rest. What are we doing here, close to Shomron?"

The Blacksmith stared at me with urgency and said, "We were concerned for our safety. A short time after you fell asleep, we drove north, but not far. The sun rose and the little donkey began to bray. We looked back at him and spotted many riders behind us, so we pulled off the main road into an olive grove. I think it was Yehu with a regiment of men. It must have been. He rode with fury! We feared trailing the group, so we drove south."

"Yehu! Afraid of Yehu? He's a child! I have no fear of Yehu. We are on a mission to wipe out idolatry and promote social justice in the north. Drive! Drive north at once!" With that, I thrust my sword to the north. But this was a ruse. I mean, well, it was Yehu.

Barak and the Blacksmith eyed each other with trepidation until the Blacksmith spoke. "See here Chava, our mission hasn't gone well. We harassed a village. That's our sole accomplishment."

Before he continued, I said, "Give me your axe." He handed the axe to me and backed off. "Don't back away from me. I want you to show me something. You hit a stone statue with all your strength. Show me where it bent the edge."

The Blacksmith inspected the axe and attested it suffered no blemish on its edge from the blow on the statue. I faced the Blacksmith and reared back in preparation to throw the axe. He ducked as I hurled the merciful weapon into a mighty oak tree.

"Fetch it, Blacksmith." I followed the Blacksmith to the tree. He pulled on the handle with all his might, but it did not budge. "Move!" I pushed him aside, grabbed the head of the axe and plucked it from the tree. "See here. Nothing wrong with your axe. It's fit for smashing idles, and you're fit to wield it. Practice throwing it into this tree. Hurl it with your heart. By the way, have you been talking to your donkey?"

The Blacksmith looked at me with a sour expression. "Chava, you're strong. I'm not as strong as you. Nobody could have pulled the axe out of the tree the way you did. You didn't even use the handle for leverage! Do you expect me to do that? And how does this inspire man to repent? Again, all we did was harassed a poor village."

"You'll see. Say your prayers and practice. I need to spend time with Barak."

The Blacksmith's face turned red as he approached me and said, "Chava, I'm done with this…"

"Unless you explain why I'm on this mission. Don't you owe me an explanation? Who cares about the axe? What does it matter?"

I looked up at the sad laborer and said, "Calm thy big flaming face. Look, I know you don't understand everything, nor do I. But there is a purpose…"

"No," the Blacksmith interrupted. "This is exactly what I mean. I need an explanation; not just *purpose* or meaningless notions.

"Meaningless? You're hurtful."

"Chava, stop trying to make me feel bad. I lost everything in Shomron. All that remained was my work, and you took that from me. Now I'm supposed to roam with you and that kid. And practice throwing an axe!"

I glanced at Barak and his big ears picking up the conversation. The Blacksmith maintained his gaze upon me. I stared into his sorrowful eyes and said, "You're correct…"

"You speak correct, rational, and balanced. But that's your fallacy. This mission aligns on the emotional domain—the heart of men, their soul. What was the love for your departed wife and child? Was it rational?"

The Blacksmith collapsed onto his knees. His body shook with unfettered spasms as tears streamed down his dusty face.

I approached from behind and hugged him. My lips grazed the back of his neck, a single soul kiss, where spine meets brain. A sharp wheel spun against my lips, nipples and pelvis as I departed my body and came face-to-face with the Blacksmith. His head transformed to skull and then, to my love, Adam. I released from the embrace and composed myself.

"Trust me in this. As sure as you redeemed that donkey and forged that axe, you shall prevail in the emotional domain. You'll come to let go of your family, build a new life, and lead others to their salvation. Let thy soul carry thy body's broken bones."

Through tears, the Blacksmith said, "Again, you speak but say nothing."

"Well, think of it this way. In your workshop you pounded away on the rational, the physical. All those tools you fashioned were mundane until you fashioned the axe of mercy through the redemption of the first-born donkey."

With that said I walked over to Barak. When we were but a breath away from each other I smiled, poked him in the chest, and whispered, "Fig. You little fig."

Barak inspected me with a nervous smile then timidly lowered his gaze to the ground.

I'd study with him. "Show me your scrolls. How do we promote the welfare of the widow and the orphan? What of the poor that rely on the corners of the fields?"

We stayed a few hours in that place before driving to Tizrah. The boys needed baths and a hot meal. The Blacksmith became dirty and skinny since taking on my company. This brawny man required heaping quantities of food to maintain his form. I loved him as I did many men I encountered over the millennia. He is my son, like Abel or David. Each being a wonderful creation. This Blacksmith! So corporeal. It's too simple and ridiculous to describe his appeal. I enjoyed watching him eat.

A bear ate less! I smiled and laughed. What did he do with that food? He breathed, sweat, and stumbled on the quaking ground. But he said things that forced me to observe the world through his eyes. My awkward affection for him manifested as bullying. He'd stare at me with a furrowed brow and say, "I'm hungry." I'd always smile and respond, "You don't appear hungry." Still, I grew frustrated he fell short of his potential.

We spent two nights in Tizrah to refresh the boys. Barak spent the days with his nose buried in scrolls whereas the Blacksmith dwelt in the inn's courtyard steeped in meditation and prayer. I ventured throughout Tizrah and accumulated provisions for our journey. The boys slept in one room. In the evenings I sat with the wind on the rooftop. As always, I sang psalms to keep me company.

One bright morning we packed ourselves in the wagon and drove north; two donkeys, two men, and a woman. We drove the entire morning. The Blacksmith wanted to stop for lunch. I grew tired of his complaining and asked him to sit in the wagon with Barak and eat bread. They ate and fell asleep as I piloted the wagon northward. In the evening I received more complaints from the donkeys. I obeyed their pleas and pulled to the side of the road for forage and rest. We carried a stock of barley but were always on the lookout for water.

I spent the evening under the stars with soft songs of His benevolence. The boys woke, and we journeyed once more until afternoon. I announced, "There, a village ahead. We will camp here today. After night falls, we'll visit the village and bring tidings of His wrath."

"I'm hungry."

"Blacksmith, I know you're hungry. I'll bake cakes."

"Cakes? Those aren't cakes you make. It's coarse barley flour. They're hard as a rock and taste like dirt."

"You don't love my cakes? I'm the original baker. The best baker in the world! My cakes are manna from heaven!"

"Chava, take a rest. Barak and I will bake cakes."

"OK, suit yourself. I'll gather wood for a fire. Do you want me to mix the dough?"

The Blacksmith responded, "No, don't mix the dough! We'll do it. Yes, please help with the fire."

I set out to gather wood, but I became overcome with sorrow. Why was the Blacksmith mean to me? I know how to bake. I understand baking; and, I know why to bake! He appreciates none of this!

I sat with dejection until Barak approached from behind. His sweet presence encouraged me as we gathered wood together. They built the fire; they baked the cakes.

Once the boys were tucked under the wagon, I allowed myself one of the fresh cakes. A little too soft but not bad.

I laid on top of the wagon listening to the boys sleep while watching darkness roll in. When the darkest dark congealed the heavens, I closed my eyes, consumed with gratitude for His blessing. My body tingled and went numb as I reached for the highest heights, but then the jack discharged a juvenile bray and I fell back to earth with a smile across my face. Again, I rose to the waters, grabbed wisdom, and pulled down. I fell back to earth with the descendent fog beading upon my face. Wet eyelashes fluttered away at the moisture as my lungs breathed the cool waters. His waters soaked my eyes; pulsed through my bloodstream and set my brain awash in a cloud of glory.

I crawled to the back of the wagon, bent over the end, and woke the boys, "Fig. Hot Cakes. Wake up. We go now." Soon after, the boys emerged unenthused and sleepy.

"We go now."

With donned masks we walked through the fog as we did on our first mission. We were more experienced now as we snuck into the village. Once inside we made a great noise. Barak proceeded:

"Thou have been safeguarded by His shield. He looks in disdain at your grain offerings. Of what value is this offering? You built an offering of deceit. You, fat cows…"

I stood by Barak's side as the Blacksmith began smashing idols in the village. The first people streamed outside as I prayed for this mission to be a success; a prayer One could hear.

"You, fat cows grow corpulent gnashing teeth on fatty flesh."

I whispered, "Come on Barak. Get it together."

"Thou feast on a venal banquet and longed for the Sabbath to speedily depart. For what? To persecute those less fortunate! The widow and orphan cry out in misery. Their father sells himself into servitude for a morsel of bread."

So far it wasn't too bad. He made mistakes but improved since last time. But his rhetoric bore dull. Where does inspiration flee? Why wasn't he rallying against the idols? I listened to him practice and knew he'd improve. He continued, but it grew unbearably difficult to pay attention. Part of the problem was the rampaging of the Blacksmith. The crashing noise and shouts of people competed for the attention of Barak's holy words.

At long last the Blacksmith emerged, and we departed. We returned in silence to the wagon and drove off, taking our ministry to the wetlands. From there, we planned to take our ministry south to the many communities on the shore of the Kinneret. I sat in the back of the wagon, alone, staring complacent at the two trailing donkeys. Dread built up inside of me with the first morning light. It didn't help that Barak complained to the Blacksmith about our work. The boy prattled on to the Blacksmith, "The main problem is corruption and lack of social justice. Idolatry, a scourge, is a symptom of the underlying sleaze. The root of the problem is where we should focus our efforts. The root is the corruption."

I argued from the bed of the wagon, but they appeared to ignore me as if I wasn't present. All the while dreads creeped. My body puckered. My spirit wished to run away. I yelled at both through tears, but they paid little heed. At one point the Blacksmith turned his head and smiled at me. I raged with sadness at has patronizing smile, wishing to stand up and smack him but became overcome with spasms in my belly. And then, everything stopped. I lay confused and tired.

Impossible! It could not be! I pulled my robe aside and placed an unsteady hand below. A wet sticky touch, I do not believe! With trepidation I brought my fingers to my closed eyes. I opened my eyes and let out a muffled shriek. The sight went from red to black as I drifted off to dream.

***

A dream of babies crying, screaming, in a steamy bath chamber. Fine linen hangs throughout. I pulled at the maze of linen until spotting a large gold basin in the center of the room. Inside the basin, a dark red pool—drawn from living souls—began to congeal. And me: I backed away from the horrible site. Again, I'm lost in a maze of off-white linen curtains and milky-white steam. Pulling curtains, a glimpse: the naked leper flanked by young servants. I retreat into the linen, but there's no escaping Pharaoh's glare peering beneath red wrinkles.

***

My eyes open with thanks for the stars above and wagon below. What happened to me? I pull my robe and touch myself below. There's nothing. Had it been a dream? I hear the boys talking nearby and leap out of the wagon.

"What happened? Where are we?"

They looked surprised. The Blacksmith replied with caution.

"We are north of Megiddo."

"Why? How did we get here? I told you to drive to the Kinneret!"

"We were concerned for our safety. A short time after you fell asleep, we drove north as ordered. We did not go far. The sun rose when the little donkey began to bray. We looked back at him and spotted many riders behind us, so we pulled off the main road into an olive grove. I think it was Yehu with a regiment of men. It must have been. He rode with fury! We feared trailing the group, so we drove west."

I screamed with contempt "Yehu! Afraid of Yehu? He's a child! I have no fear of Yehu. We are on a mission to wipe out idolatry and promote social justice!"

The Blacksmith continued, "What's with you and Yehu? Go fight Yehu and his army if you wish. I'm not. Barak isn't either. Why did you fall asleep these past two times when Yehu approached? You want a chance to fight Yehu? Don't fall asleep before he happens by! But you understand it won't happen. That crazy prophet anointed him. He's the king."

I had questions. What transpired while I lie on the wagon? Did I bleed?

"Blacksmith. Please explain what happened when we finished ministering? I instructed you and Barak to drive north, and then went into the bed of the wagon. What happened after?"

"You laid in the wagon and fell asleep. Barak and I drove north as you ordered. A short while later…"

I interrupted, "So, I didn't talk to you from the bed of the wagon? Was I not awake while we journeyed?"

"No, you fell asleep as soon as your head hit that sack of barley. We hadn't started to drive. You spoke not a word to us."

It was only a dream. I hadn't bled. Should I be grateful? Do I need to depend on the Blacksmith to help me distinguish dreams from reality? And Yehu. He knew where to find me but rode away.

I continued, "Thank you Blacksmith. Barak, is this true?"

Barak stared at me and said nothing. "Barak, I asked you if it's true?"

"It's true Chava. You fell asleep at once. You spoke not, but I heard your voice in my head while I complained to the Blacksmith about our mission. Your protests rattled around my skull. I told the Blacksmith that the main problem is corruption and lack of social justice—idolatry, without a doubt a scourge, is a symptom of the underlying sleaze. The root of the problem is where we should focus our efforts. The root is venality. While I explained this to the Blacksmith, you slept and spoke to me."

"You sense. How much do you perceive? Did you listen to me bleed and the cry of babies?"

Barak stammered, "I'm not a prophet."

"Yes Barak, I agree, you're not a prophet. You're only hope is to slaughter helpless figs. To idle away your days sitting under the shade of the sycamore fig tree."

Barak continued with a hint of sorrow, "I listened to protests in my head. Nothing more. I know not about bleeding or babies crying."

"It's ok Barak. Little gained through sorrow. Be cheerful for thy good words, which shall outlive the memory of any priest. The Almighty created you for this important mission."

We lingered sufficiently for the donkeys to rest. Much before dawn I climbed the driver's seat and steered toward the wetlands while the two boys rested in the wagon bed. More than once I reached under my robe to inspect my condition with glad relief it had been a dream. But Yehu wasn't a dream. The connection between us, not wished away.

We rode to the east on a rocky road as the sun peeked over the horizon. I squinted under a floppy hat as His host made a noble effort to burn my eyes. The first birds of the morning sang shy greetings to one another. They reached a loud crescendo as we came near the wetlands. I'd water our donkeys here before heading south. The boys laid in the wagon, semi-asleep, fighting a fierce battle to stave off the day.

I strode along the boundary of the shore until I found a pool absent of stalks and debris; a pool designed just for me. On this shore, all alone, just me and Father. It could've been a thousand years past or future. Even though I only dreamed my monthly event, I still felt compelled to immerse myself. I threw my robe on the ground and placed my jewelry in the floppy hat. The pool remained clear as I descended deeper, all alone, the only soul in the world.

I sensed the evil men lurking after I immersed. Rage welled up at this disturbance timed exact with my moment of privacy and peace. If it wasn't for the safety of the boys, I could linger here. This frustrated and angered me further. I began to emerge from the pool. With each step to shore my body separated from the living waters; from wisdom to fury. Out of the watery womb my flesh emerged and drops descended as I stepped on dry land naked but not alone. Intruders. They were here on behalf of a king, Yehu.

***

I'm a king. What does it mean to be king? King Yehu. As a child, I thought it was the best thing to be king. The king has everything, an entire kingdom at his disposal. This was before I met Chava. Before Chava enslaved me and brought me to the north country. I pledged to be her slave forever, and she pierced my ear according to the law. After, I rode away and became king, but I am still her slave. I enjoy women, advisors, an army, and slaves of my own but it's Chava, my Master, that commands my thoughts. I am Yehu; King and Slave. How can I reign while Chava reigns over me? I know where she is, but I cannot approach her. It cannot be revealed.

***

I stand naked and wet in front of the armed man. He clutches my gold earring between his thumb and forefinger.

"I only came for this."

I laugh and say, "You want my earring?"

My naked flesh transforms to a darker shade before he can respond. I get dressed and adorn myself with the remaining jewelry. I walk toward the wagon while beckoning the stunned Moabite to follow. By the time we reach the wagon my skin goes mundane and his stupor ceases. He lifts the earring high so that his cohorts may gaze upon his victory.

The four mercenaries standing watch at the wagon didn't harm my boys. That couldn't be tolerated. Yehu knows. Yes, Yehu. These are his mercenaries out to collect his trinket. None have yet to summon my wrath.

"You got what you want, Moabites. Go to peace."

They glance at each other confused by the ease in which they accomplished their mission. "Is there more for us?"

Such insolence! Expect this for obliging ruffians.

"Yes, I have something else for you. Please allow me to retrieve it from the wagon."

I go over to the wagon and rummage around muttering. "Hmm, where did I put it?" I smile at them and say, "Please forgive me. I misplaced it."

One of them says, "What is it? Be quick. Perhaps we'll take whatever we want."

"Be patient little boy. It's good, you'll love it. Here it is!" I stand up on top of the wagon with the drawn sword above my head. The Moabites glare at me with reticence. One of them reaches to draw his sword but is cut short by the Blacksmith's axe which splits the back of his head. The pandemonium ensues when the donkey emits a loud bray unleashing a series of hind kicks cracking a Moabite rib. The remaining three men retreat in a semi-circle to defend themselves.

"Moabites, you got the earring. That was your mission." I jump off the wagon with my sword and face the semi-circle. "Sheath your swords and go."

One lunges with crude swordplay. His expert swipes don't strike me. I poke his thighs with my sword each time he tries to stab me. His cohorts stare unengaged, spellbound while the man flails at me until collapsing from exhaustion.

"You're finished here."

I turn my back on them and throw my sheathed sword into the wagon. "You go now."

I nod to the Blacksmith and Barak to climb aboard and drive. The Moabites look on as we head back to the main road, proceeding south to Rakkat. On the open road my mood becomes sad, neglected, and angry.

"Blacksmith, you don't care for me and my friendship." The Blacksmith hands the reigns to Barak and peers back at me. "That's right, you take me for granted. I'm trying to take care of you, but you won't let me! You always criticize or ignore me."

"Chava, I don't understand your complaints. I put my future in your hands and do everything you ask. It's difficult and dangerous, as you can see. When did I criticize or ignore you?"

"Don't throw my words back at me. You know how you feel. Do you think it's easy to bear this responsibility? See what's happening in Israel? Yehu is an inexperienced boy. And in Yehuda it's worse. Atalya, Jezebel's own daughter, rules Yehuda. It's a disgrace. I'm asking you to care about what I'm trying to do. Live up to your name."

"You speak in riddles. I don't know what you want or, more to the point, what you're trying to do. You're upset at something I did or didn't do but I don't understand. I am a simple blacksmith who never left the city of Shomron for very long. For whatever reason, I came with you. I didn't have a choice. You control me and Barak. What else do you want from us?"

"Oh no, leave Barak out of this. I'm talking to you, not him. Just turn around, speak not, and drive the wagon. Can you do that for me?"

We drove south toward Rakkat in silence. My ear felt naked without the earring, a gift from Pinchas many years ago. Pinchas himself took it from a Midianite princess in the wilderness, but that's a different story. The earring is a trivial relic. Sometimes people own things. Sometimes things own people. I owned the earring because it gave joy to the giver in giving. This earring; possession an impossibility, ownership not. A futile mission to grasp the earring. The earring, and what it represented, owned him.

Yehu the king willingly surrendered his body, and liberty. A sovereignty scorned with ingratitude to his Creator. How was it so easy for me and so difficult for mankind? I had everything because I held nothing. The gifts from Father ran through me like a blessed river—an eternal, timeless instant; infinite nothingness un-held.

The Blacksmith was not forthright and open with me. These two times I saw the Blacksmith drive his axe into a living skull. He did it with regret, without hesitation. Even now I sensed he felt dirty from slaying the Moabite. He hid his person from me. His instant and eternity, simply the loss of his precious family. I shed a tear for his gloom and harassed him for the duration of the journey. The madness I'd inflict on him, his salvation. Soon, instead of seeing me he'd see himself in the mirror. The Blacksmith was not the first. The first man I tormented; Adam. I vexed him much worse than Yehu.

But now, Yehu's lust invites me.

***

I set camp in the north.
I'm near to her. She knows as she knew me.
I sit alone in my tent waiting for my prize.
"King Yehu, the Moabites arrived."
"Send them in."
"You have the earring?"
"Yes, we have it. We lost one man. Two are injured and need medical care. Why is this earring so special? That woman is a witch. Who is she?"
"Further questions and I'll pour hot coals into your mouth. We made a deal. Give me the earring."

Oh, how I expected this moment. I fought to conceal my excitement from the mercenary as he reached into his satchel and pulled out a small linen bag. My face flushed and my head pounded when he opened the bag and displayed the earring. I couldn't contain my hand from shaking as he extended it to me. I did my best to feign control.

"Put the earring on the table and go. I'll pay you later. You can stay in our camp for three nights to rest and recover. After which you shall ride back to your land. You'll mention this to no one. You go now."

Everything went fine. Their mission complete. But their leader looked at me with curiosity when I told them to go. I said too much. He knows she talks that way. They know too much. What does it matter? Here lies the earring. But why can't I shake that face from my mind? It's as if she's in the room. He touched the earring, didn't he? They'll never arrive in their own land.

It's mine.

It sits alone on the table, smiling at me.

Not yet.

***

I laid on the wagon staring at the bright sky as we plodded along on bumpy ground. The sun burned the smile on my face into a mocking exaggeration. I contemplated the busy months ahead. We must stay in Rakkat for the coming days. After, the boys will go to Jerusalem on pilgrimage. I'd not go with them.

I lay on my back, without the slightest movement, during the heat of the day. The smile painted on my face until mid-afternoon when we pull off the road to set up camp. We sit speechless the eternal afternoon and evening.

At bedtime I say, "Blacksmith, Barak, travel to Rakkat without me. I must take care of an affair before joining you."

"Where are you going? Don't you need a horse or sword?"

"No, I don't have far to go. Just my hat."

I sprint to the meet-up.

***

I gaze at the earring as it lay on the table.

Soon, master and slave will reunite.

I walk outside to inspect my soldiers. Two hundred of my most loyal men camp at my side. I paid the Moabites earlier. They must be silenced.

But where are they? I approach my captain and ask, "Where are the Moabites?"

"My Lord, they departed while you were taking your nap."

I began to speak but stilled myself. This is a grave sign. They fled with fear. What should they fear here? I offered sanctuary and medical care.

"Captain, how did the two injured men ride?"

"My Lord, their injuries were a secondary consideration. They were intent on a swift departure. Is there something amiss? I'd have kept them here if ordered."

"Yes, something is amiss. Gather two groups of ten men. Hunt them, kill them, and bring their heads to me. You go now."

Curses! Again, I spoke her words. I'm shocked by the reaction of the guard.

"Is this amusing? Stop smiling and go, now, Azazel!"

***

I stop running once I reach the ideal juncture, then sit in the middle of the road. Stingy moonlight illuminates my form. I'll take the most passive approach possible when making a proposal.

I don't wait long. Riders advanced from my rear; creeping cautious. One rider dismounted and approaches with drawn sword, raised to strike, and I say, "Don't do that. I'm trying to help you. You have no guardian other than me."

The Moabite walked around to face me. He pointed the sword at my neck and said, "I thought we saw the last of you."

I pushed the sword tip to the side and said, "There's no time for talk. Yehu's men are in pursuit."

I motioned to the injured; "They'll slow you down and get picked off. You'll all be killed."

I faced the others and say, "Take your chances scurrying like easy prey back to Moab or come with me. That's your choice. If you join me, you must follow my orders without question, and you'll be beholden to me as your master evermore. Choose now. Die free men or live as slaves. Ride away or bind yourselves to me. No horses. We go now."

One, most clever, pays careful attention to my words. He heard Yehu and me uttering the same phrase. He knew not what it meant, but he believed in the truth of his predicament; death awaited. He followed me. The others fled. They had no chance of survival.

The two of us descended from the road and sprinted across a rocky field. Once out of sight from the road, we slowed. Yehu's men would track the horses. I doubt they'd notice that the gait of one horse changed but they'd try to hunt for the short head once it became evident. They'd leave men to track their missing head and find us if we didn't make haste. The main burden was taking care of Barak and the Blacksmith. And my new slave and the donkeys.

As we neared the wagon, I set rules.

"Don't tell me your name, slave. You must abandon your past. Here forth your name is Omid. That's your name. Give me your sword, gold, and everything else you have. Don't object or I'll take your shoes."

"I won't protest. We made a deal. I'm your slave but you're responsible for my security."

"Omid, you're incorrect. I removed you from the immediate threat and certain death. Yehu's men will come up short. They'll be looking for you."

"Who are you and what is your relationship with Yehu? You appear to be a normal woman, but you're not. What are you?"

"What am I? No, what are you? You are a slave."

***

I longed for this moment, but I let it linger, a king, alone in his tent while the camp sleeps. The earring sits on the table.

I came into this tent as Yehu the king. A man. Who will emerge from this tent?

Chapter 9

נצח (Eternity)

Jezebel's Daughter

I acquired a Moabite slave. Here's the truth: one who acquires a slave gains a master for himself.
Another truth: Yehu the slave has trouble severing the relationship with his master.

"Omid, the questions will wait. I'll answer what I answer, but you must serve me as is your duty. Dawn beckons and we approach my comrades."

Although I tormented them aplenty, Barak, and the Blacksmith were sincerely relieved to see me. I introduced my slave and instructed them to make haste for Rakkat. They prepared for the journey chagrined about Omid.

"Omid, you'll walk while Barak and the Blacksmith will sit and drive the wagon."

"Why must I walk with plenty of room in the wagon? Or I can ride the donkey."

"Enough questions. First, I need to be alone in the wagon. Second, those donkeys are not for riding. Don't try it. Those are the Blacksmith's donkeys, and if you mistreat them, you're likely to get an axe buried in your head. Remember?"

"We go now."

And we went. I lie while the wagon bounced closer to the banks of the sweet water lake.

***

Candles burned bright in my tent. The flames illuminated the earring as I held it between my fingers and, with surrender, placed it in my ear.

Before reaching my bed an interruption of riders intruded upon my solitude. Who disturbs me at this late hour?

***

The slippery serpent continues my tale (believe what you will)…

The woman, Chava, sleeps in her wagon. Yehu, stares mesmerized at the door as green mist peeks its nose under the tent.
A regal woman and an elderly man enter the tent. The woman is Atalya, queen of Yehuda, every bit the speck of Jezebel. Green eyes pulse with pinpoint spirit of Lilith. Auburn tresses of hair, streaked with grey, draggle on her soft bark complexion. Small crinkles outline her smile.
The man, Seti, is an Egyptian magician and necromancer. A short stocky man with painted eyes and thick black hair atop a tiny head, appearing too small for his body. Finger bones attached to his belt rattle unnerving clickety-clacks with every step.
Yehu's eyes follow Atalya as she circles him while speaking. Seti, with eyes rolled to the back of his head, chants in low tones.

"Yehu, no refreshments for the queen of Yehuda? I travel far. Pour us wine. Don't mind my friend, my ally from Egypt. Seti accompanies me on this mission to ally with you, Yehu. Our kingdoms shall align. Yes, you killed my son, but I don't bear a grudge."
Yehu pours two cups of wine and walks toward Atalya. She looks at him with a thin smile as she takes the cup and raises it to her lips while nudging the bottom of Yehu's cup with patronizing encouragement. Atalya's condescending stare does not waiver. All occurs amidst the reverberating chants of Seti (a most repulsive diplomat) in the austere tent. Atalya puts her cup down and begins teasing Yehu's chest and neck with her hands. She lifts his robe as she pushes him back onto a chair. Yehu sits exposed and complacent as Atalya walks to the table and refills a cup, turns to face Yehu and disrobes. Yehu stares through her while she walks to him and lifts the cup to his lips. The wine spills from his

chin undrunk. An annoyed Atalya drinks the wine and tosses the cup to the floor.

Atalya sits, straddling the complacent body of Yehu, who sits without expression while Atalya kisses his lips, trying with futility to arouse Yehu. Atalya doesn't realize who controls the man, this loyal slave. Atalya sits up straight and stares at Yehu with a curious grin and says, "Are you not a man?" She reaches for the earring; a pinch between thumb and forefinger. In an instant the air is sucked from the room and Atalya is thrust off Yehu's lap and propelled onto the floor. Seti looks in stunned silence as Atalya lies naked gasping for breath. One candle remains burning in the large tent; dim light vanquishing much darkness.

Yehu stands and says, "Yes Atalya, we'll become allies. In due time, I'll visit Yehuda so we can discuss an alliance. Please leave as I destroy yet the house of Ahab."

That is the voice of Yehu but words of another.

Atalya struggles to catch her breath, straining her eyes in the dim light to discern the man behind the words. The anger provoked her at the mention of Ahab—a reference to her mother Jezebel—increases with each hard-fought breath of air. Yehu gathers her clothes and smells the trace before casting them to the homicidal queen.

Yehu says, "I got your scent. I'll find you with the steeds of Jerusalem. You may go now."

Atalya and Seti depart in humiliation for the long ride back to Yehuda with their cadre of Yehudi and Egyptian forces.

A short distance south of the Israelite camp a crazy man walks along the center of the road for a meeting with Yehu. The man complains of prickled flesh in harsh daylight. Why else did he travel alone in the dark of night? It's a crazy man who misses the solitude inside the belly of the great fish. A man so crazy that he has the power to stir the nations to repentance.

The crazy man marches onward, lost in prophecy, paying no heed to Atalya's cavalry barreling straight at him. The riders narrowly pass on Yonah's left and right. None of them spot Yonah even though they see him. Atalya too, rides on oblivious, but Seti detects Yonah and veers too far to the right. His horse kicks up gravel on the side of the road as hooves scramble to maintain balance. Riders behind Seti struggle to pass amid Yonah's curses. And then, a divine still-sound greets the errant mutterings of Yonah as he approaches the outskirts of Yehu's camp.

Silence flees in the wake of Yonah's shouting...

"Where is the King? Come out, slayer of heresy! Savior of Israel!"

Miraculously, the entire camp sleeps through the commotion except for a few weary sentries who try in vain to suppress the crazy one. Not knowing what to do, the sentries lead Yonah to Yehu's tent and scurry away for fear of a reprimand or worse. Nobody wants to hold the bag. All alone, Yonah barges into Yehu's tent.

Here is where Yonah transforms. Yehu stands in the middle of the tent with a faint smile directed at Yonah. Yonah approaches, takes Yehu by the arm, and says, "Come old lady and sit."

Yonah sits across from Yehu and speaks, "Who's inside? The anointed one? That's who you are, not a woman. In fact, you are not a man nor slave but a divinely anointed king. You have no power outside of serving at the privilege of His divine authority to exercise justice and virtue.

"It was you, King, at your behest Jezebel plummeted to her death. The ground of Jezreel drank her blood without protest. Many years earlier Ahab and Jezebel perverted justice against Naboth by seizing his property in Jezreel. Take warning. You aren't a man, woman, or slave. You are King."

Yonah's affection mesmerized and left me, the serpent, spellbound. He held Yehu's hands and stared with loving eyes. This so certain a personal matter to Yonah: anointer of Yehu. Yonah walked to the door and said, "Remove the earring and return it to the owner."

And Yonah departed.

Who sat alone in the king's tent? While the earring remained in place, I couldn't determine the identity: king or slave; man or woman. It didn't matter. A creature without free will; he, an anointed king. I, the serpent, saw it remove the earring from its own ear and saw the anointed one appear.

***

Serpent, it's not your story to tell. Nor is it Yehu's story. I must tell through my perspective since it's my tale and my dreams. How now do you possess the power of speech without my permission?

***

The holy can never be evil, but evil can be holy. The Fount of holiness said: *"For men shall not see me and live."* Evil was brought into the world for a man to live and exercise free will. Man lives among evil, striving for holiness. This is the paradoxical gift of the Almighty that is my motive force. Haven't I served the Almighty by making this happen?

I slept in the back of the wagon while we traveled hours on rugged roads. Barak and the Blacksmith drove the horses. Omid and the two donkeys trailed.

I sat upright at the conclusion of the dream. Omid and the donkeys returned my gaze. His long face appeared far more fatigued than the donkeys. Oh, how weak are these post-diluvian men! I hopped off the wagon, urged Omid forward, and helped him climb aboard. Omid sat with relief as I walked next to the donkeys on our way to Rakkat.

I bore no guilt about the dilemma of Yehu even though I was liable. He hired mercenaries to bring him my earring so he could assume my form. But I had released Yehu from my service, so it was no longer possible to assume my form. Although he was now a free man, a king no less, he never considered emancipating himself from me. Was it my fault he preferred to be a slave? Should I take pity on him for his preference to be an old lady? The King shall be wise with understanding and know to discard these fantasies.

Every event is meant, so do not deny the indestructible truth. One man can spend a lifetime attempting to fell a mighty oak with a feather.

On that day I saw the mercenary holding my earring, I realized Yehu was in trouble. I could have sent the mercenaries away empty handed.

But I let them go with the earring to attend the meeting with Atalya and protect Yehu. After that, Yonah could influence the king. So yes, I emerged from the pool and allowed the mercenary to take it. Naked and alone, roaming a faithful journey confident of Yehu's protection and redemption. That's a brief explanation. But it was Omid, now enslaved, that brought the earring to Yehu. Oh, you naughty earring who twists circles of slaves.

We were not too far from Rakkat when I instructed the Blacksmith to detour off the main road. He grew impatient with the journey and me. Well, he was impatient with me before we even met.

The lack of order and unpredictability in my company, a stark contrast to the predictable workshop, subverted his need for control. A man with tempered dreams of a fiery workshop on a frigid road, reality asunder, under His watchful gaze. Oh Father, do not show me Thy wrath of vexation! How a soul is cast into the scorched crucible of turmoil.

The Blacksmith gazed from his perch and said, "Chava, I thought we were going to Rakkat. I looked forward to sleeping in a proper bed and having a hot meal. Where are we going now?"

"I know a better place. A farm. The only person living on that land is an old lady. A widow. It's comfortable, and you'll get hot meals, but there'll be work aplenty. We'll hide on the farm until Yehu's men stop looking for Omid. Or we might stay longer."

The Blacksmith looked at Omid who lay sleeping in the wagon and said, "Why did you bring this one? Those Moabites tried to molest us. I don't trust him."

"You shouldn't trust him. But I saved his life for his servitude. Yehu's men killed his cohorts. Such a waste. Omid is a Moabite it's true, but he has no friends here or anyone to rely. Without a doubt he'll be handy on the farm."

I walked alongside the wagon as we traveled the narrow road. The valley stretched before us in stark contrast to the slopes east and west. Now that we sank into the valley, we no longer saw the sweet water of the Kinneret.

The grass was brown from the parched summer but ripe fruit for harvest abounded. It was a farm with no shortage of work.

Once again, the Blacksmith's cultivated apathy, and I began to cry.

He said, "What's wrong Chava?"

Through tears I said, "You are what's wrong. What do you think? Why did you come? All you do is complain and make me cry with..."

The soil shuddered as I struggled muddled words, gasping breath through choked tears upon drenched muck. He refused to understand the mission or himself. Once more I tried to speak, "You don't understand me even if you hear what I say. How many times do I tell you? And nothing ever changes."

Throughout this episode the Blacksmith held the reins and stared straight ahead without speaking a word.

Barak turned away trying to hide. Omid from the back of the wagon began to cajole the Blacksmith: "Hey Blacksmith, why don't you be a good slave and treat the lady with respect?" The Blacksmith leaped over into the wagon, grabbed Omid by the neck, but lost his footing and tumbled off the edge.

Shocked, I shouted at the Blacksmith to stop but he didn't listen. The Blacksmith tried to climb upon the wagon, but Omid kicked him in the chest. This provoked the Blacksmith's fury. The lumbering brute rounded the wagon and mounted the seat to approach as before. By this time Barak had hopped off his seat and scurried behind me. As the Blacksmith jumped onto the bed of the wagon Omid jumped off the back and ran up the road. The Blacksmith leaped and gave chase.

Barak and I watched the swift Blacksmith pursue Omid. I presumed Omid was swifter, but such was not the case. The Blacksmith caught up with Omid, grabbed him by the collar and yanked him to the ground. I did not wish to interfere even though Omid might die or be crippled. Still the same, I yelled, "Blacksmith, stop now!" The crazed assailant pulled a knife from his boot and stared straight at me. I returned his stare with a smile and lifted my palms skyward. With miraculous rationality he continued staring at me until his scowl transformed to a grin. Oh, the rapid mood swings of the Blacksmith. Omid hurried back to the wagon, reluctant to provoke the Blacksmith ever again.

With convenient normalcy we reassembled and continued our journey to the farm. The pleasantness of the day dispersed the tension. And, the boys were excited to go to the farm and cease roaming for a change. Still the same, I foresaw Omid faced additional danger. But it didn't matter. I saved Omid's life these two times. First, from Yehu's men and now from the Blacksmith. Indeed, I spared Omid the first time we met at the wetlands. An impervious man needing not my protection or mercy from an earthly power. He could walk through a battlefield without suffering a scrape.

At last we approached the outskirt of the farm. The ground lay fallow and brown from the heat of the summer pleading for human toil and heavenly Grace. Vines held grapes but needed a good pruning, come winter.

Amazing that the structures stood: two houses and a barn in a state of disrepair exhibited years of neglect.

The wagon lurched to a halt. I spoke with pride, "Well, here we are. Welcome to the farm."

Barak glanced around and said, "Where's the old lady, the widow? This place appears abandoned. No dwellers in the past hundred years, I'd say."

I said, "It's me who is the old widow. It's my farm, where I live sometimes, although the farm has stood idle for many years. There are two houses. The small one is mine. You three can take the large house. Check the barn for wood and tools because the roof needs repair."

The group looked around with grim faces at the neglected farm. For me, nothing to do but feign normalcy. Before they inquired further, I said, "I'll get food prepared. Let's make a proper accounting of supplies we'll need. Barak, you can go to Rakkat tomorrow with the Blacksmith to load up on provisions. I'll give you money. Put the donkeys and horses in the barn. No, put them out to pasture first. Omid, fetch water from that well. There might be a rope in the barn. Lots of work to do. No time for rest. We work now."

Did they grumble complaints in the face of Chava's trickery? Yes, but they'd nowhere else to go. Besides, a dilapidated farm is better than being pulled by one's nose ring on the open road.

The four of us toiled all day to produce an inhabitable farm. I was most grateful for the well which provided plentiful water. I instructed Omid to draw buckets for the livestock while I gathered roots, herbs, and fruit. A dry winter had given way to a sparse summer and stingy farm, but we endured that first evening. Barak and the Blacksmith conducted repairs on the big house and a proper inventory of tools and supplies we'd need.

We finished eating and set our backs on the coarse ground. Stretched out above us was a dazzling blanket of stars. His grace rolled away the hot afternoon, and I prayed for the land and declared His faithfulness in the night. Life sustaining dew rolled with His loving kindness in the morning.

Oh, if I could stay here on this farm and evade the schemes of thy people and their folly. I have no hope of saving the Northern Kingdom, do I? A pure delight on this farm with a donkey for company shall be my prayer. With that in mind, I asked the donkey to lead the beasts into the barn to retire for the evening. She responded with a loving bray and walked into the barn with her cohorts.

The Blacksmith looked at me and smiled as he pulled his axe out of a tree. He practiced throwing that merciful weapon most evenings and became an expert. Soon he'd need to summon that skill on a target other than wood.

The boys retired to their house while I wandered the property before entering my house. Earlier in the day I formed a crude bed of straw stuffed into a dilapidated sheet of flax linen. I laid on that bed and closed my eyes.

In a moment I entered the world of dreams. I sat on the banks of the Nile and eavesdropped on a conversation between two men. They talked as if alone.

***

"We hold important positions and continue to contribute positively to the country. Why are you worried?"

"Our merit and past are of no account. We'll always be *others* with another loyalty. Suspicion and blame pursue us. People will project upon us the source of their evils."

"This is nonsense. Pharaoh's own daughter has an affinity for our beliefs. The girl became one of us! Do you think Pharaoh would condemn his own daughter? Pharaoh shall not cater to the ignorant rabble."

"Our success is conspicuous. Worse yet, our numbers grow in tandem with this illusion of stability. A reckless folly to believe we are endeared by the government or the population it rules. Joseph, the exilarch, is no more. Even during the time Joseph led the government we were aliens. Of Pharaoh's daughter you ask? Pharaoh holds the reins of a beast. A god whose control is not absolute. The regal deity answers to the population, the priests, and members of his government. Pharaoh's daughter has provoked the wrath of those elements. Pharaoh's affection for our people through his daughter's attraction to our laws and customs is a dangerous fantasy. Do you think Pharaoh is a frivolous monarch? He sees the danger of his daughter's epiphany and the specter of weakness. It'll drive him mad with resentment. This is the new Pharaoh rising that does not know Joseph. Batya, Pharaoh's daughter, has given birth to this *new* Pharaoh."

***

The dream was a reminiscence devoid of symbols or allegories. An unadorned dream of stark and devastating simplicity.

I awoke to the enmity of exile and its dehumanizing rationalizations. How could I, could anyone, prevent it? We couldn't. Not I or little Barak. But this old lady has learned to try even when the circumstances are dire. On my farm I sow the fruit of futile hope and demand a bountiful reaping.

The Blacksmith and Barak needed to set-off early to buy provisions in Rakkat. I was pleased they emerged from the house without need to clamor at their door.

"Good morning. Take these coins for the goods."

They mounted the wagon, and I said, "Goats, we need goats for milk and cheese. Buy an additional wagon and a team of horses for hauling lumber and tools to build a self-sustaining farm. We'll be here a long time."

They departed as if making their escape, so happy to flee crazy Chava, as I sputtered the last requests.

The Blacksmith and Barak departed for three nights. During their absence Omid and I repaired in order of priority. I worked without interruption, steady as a flour mill, in contrast to Omid who woke late, retired early, and took frequent breaks. Whenever I looked up from my chores, I spotted him resting in a shady place. I complained, but he wasn't accustomed to farm work and lacked stamina. Already he was too old to be a productive laborer. One afternoon I asked Omid to draw water for the donkeys, and he purposefully let the bucket fall into the well. Without complaint I rigged up a rope with a hook and fished it out while he lounged nearby. His behavior and work ethic needed correction. I requested him to be more attentive, but my lecture produced the opposite result I sought. Neither reward nor rebuke influenced a better effort, so I shut my mouth.
    By the third day I had completed many chores on the farm. I expected Barak and the Blacksmith to return the previous day but gave it no heed. Finally, they returned in the late afternoon with abundant supplies. I welcomed them back with joy and bid them to relax while I penned the goats and put the horses in the barn after watering them. Additionally, there were tools, wood, and grain to stow away. I worked well into the evening with the Blacksmith. Omid and Barak had gone to sleep.
    The two of us finished working and sat on the parched ground. I turned to the Blacksmith and said, "What took you so long in Rakkat? I expected you to return a day earlier."
    The Blacksmith gazed out on the horizon and said, "It was Barak. Each day he went to different places in town and preached to the people of corruption and righteous justice. He spoke most of the day although I cautioned refrain since our plan involved an anonymous approach. But he was a barrel ready to explode. And Chava, he spoke with authority and conviction. An inspiration to the people, divine rhetoric, amazing to see him transformed from that boy who muttered incoherently in villages in the dead of night. This method is worthy."
    This was a bright development. Of note, the Blacksmith finally exhibited some passion. This must be the way! Why had I been so heavy handed in my practice? I understood little of leadership and inspiration. Even getting an honest day's work from Omid was beyond my capabilities.

The Blacksmith stood. I offered him my hand, and he pulled me upward. I smiled and said, "That's good. The two of you have a mission. On the first day of every week go circle the Kinneret. You'll take care of Barak while he spreads the word, but please return before each Sabbath. Two horses, and the donkey to carry supplies, shall suffice. Keep your axe handy and practice throwing every day with perfect accuracy and power. One more thing. Return with a beast so you men can enjoy meat on the Sabbath."

Four years passed. Omid and I worked on the farm and profited from the surplus and gave to the needy. Barak and the Blacksmith journeyed each week. Barak preached to the Israelites and returned with the Blacksmith before the Sabbath. The veil of the mundane lifted on the seventh day, and we rested.

Each year I sowed and reaped a larger field with wheat, barley, spelt, rye, and oats. And fruit, beans and vegetables. During the conversion of a field to farmland I harvested eminent stones to build a granary and guest house. I worked for the sake of work and without care that time etched away my creation. A labor of joy, and few tears except on those rare occasions in provocation of the Blacksmith. Omid's work ethic improved or perhaps my expectations lessened, but he transformed from a delicate mercenary into a burly farmer, a laborer who grew bored and asked frequently for his freedom.

One Sabbath afternoon a puzzling wind descend upon us.

Barak turned to me and said, "Is it an evil portent?"

I looked to the south and said, "Travails of birth. Our time here is ending. Silence, lest we speak of this on the Sabbath."

The veil of the mundane replaced the Sabbath. A new era was upon us. The corporeal land pinged with birth convulsions. I faced the boys and said, "An affair stirs in Yehuda. The land will shake. Tomorrow we prepare. I must retire to my bedchamber now. Goodnight."

I sat alone in the dark house with my eyes shut and slowed my breathing as the temperature of the room equalized with my body and I let my physical form slip away until my skin transformed from deep black to primordial translucent. I exhaled across the breadth of the universe synchronized to the eternal breath of the Creator.

A sensation tingled my lips and nose. A force field like a vibrating wheel spun inside my womb. The wheel spun and scraped against my lips, nose, nipples, and groin as my body and consciousness subordinated to the wheel. With revolve, the wheel vibrated through space and hovered above Jerusalem before descending on the temple and resting atop the flames of the menorah.

Yehoyadah, the head priest, looks face to face with Yoash the boy. The light of the menorah illuminates their faces. A lady with long white hair sits nearby in the darkness. She is Sara no longer. A transformation from Sara to Sarah; nursemaid of Yoash these past five years in the Holy of Holies. Yoash is the remaining seed of the house of David; saved from the poison of the wicked queen, Atalya. The time for the boy to be weaned had passed. The ascension to the throne is at hand. Yehoyadah gazes at the menorah, exploring my presence as the flames flicker with the vibration of the wheel, while speaking to Yoash of kingship. The three gaze at the menorah.

The wheel ascends to the heavens, descends and hovers on a lone candle inside an imperial chamber. Queen Atalya sits on a throne while Seti stands nearby. They cease discussion, sensing the wheel, and stare in unison at the candle.

The wheel ascends to the heavens, descends and hovers at the end of a long table in another imperial chamber. This chamber is not as richly appointed as the previous chamber. At the opposite end of the table sits Yehu, flanked by his brother and uncle. They eat and drink, undisturbed by the wheel as it glides across the table hovering between the three men. Still, the men continue to dine without noticing the wheel. Yehu's uncle turns his gaze toward Yehu and begins speaking.

"Yehu, if you aspire to protect the throne and wellbeing of the citizens it requires consolidation of power. Two things. First, distract the population. Second, get yourself a valuable ally. The first is simple. We cannot allow the people to serve the whims of the prophets. Do you want to share power with the prophets? Do you want them to undermine your sovereignty? No, of course not. You need to undermine them. Destroy the prophets and give the masses a banquet of Baal to feast upon. It's drastic, but for their own good. To share power with the prophets is foolish."

I'm working on the partnership. Queen Atalya comes in a few days. I advise you to be cordial with her. Shomron will work with the kingdom of Yehuda and ally with Egypt. This is the defense against Assyria; a bulwark with the addition of our friends in Sidon."

Yehu showed little interest in affairs of state. He stared off into space provoking the indignation of his uncle.

"Yehu, I hope you're listening because your actions will have consequences for you and the people of Israel. Without allies we'll crumble. Would you face Assyria alone?"

Yehu glanced at his uncle with a dazed expression as he drained a cup of wine. He set the cup down and grabbed the earring in his pocket. Yehu looked at his brother and said, "Where's father?"

Yehu's brother laughed nervously and said, "Father is dead."

A royal slur, "Yes, father is dead. If only he was here with us now. Instead, the lesser brother is my advisor." The uncle's face burned with hatred as Yehu continued.

"This is your plan? Inspire worship of Baal and join forces with Atalya? Dear uncle, whose throne am I protecting? You repeat the same thing since I destroyed the house of Ahab and priests of Baal. Shall I ascend the tower and paint my eyes? Who will fling me from that tower?"

"Yehu, get a hold of yourself! You speak like a woman. It's true, your father was a stronger man than I. But he'd give the same advice. These are different times. Assyria grows stronger each day. With a voracious appetite they'll extract tribute until we bleed to death. Then they'll invade, resettle your subjects to foreign lands, and import a foreign population. Expect it."

Yehu paced the room and said, "Yes, I speak like a woman. If only. Uncle, Yonah told me it's simple."

"Yehu, don't waste our time discussing the incoherent mutterings of an idiot."

"Uncle, Yonah says nothing has changed since king Shaul or since the first judge. To have faith in the Almighty and pledge our fidelity to the dictates of His law is our shield. That's what Yonah says."

"If you insist on quoting Yonah, please indulge me with an explanation of his actions. For instance, it's known that Yonah is a false prophet. He called people to repentance under the supposition that they'd be destroyed. And then they weren't destroyed!"

"Uncle, they weren't destroyed because they repented."

"Yehu, what is this folly you speak? Repentance is nonsense. Who repented? And if they pretend at repentance, it's a sham that alters not a decree from on high. And another thing. Yonah should be indicted on charges of sedition. He's an Assyrian spy. What did that idiot do in Assyria? Does he love them?"

"Uncle, Yonah anointed me king."

"Yehu, the crazy man didn't crown you. You yourself seized the crown from the house of Ahab with no help from Yonah. Don't make a mistake by empowering these so-called prophets and relinquishing your own power. Wield it wisely or you'll lose this kingdom."

"I'm retiring for the evening", Yehu said as he set the cup on the table. He didn't spot the earring that lay next to his cup.

***

The songs of the birds pulled me out of a deep slumber. I identified each bird on my farm by their song. A familiar joy of melodious news delivered each morning. A few of the birds sang soft songs afore first light. More joined as the light intensified. Finally, they all joined; yelling at each other in a cacophony of furious songs until accepting the dawn of a new day with a softer tune, trailing off to do their work.

I laid down and scanned the details of the familiar ceiling while thinking of my work, and results, without consideration of failure or victory. Trudging along, a blind conduit of people across the centuries who lived in the world of my choice, subjected to a reign of caprice. Yehu talked well to his uncle but possessed dwindling strength to prevail. The ascendency of Yehu was one more chance for the kingdom of Israel while the exile tarried until it pounced on a woeful generation.

The mission to take the first of the exiles, to descend from the land without chains of bondage, fell with oppression on me.

I stood outside with Barak and the Blacksmith while Omid slept. The two remained silent as I stared at the barn and said, "You will travel no more. Good service you did these years. The message you planted in those receptive hearts will flourish throughout the ages. But we have gleaned all we can upon this land."

We must sack the surplus grain for a mission. I'll take a group of people. They live in a village near Shechem. Once we finish our work, I'll go to their village and bring them here to load up on provisions before journeying north. Barak, you'll stay on the farm with Omid. The Blacksmith and I will fetch these pious villagers."

For some time, we worked the farm. His blessing manifested in plentiful winter rain produced an abundant crop stacked high in bulging sacks. One morning the Blacksmith gestured at Omid emerging lazily from the house and said, "Is he your slave or are you his slave? He sleeps and eats more than he works. You bring him his meals and ask little of him."

I smiled and said, "Sometimes he works hard but he's accustomed to a soft life, not farm work. I'm his master, responsible for him and have kept him safe. Never did I believe Omid might serve with vigor. He serves commensurate with his stamina and yearn to work. I try to encourage him."

With a puzzled expression the Blacksmith said, "The slave will be for nothing else but serving the master."

"Blacksmith, what of the freemen that you and Barak meet during the week? Do those men serve their master with longing? The Almighty is their master. How do they serve Him?"

The Blacksmith kept quiet while I whimpered. He looked at me and rolled his eyes in frustration. I composed myself and said, "I had a vision of Sarah. Her time of service will end soon, and she'll be free to leave Jerusalem. But now we ride to the village near Shechem. We go now."

The main roads from Rakkat to Shechem teemed with farmers, merchants, and soldiers. Dry dust mingled with bleating flocks and parched travelers on the hot thoroughfare. Burning eyes disseminated grievances against a cloud of culprits.

With me: four horses, two donkeys, and a big blacksmith. By late afternoon the congestion eased, and the heat abated. By evening we reached Jezreel and a suitable place to rest and water our beasts. The exhausted Blacksmith slept under the stars while I sat nearby with soft songs.

What did I discern? I tried, as always, to ignore those questions since it provokes endless inspection and presumptions of power rather than simple action. A preference to remain ignorant was my way. This world is a world of action wherein I was most content doing simple work on the farm in austere fidelity. Prophecies baffled my head and unfairly interfered with free will. A laugh of abject consolation pierced my lips at the prospect of running away like Yonah before I shut my eyes in expectation of the painful visions of destruction and exile.

But the vision of exile loomed deficient. Instead, I pictured a compliant Yehu sitting at the dining table with the wicked queen. Atalya sat at the table wearing my earring.

I came closer to her face with shock as she stared into my eyes.

She saw me and my environment. I too, panned my gaze searching the room and came face to face with Seti, his eyes rolled back behind his head, returning my glance with white globes protruding from grizzly eye sockets. In an instant his eyes righted themselves and stared into my eyes. In another instant, I woke from the vision. They know my identity.

Unless one has prophecies, one should not judge Yonah. You'll never comprehend what that crazed prophet saw that inspired him to flee by ship. Those visions pulverize one's will. Therefore, it isn't fair, even for supra-woman.

I wished to depart for the village at once, but the animals needed their rest. At dawn I rummaged through our camp making enough noise to warn the Blacksmith and the animals that sleepy time ended. I was nervous to wake the Blacksmith and asked the donkey for a bit of restive braying. The donkey accepted the scolding she'd receive from the Blacksmith and let off a series of sounds.

Dawn greeted us in its full glory on the road. Soon after, the heat of the day and fellow travelers received us with wrath on the dusty highway. Foot traffic, flocks, and wagons flowed along the busy road. By afternoon we bypassed Shomron and headed south toward Shechem. As we drew close, I became excited with anticipation of reuniting with the village I'd departed years earlier. How were Mara and Adam? What of the Prophet and his son Joseph and the others? I purposefully did not reckon time passed. Why should I?

The road between Shomron and the village was deserted, but I grew certain we were being examined. It mattered not. The village, a haven no more, was meant to expire. A soon-to-be traumatic experience for the villagers, but I suspected the young ones—who never experienced the outside world—might cope well. In its lofty excellence it was an unnatural existence, suspended from the laws of nature.

What is it that tethers the simple man of faith?

The entrance to the village hid from the road, impossible to unearth with the eyes, but only by sensing a void within the orderly fabric of nature.

The Blacksmith and the beasts followed.

The dusk of the exterior world took on a different hue as we embarked along the edge of the valley: Purple.

I walked toward the familiar houses and gazed at the expansive wheat field, which provoked the same unsettling sensation experienced years prior. Several children ran toward us with excitement. I smiled to them as we walked toward the houses, but the children paid little heed to me. They were much more interested in the donkeys and horses.

A woman spotted me. Mara's red hair bounced in the diminishing light as she ran toward us. I raced toward her with a gleeful collision and embrace.

We stared smiling at each other. I placed my hand on top Mara's big belly and said, "How many children will this be?" Mara said, "Only my second", as she caressed my hair and face with her hand. "It's difficult for the women to conceive here."

I took a step backward and said, "There's not much time", as I held Mara's hands. "Atalya, the wicked queen, has joined forces with Yehu. Do you hear the happenings of Israel and Yehuda? Never mind. Israel will be exiled. This village is not safe. The Blacksmith and I will carry your village to the north."

Mara let go my hands and said, "Chava, are you crazy? Why shall we leave? This is our home."

I smiled and said, "Only a few years ago you were apprehensive to leave Shomron. You've been here a long time and are scared to go, but this land will always be home even as your progeny wander the earth in exile for the ensuing millennia."

Mara stared at me with a blank expression and said, "Come meet my child."

Too much, too fast. Mara appeared numb.

I grabbed Mara's arm and said, "There's no time for this. It isn't safe here."

A short while later we gathered the entire village of some forty people, including ten parental units and their children, in the area between the houses.

I spotted Adam, the one I kidnapped from Jezebel's priests as an infant. Adam knew me not.

The Blacksmith stood by my side like a statue. I glanced over the crowd and said, "All the workers of iniquity shall be scattered."

I continued looking over the crowd as they stood uneasily. Finally, the silence was broken by Mara's husband. Joseph said, "You return after many years—ordering us to abandon our village—and declare but one sentence from a psalm? We were brought here to preserve a community of the devout and have behaved with righteousness these past years. Do you presume that we are workers of iniquity? Without exception, we are not workers of iniquity and will not be scattered."

We were summoned to attention by the alarming shrieks of the donkeys. The Blacksmith drew his axe readied for an attack. I sensed it too. The donkeys were warning us. I drew my sword and took on a defensive stance. The villagers stood nervous and bewildered. They didn't understand the donkeys or sense the threat.

I shouted, "Go, run! Run inside your houses. A raid is underway." The villagers fled in disarray. Some of them thought it was the Blacksmith, and I that were attacking them. Both donkeys continued to bray. The sound echoed off the cliffs and filled the valley with ceaseless shrill.

Twelve horsemen bore down straight on us but then circled toward the wheat field. I said, "Blacksmith, stay here and defend the village", while I ran toward the horsemen.

An oddity. They stood in a group at the edge of the valley. I slowed my approach and turned my attention toward the wheat field. It's then I saw him.

Seti. He walked along a path between forest and wheat field. The wheat stalks whipped back and forth in the absence of wind. At a loss for what to do, I walked along the edge of the field, but the wheat stalks assembled, a hostile army blocking my path. It spoke a language I refused to understand. I pleaded for the field to free a path, but it wouldn't yield. I drew my sword and pointed it at the lead stalks. The stalks moved left and right as I marched forward a few paces into the field.

I stopped and glanced at Seti who lurked on the edge of the field. He opened a satchel from around his neck and poured the contents onto his palm. Without hesitation, Seti threw the contents above the field. A large cloud of dust descended over the entire valley. It tingled my skin as it coated the environment in a glittering mist.

I looked downward and saw the wheat stalks become darker, becoming black. With reluctant fingers I touched a stalk, and it crumbled into ash. The ground itself transformed to ash and the scent of burned bread hung in the air. I turned around and attempted to escape as the ground quaked beneath my feet.

I teetered as I tried to walk the few paces out of the charred field, took a few steps, but my feet sank into the earth until my legs submerged up to the knees. Stuck at the scorched edge, I tried using my sword as a cane but progressed forward in slow motion.

The donkey galloped toward me with outraged bray. His mother and Blacksmith trailed. My attention became focused on the donkey as he reached the edge of the charred field and continued to bray at me and my predicament. I didn't expect what happened next. Seti appeared and swung his sword on the donkey's neck. Blood spurted into the air as the donkey's mother screamed in agony.

The quagmire impeded mobility.

The demise of the donkey crushed my spirit.

I stared forward with blurred vision as if in a dream and saw the Blacksmith hurl his axe at Seti. Time slowed as the axe rotated toward its target. The head of the axe penetrated Seti's head and hurled him on his back beside me. I reached out to grab the axe handle to use as leverage to escape the quagmire.

Grief washed over me in a debilitating wave. The law of the first-born donkey is that its neck shall be broken if it's not redeemed. The Blacksmith redeemed it according to the law!

How could He?

Oh Father, what is this?

ETERNITY. Severity of eternity.

I screamed with grief as the donkey's mother and the Blacksmith stood over the dead donkey in disbelief. The intruders rode toward us. A rider barreled into the Blacksmith. I looked on helplessly as the Blacksmith fell to the ground unconscious.

The intruders looked at each other indecisively. These men, they were soldiers of Yehuda commanded to go with Seti to stifle a rebellion in the northern kingdom. But Seti was dead, and the northern kingdom was of little concern to them. Indeed, they served Atalya—with disdain—to protect their own interests. They were pleased with the demise of Seti.

I screamed, "You go now".

They tied the Blacksmith on top of a horse. Next, one man began to pull Seti's feet out of the burned field. I held the axe handle as he pulled but the axe dislodged from Seti's skull. The man smirked at my dilemma—stuck in the quagmire with a sword in one hand and an axe in the other.

Yehuda's intruders rode away with the Blacksmith and Seti's corpse. The men of the village came and pulled me from the mire. I rose, sheathed my sword, and embraced the bereaved donkey. The donkey urged me to mount her. This, I had never done.

I obliged the insistence of the mournful beast and bathed her neck with tears. She put the past behind her and trotted in pursuit of the Blacksmith; the hostage of Atalya. I bade her to pause a moment as we neared Joseph and Mara.

I looked at Joseph and said, *"He makes thy borders peace; He giveth thee in plenty the fat of wheat."*

Joseph said, "Again, you quote a psalm. Our borders have been destroyed. Our wheat has been burned. Your carelessness led them here."

Joseph did not know, nor need to know, that it wasn't I they followed here. It was Adam—the one I circumcised, the one that Joseph raised—that led Seti to the valley. Adam, now a young man, bore the responsibility for destroying the village. *This* Adam desired to leave *this* garden.

I secured the axe to the donkey and said, "You cannot stay here. That Egyptian poisoned the land. The pools will dry, the fish shall die. The fine oil turns to tar. Take yourselves and young ones to my farm near Rakkat with these four horses that will lead and carry your burdens. You were never meant to live generations in this valley. You go now."

I did not look back or answer when Joseph screamed with disdain, "Chava, who are the workers of iniquity?"

I answered under my breath for none to hear, "Is it those who choose not? I chose long ago, so you'd have a choice. You have a choice."

I sat on the donkey as she trotted toward the path we had entered a short time ago. However, this time, the road was visible, demarking no delineation between the forlorn valley and surrounding land.

The valley needs no prayer, it's true. We transformed the ground of Adam to a garden against its will. The ground of Adam reverts as His law of nature prevails.

Chapter 10

מלכות (Kingdom)

An Eternal Sabbath

Wonder why the death of the donkey hurt so much? Yes, I experienced the loss of many people and animals, but this tragedy was as if Father broke his covenant. The Blacksmith redeemed the donkey under the law. If not redeemed, yes, its neck shall be broken. Why did Father allow Seti to break its neck? Does He disapprove of his daughter?

I hadn't gone far on the southern road when I heard an old familiar voice. The Prophet said, "Chava, how do the people fare?"

I replied, "They look forward to moving. Bring them two wagons; more if possible. No time for talking now. This donkey takes me to Jerusalem to rescue her master."

The animal trotted south with beastly motivation to find the Blacksmith. Her big eyes pleaded with me when I pressed her to rest. Still, those eyes boiled my tears. With a shove of her muzzle to the side I said, "Stop staring at me. What do you want? You need to rest. Don't annoy me, donkey." It didn't help. The forceful nose assaulted me with savage shame. She rested a while, and then ran off without me. I chased her most of the night until she came to a fork in the road at dawn. Suddenly she stopped and beckoned me to mount her again. Here I was, the servant of a donkey.

She proceeded at a steady trot. I bounced up and down, eyes closed and visions of Seti with the axe blade buried in his skull. In a moment I entered the world of dreams; sitting on the banks of the Nile, eavesdropping on a conversation between two men. They talked as if alone.

***

"We are of pure Egyptian blood. This is an insult to our nation. A spiteful government took no pity. Forced us to sell our lands to Pharaoh under the administration of Joseph, Pharaoh's ring bearer. Joseph, the Hebrew. Now, it's those people that control huge tracts of land in the most fertile region of our country. And commerce and trade. Pharaoh too! His own daughter has adopted their customs! They multiply and overrun our homeland."

"Blood matters not. Nor does it matter where your forefathers were born. What matters, for you to make your way in this land or any other, is your own wits. What is a true Egyptian? Your esteemed lineage is an illusion. Your veins bleed red just like the Hebrews."

"It's foul play, not wits. We too stored grain to prepare for the famine. Why is it that Pharaoh's grain did not rot? A conspiracy!"

"Who conspired? The government built and safeguarded vast storage cities. What did you build? What do you know from storing grain? The vermin and the weather consumed your grain, not foul play."

"Those people poke their fingers into agriculture, trade, artisanship. Don't you see they control everything? They lend to the vulnerable and ensnare them. Do you see how they treat their livestock? These beasts are holy, but they treat them like mundane property. Those people multiply but do not marry our daughters. They keep their own names, dress, and customs. Shall we call it but any other name than dual loyalty? Or no allegiance to Egypt! A new Pharaoh will arise.

***

I drifted back to consciousness nearby Jerusalem and pleaded with the donkey to stop and allow me to walk. She brayed with exhaustion in response to my pleas but agreed. We ascended near the Temple Mount where I stopped her and said, "That's enough donkey. The Sabbath is coming, and we need to find a stable for you to rest."

The donkey turned to me and said, "I'm not resting until we take care of our business. Climb back on top. We go to the royal stables."

Her speech did not surprise me, but I felt elated that a restoration to the dynasty was about to ensue, so I agreed and climbed back on top the donkey. She took narrow alley ways and shortcuts to the royal stable. I dismounted once we arrived and retrieved the weapons. Both axe and sword I held at the ready. The donkey asked for a stall. I obeyed her instructions and penned the beast. My sweet friend bent down and grabbed a mouthful of oats, lifted her head, and stared with an innocent gaze while she chewed the meal. The simple expression on her face, as if nothing eventful transpired, charmed my heart.

I stared toward the other end of the stable and saw the majestic priest, Yehoyadah, approaching.

I was overcome with awe and comfort as Yehoyadah came near. He was the eminent scholar of the generation. The one who protected the infant king, Yoash from Atalya. It was Yehoyadah that taught the king in the holy sanctuary. Yehoyadah was everything in one; the scholar of the generation, high priest, and king. These were separate roles, but this man wielded all three crowns. The Almighty's exilarch upon the physical realm.

Yehoyadah, appearing to stare through me, said, "Yoash shall be anointed soon. She will come whence I came. Atalya. Wait here for her."

Yehoyadah placed his hands on my head and said, "I bless you, first daughter, to execute judgement on the wicked."

His words coursed through my blood and transformed me into an executioner.

Yehoyadah went back the way he came. His silhouette gliding to the end of the stable. Even though he walked toward the light, his shadow refused to lie on the floor of the barn which was scrubbed clean prior to our meeting. Nervous anticipation streamed into the barn with the fading glow of the day and the approaching Sabbath. A lone fly buzzed nearby, confused by the lack of filth.

Yehoyadah's faithful began their surreptitious assembly. The priests and Levites that completed their shift assembled at one gate. Their replacements, the fresh shift, along with faithful soldiers, stood between the palace and the temple. Swift warriors marshaled at another gate. In this way, Yehoyadah armed and stationed his faithful so there'd be no interference with the coronation of Yoash—and no salvation for Atalya. The weapons themselves were infused with the holiness of the temple. The shields bore the crest of the house of David, which would be restored. A holy aura leeched from the temple walls and soaked the air, infecting the swift and faithful.

I waited outside the barn and joined song to the onset of the Sabbath. With my eyes closed I probed the temple and its surroundings. The coronation began as soon as the swift warriors formed a perimeter around the temple. Yehoyadah emerged from the holy sanctuary with Yoash the boy. The two of them were past the altar when Sarah, unnoticed by the gathering, departed the holy sanctuary and lithely faded into the recesses of the courtyard. She glided ghost like, adorned with pale skin and long white hair. Her days in the sanctuary had passed. Now she strolled free from the blessed confines.

The crowd remained disciplined in their silence despite the buildup of anticipation for a new era of righteous sovereignty. Yehoyadah harnessed the Sabbath—His calming gift nourished the righteous rebels before the coronation.

Yehoyadah gave the scroll to Yoash the boy and pronounced him king as he anointed him with oil. At once the righteous rebels exploded with a jubilant noise.

The crown miraculously fit on the small boy's head as a sign that Yoash was the true king. It was done. The commotion grew with affirmations of joy. Suspicious ears from within the palace perked to attention.

Atalya summoned her guards and ran with haste to the temple to investigate the source of the noise. She arrived and saw the small boy with the crown standing next to Yehoyadah. "Rebellion!" she cried twice: once for the rebellion itself and once for negligently letting this boy slip away when she herself poisoned the descendants of David and took the throne. With an oath, the boy became King.

Atalya's rage turned to fear when she recognized the preparedness of the rebel force. They amassed and channeled her retreat to the palace through the stable. It was well known she should not be executed in the Temple environs.

I transformed my thoughts into speech; a contract. "Hurry harlot. Come through the stable and meet Chava. I wait for you with my axe and sword. With patience I stay out of sight until you and your entourage are well within the long stable. You come now."

Atalya and her entourage ran into the barn. The faithful militia slammed and locked the door behind the fugitives. I came out of the shadows and stood in front of their path. The lead guard smirked and said, "A little girl holding such a big axe and sword."

I stared deep into his left eye and gazed at the nerve leading to his brain. The footman flinched and put his hand to his head as I pinched the nerve. I threw the axe down the long corridor which struck below the man's neck. He lay on the floor dying as I walked forward with the sword in hand.

One man charged me, another, and another. All of them were out maneuvered with ease. I slaughtered each of them with a merciful slash across the neck. At last, Atalya remained alone. The former queen backed away from me until her back pressed against the stall. She whimpered incomprehensibly and looked down as if she expected salvation to rise from the floor of the barn. I raised my sword and said, "Look at me, Atalya. Look at me."

Atalya shook with fear, raised her head, but refused to gaze into my eyes. I examined the donkey who stood in the stall a mere hands length from Atalya. The donkey lunged forward and grabbed a bunch of Atalya's hair between big boney teeth; holding her tight. I lowered my sword and closed the gap between us. She gazed with fear and hatred. The blood of Jezebel pulsed behind her eyes. I stared into the green mist and perceived the spiritual remnants of Lilith.

With my free hand I plucked the earring from her ear. "This is mine. It has no power. A trivial gold earring. It's only my will, attached to Him, that has power. You could never win. To what ends do you exercise your will? Your will is restricted."

Why did I bother with meaningless discussions? Am I angry at this harlot?

This derivative of Lilith—the evil that seduced my husband.

This disgrace that poisoned with cruelty. It didn't matter now. I took my sword and thrust it into her heart. At last, we destroyed the house of Ahab.

I looked at the big eyes of the donkey and petted her muzzle. The opening of the barn doors interrupted the quiet. The faithful guards streamed in and carried the bodies to the palace. Another strode into the barn: The Blacksmith. For those same guards released the prisoners of the wicked queen. I smiled as the donkey brayed with loving joy at the sight of the Blacksmith.

The burly man smiled at his donkey, grabbed the axe, and marched out of the barn without saying a word to me.

"How many times will you ignore me? I traveled far with your maddening donkey to rescue you."

The Blacksmith gestured with the axe and responded, "I will do what you trained me to do."

I smiled and said, "Very well. I'll come, too."

We rushed with slow progress amidst the masses of exuberant revelers. Word of the wicked queen's demise spread quick. Vigilantes sought loyalists and servants of Baal. However, the Blacksmith and I were first to approach the Baal palace. I stopped the Blacksmith from smashing the front door. Instead, we took a side entrance and proceeded unobserved into the main sanctuary. Mattan, head priest, stood alone at the disgraceful altar with a sword in hand. I ran toward Mattan and leaped over his head. Before he raised his sword, I sliced his neck.

I stood on the dais above the altar. Mattan turned to attack me before realizing the extent of his injury. He stared at the blood on the altar and took notice of the fount emanating from his neck before dropping dead.

The Blacksmith walked to the front door and opened it. Masses of people pushed inside and began to destroy the place of Baal. Screams of horror and death filled the air as the mob pursued and slaughtered the practitioners of evil. I struggled through the crowd to join the Blacksmith at the front door, but it was too difficult to move against the crowd. At last, the Blacksmith came for me, took my hand, and led us away from the carnage.

We stood on the street as mobs stomped Atalya's legacy. I closed my eyes and put my palms on my ears to escape the chaos. The Blacksmith's hand touched my shoulder. With startled anger I said, "Why did you open the door so soon? You didn't wait for me. They trapped me, the people, rushing into the hall. I hate crowds." Once again, the Blacksmith put his hand on my shoulder. Then I began to cry. The Blacksmith said, "You're stronger than I am. You can push people out of the way with ease."

"Push people out of the way? What if they fell to the floor trampled underfoot? Have you no consideration for the surrounding souls? You know not thyself!"

I could speak no more. Only cry and run away from the Blacksmith toward the palace. As I approached the palace, I glimpsed her. Tears welled in my eyes interfering with my vision, but the hair and the gait of her walk were distinct. I gave chase along an alley, rounded a corner, and came face to face with Sarah. She looked at me with a soft smile. I came close and cupped her face in my hand and said, "Sarah, do you remember me?"

Sarah's white hair and skin glowed in the meek light of the alleyway. Imperceptible to most, her physical form was translucent. The untarnished soul of a baby burned beneath her physical husk.

"Sarah, you are a harvest, a bountiful harvest."

We stood staring at each other for a long time. I stroked her shoulders and caressed her face with wonder. The woman who nursed and weened the King in the Holy of Holies; an angel who had performed one mission underneath His cloud of glory. I begged myself to cease looking upon her radiance.

"Come Sarah. Come with me, daughter."

We walked back, a single rectified soul, the way I had come. Crowds thronged the streets, some of which I maneuvered aside to protect Sarah. Most people did not notice her. However, occasionally, someone astute stopped in their tracks mesmerized by Sarah.

Years before, on her balcony, I did not recognize my own soul.

Sarah hesitated when we neared the place of Baal. "No, don't worry, Sarah. It is being destroyed. The people are tearing it apart."

It was Sarah who saw him first. She set her eyes on that big man with the axe and spoke her first word: "Abraham". Relief and joy spread through my body. My spirit rose off the ground. From on high I watched the two of them walking toward each other: Sarah and Abraham. I winced at the name "Abraham." Oh, how I hoped I'd call him by that name. To me he was always Blacksmith.

My spirit returned to its body content to watch them hold hands and speak to one another. The night ebbed on, but Sarah and Abraham stood together like a statue that resisted time. It was sweet, but I lost patience before dawn. With a brief goodbye I told the two of them they were on their own until after the Sabbath when we'd meet again and travel north.

The walk to the stable was less congested with crowds. The donkey was fine. Dead bodies were gone, but the dried blood of Atalya and the others stained the stable floor. I exited the stable and walked toward the temple. The guards had been reinstated, which made it difficult to wander the temple without being accosted. A suitable place was found to linger in anticipation of the morning incense.

Finally, the house of Ahab is destroyed, and the physical manifestations of Lilith are neutralized. A moment's aroma of savory goodness and city steeped in spices of cinnamon and spikenard. No ungrateful pondering for the possibility of Lilith's return. A time and place for simple gratitude that the people were happy and Yoash sits on the throne. Yoash, the King, eight generations after David. Serenity shall descend on Jerusalem once more.

The three of us departed Jerusalem with Abraham's donkey, two wagons, and four horses. At Shomron, I said goodbye to Abraham and Sarah. The two planned to get married and strike out on their own. Sarah harkened to a vision, a place for her and Abraham to go for themselves. A place their forefathers departed many generations ago.

The markets of Shomron teamed with people and goods. None remembered the severity of the dreadful famine years earlier. Young ones didn't know of the famine. Old ones forgot.

An old merchant stood behind a table. On that table was a solitary sack of fine flour. I approached the merchant and said, "One shekel for that seah of flour?" The man nodded in consent. I gave the man his shekel and asked, "Does anyone remember the great famine?" The man replied, "I remember my daughter."

A famine ended, but the memories of the living for those they lost endured.

***

The search for a replacement took time. This new donkey was a magnificent beast. A small jack with the strength to dislodge a millstone with a single kick. When I first met him, he brayed so strong it shook my bones. The thought of being without a donkey was too sad to contemplate. He was the perfect companion. Although, nothing filled the void left by the Blacksmith. I spoke out loud to the spirits of malice descending on this land. "Oh Abraham, I never even called you by your name. You see how hard it is to part? Blacksmith, Abraham, I loved you like a husband and you cast me off like an old mother."

Mounted men approached from my rear. The donkey brayed, and I said, "Yes, I recognize them." The riders closed the gap and followed close behind me. One rode past, turned, and blocked my path. We faced each other. I spoke first.

"Yehu, a new king reigns in Yehuda. The rightful king. We, you, destroyed the house of Ahab. Yonah anointed you to destroy his house in the Shomron. Do you remember what Jezebel said from the tower? Is it peace, Yehu?"

The throne depleted his energy. Yehu looked gaunt and tired. The strong boy traded his virility for that of an emasculated king. What lies had he feasted upon in the dining chamber with his uncle? To pursue peace through evil. He sat on his horse now and stared at me without speaking a word. I spoke again, "Is it then? Is it peace, Yehu? That's the question for a king! Why did you come to meet me on this road? Do you want a beating?"

Yehu approached and whispered, "You never gave me a chance. You tricked and took control of me. How was I supposed to stop being your slave?"

"Yehu, every morning you shall bless Him for not creating you a woman."

"Yehu, Lilith was the root of Jezebel's and Atalya's power. It was you, destined to prevail over this evil. A mission to destroy the house of Ahab in Israel. But not alone as a free man without a strong connection to the Almighty. As my child and my slave, you prevailed over evil. Through my link (to Him above) you rose to the task. I am a slave to my Father. You are a slave, but not mine. As a king you are a slave to your people. Serve them with fidelity and faithfulness. Bring them to serve my Father, your Father."

Yehu looked at me with a slight smile and started to ride away. Before he rode off, I handed him the sack of flour and instructed him to keep it beside his throne. "When you gaze upon it, you'll know knowledge and be reminded of serving your people. A simple sack of flour and a simple people of faith."

I took the earring from my ear and said, "Take this as a reminder you are released from serving me. A king, not my slave. Go to peace Yehu. You go now."

It is written that Yehu served twenty-eight years as king.

***

I received a tepid welcome at my farm. The former village inhabitants were familiar with the soft life. The shock of losing their Eden was profound. Although, young Adam seemed pleased with the change. I gathered the group together and presented the choice.

"All of us have a choice."

At once, I laughed to myself at the irony of choice and almost shed a tear for the King.

"I will take you people, who choose, to a new village; a special place; a protected place where you can live your days in predictable peace and plenty. The rest of you can go wherever you wish. I'll give you money to start. Tomorrow morning, we go. Decide by then. If you go to the new village, please help load the wagons with grain, fruit and vegetables."

After the group dispersed, I confronted young Adam. This is the one I had circumcised years ago. The one I saved from the fires of Baal. He was now a man with his own will. I walked up to him and said, "You don't want to go to the new village, do you?"

"Maybe I'll go to the new village. Otherwise, I cannot decide where to go or what I'll do. Joseph and Mara are parents to me. And the others. I have no family or friends other than these people."

"You didn't answer the question, Adam. Again, you don't want to go to the new village, do you?"

"Where else am I to go? Who else will be my family?"

"Adam, I believe it's best for you to treat those questions independent from one another. The new village is like the old village. The new village will protect and insulate you, a sequestration from the outside world. You know this. Now you have the choice."

Adam stared off into the distance and said, "I cannot decide."

"Adam, shall I decide for you?"

"It depends what you decide."

"Adam, I'm done talking, and I already made your decision."

"What did you decide?"

I walked away from Adam with these last words, "No, you decided."

Adam grabbed my arm, the same arm I used to seal him into the covenant, and said, "What did you decide?"

"You already decided Adam! You aren't capable to live in sequestration. It was you who led Seti, the Egyptian, to the village. Did you expect the destruction of the village and the upheaval to the lives of those you love? It mattered not to you, a man that could have exited that village through his own choice. You always wanted to leave the village but feared to execute the choice. You committed a sabotage and cursed the others when you summoned Seti. In the morning, you'll say goodbye. I know a different place for you to dwell—it's with the children of Eden. Don't cause trouble for the others. They are going to a new village to the north. You go south."

Omid and Barak inspected the exchange from a distance and moved forward after Adam took leave. Barak had transformed from a timid young man to a sage these past few years. With (my) staff in hand he walked with regal humility. I smiled and asked if they'd miss the farm.

Omid replied, "Don't urge me to leave you or to turn back from you. Where you go, I will go and where you stay, I will stay."

I winked at Omid and said, "Ruth you are not, but you have been a faithful slave and I'll miss your jokes, Omid. Grant this day to you, do I, your freedom. Please travel with Barak to Tekoa so he can guard your safety. From Tekoa you can journey to your land. You'll drop off that boy, Adam in the shadow of Gilboa for the children of Eden. He'll work now."

I turned to Barak and said, "Fig, you'll watch after Omid. Per chance he can help you this season in Tekoa with your figs. The Almighty will bless you with bountiful yields of exquisite figs. This land needs prophets and you will teach the prophets beneath thy fig trees; more prophets than seeds of thy fig tree. Go forth with thy staff in hand."

It was a joyous goodbye to Barak, my precious Fig. I took leave of them and wandered the farm in solitude till prophecy intruded on my serenity. The vision of an aged Barak sitting under the shade of a fig tree with a young acolyte burned my eyes. This simple vision would be the seminal portent of all I experienced this past generation. A small shoot will emerge from the soil of Tekoa. Nothing will be reckoned other than this matter. Amos. But that's a future story.

The familiar birds welcomed the morning with their routine while the men assembled in prayer. Afterward, Adam said goodbye to Joseph, Mara, and the others before departing with Barak and Omid. Joseph shed tears for the boy he raised from a baby. I suffered no patience for sentimentality and long goodbyes.

I pushed everyone to assemble with haste. With finality I abandoned my farm and cried to the villagers, "We go now."

A mixed multitude of righteous joined our northbound caravan. Who knew where they came from or how they learned of this journey? By the time we exited the kingdom of Israel we numbered thirty-two men with their wives and children: horses, wagons, and livestock. For most of the trip the little donkey walked at my side. Highway men and soldiers of Ashur paid us little heed as we circled around the great city of Nineveh. A question crossed my mind about the time Yonah entered this great city, but it would remain unanswered. Why should it matter if the people of Nineveh repented? What matters is the inevitability of war between Ashur and Israel. The echoes of Yonah's call to repentance decay on the surface of those massive walls of Nineveh. But even so, ears crave that still sound.

We reached Baku's village and experienced the warm hospitality of Shirvan and his community. Our group spent two days resting in the village. Some even consider staying in this generous land with its gracious people, but we move onward. Before we departed, Joseph blessed Shirvan and his people. The blessing conjured a vision of peace in my consciousness as I drifted into the future; a future of cooperation and affection between neighboring nations. My passion was provoked by the prospect of neighbors bonding, not from venal power dynamics and alliances of convenience, but in brotherly love of shared principles. But if the principles do not emanate from the same source, then what? I could ask Joseph and Mara, "What is the source of your principles? On what foundation do they stand?" The foundation is His indestructible truth. If I ask Shirvan the same question, I'll get a different answer. And to be sure, Shirvan's principles rest on a foundation of sand. This then, is the place Yonah should have come! The wide-world needs Yonah: savior of the nations. Oh Father, why did Yonah not travel onward from Ashur?

Shirvan's men accompanied us to the Scythian border. I left my prized possession in Shirvan's stable. The beast brayed complaints, but I wouldn't be persuaded to take him for a slog across the vast steppe. My heart pounded with embarrassment from exasperated looks of all who suffered the incessant beastly song. I thought, that's it, short of making an oath, I will not obey commands from a donkey again. Cursed mortification and rage!

In this land, the summer rains bogged down the journey to the new village which transformed us into a procession of mud folk. That was the choice, travel in the winter on frozen ground or on summer mud. It was not much of a choice. These people would freeze on a winter's steppe. Winter was also the time for warring Scythian tribes to maraud, but we encountered no violence on our week's journey east. The Almighty led the children of Israel on sodden ground across that muddy steppe with no glad songs of gratitude to Him or your humble servant Chava. The mud people gave me a soggy regard when I pointed to the distant cliffs that camouflaged their new village.

"We are here," I said with a big grin.

Joseph responded, "Here what? We are lost! Why did you bring us to this dangerous wasteland? We could have died just as well in Israel."

"Joseph, when will you see? Do you not remember David's words?"

"What words?"

"Our fathers in Egypt gave no heed unto Thy wonders; they remembered not the multitude of Thy mercies, but were rebellious at the sea; the Red Sea."

"In the shade of those cliffs is your new village, a place of security and plenty. All the colors transmit with purity from the Source. Thy sole task in that place is worship of the Almighty. And study His law. You cannot see the blessing concealed within those cliffs. There's no need to send men in advance to spy the village since we will arrive soon. And you know, we don't need irksome spies to carry back evil reports."

Joseph shot a glance of disdain in my direction and then held his hand to his head as if he were experiencing a headache. The others were enjoying the change of landscape from steppe to forest. We set camp under the kind trees and set out for the village the following morning. The pleasant dawn transformed to a foul afternoon of bitter complaints as I led our multitude alongside the edge of the cliff in a futile search of the valley. I laughed apologetically the entire time I led the bitter lot around in circles of vexation. Mother's milk and mother's torment were the same.

At night the men approached me with Joseph as their spokesperson while I sat with Mara.

Joseph said, "How much longer shall we search for this village? At some point we must return. Is it possible we seek what cannot be found?"

I stood up and replied to Joseph, "With my whole heart I sought Thee; let me not err from Thy commandments."

"Chava, please spare me the psalmist allegories. We are not robust people fit to roam this land. If you cannot find the village, we shall return. Think of our frail youth dependent on our protection."

"You are frailer than your youth. Perhaps you'll die here while the youth enter the new village. Dare to provoke my anger and you'll be forced to make your own way."

I walked away from the camp to search for the village. The night was dark and devoid of wildlife and companionship. Even the wolves refused to beckon to my call. Oh, dejection. Why did I not take my donkey for companionship? Maybe I should flee from these stubborn people and escape their endless complaints. As soon as the thought entered my mind, I heard the roar of the raging river in the distance. Relief and disappointment coursed through my blood.

With laughter I ran back to the camp which was in a frenzied panic by the wolves I summoned earlier. The men kept the wild animals at bay with torches while children huddled nearby their mothers. I chased the wolves some bowshots distance from our camp until the wolves turned, encircling me. The large green-eyed female leaped into the circle and attacked. I fell to the ground, and the wolf began to nip at my neck and back while I laughed. The wolf, failing to control her affection, bit hard and breached my skin. Still, I laughed as she mauled my neck and face until I fell asleep.

That was the last I remembered until a face appeared above me in the morning light. "Yehu,", I screamed. My addled soul struggled to remember. My head wobbled as I sprang to my feet and stared at a group of people I did not recognize. I fell onto the ground wondering how I became caked with dry blood. Shaking hands explored lacerations on my face and neck. Again, I cried, "Yehu,", and sobbed until I noticed the figure standing by my side was Joseph, not Yehu. My body began to shake with laughter at the recollection of the wolf and the realization of who I was and why I was here.

I stood up and returned the stares of Joseph and Mara. Mara said, "We heard the wolves howling and thought they killed you. Are you strong enough to walk or should we carry you?"

"No, I'm fine. Let's go back to the camp. These are only scratches."

Stares of horror and revulsion greeted me back at the camp. The picture of blood on my body appeared as if I had escaped death. A splash of water revealed that the wounds were shallow and inconsequential. The wolf with eyes like Lilith had a pure animal soul, but she wished me no harm.

Mara asked, "Do you want food or water? You never eat."

"I'm not hungry. I just want to bathe my hair and body."

Joseph interjected, "Baths! Our water will last a day, two at most.

Mara looked disapprovingly at Joseph as she grabbed a bucket with water and began to clean me with a wet cloth. Joseph began to walk away, and I said, "Don't go. I want to show you something. There's no dearth of water."

The three of us mounted our horses and rode north east a short distance. The sound of the raging river grew louder as we approached the new village. We crossed the bridge on horseback and dismounted. Joseph and Mara looked with disbelief at their surroundings. This is what I had described, but their faith had so diminished they stood with doubtful delusion. I laughed at the thought they were disappointed that the existence of the village was real. The past day of our futile search was too frustrating to bear, and this was the result. A good thing I caused them to tarry about.

KINGDOM. The bride.

Joseph remained silent but Mara spoke with boundless joy. "Oh Chava, it's beautiful, everything you said. How'd we ever doubt you? Quick, let's go back and bring the others."

I mounted my horse, crossed the bridge and waited a few moments for Mara to pull Joseph out of his trance. We returned to the camp and announced our immediate departure for the village. With excitement the yearnings of our community mobilized to the north east. By late afternoon we crossed that ancient bridge across the raging river: the Shabbat River. I lingered on the bridge and indulged tears of loneliness for my Adam. A bridge (of choice, of knowledge), not made by human-hands, between two worlds.

I sprinted with glee to the grain room; to be first to bake bread from this wheat. Everything was provided and arranged with divine order. I took milled fine flour from a sealed earthenware pot and poured it into a kneading trough with water. Next, I mixed living dough and salt into the shaggy mass. After combining the ingredients, I ventured outside to inspect the upright oven. All night I toiled, and all morning I baked until loaves were stacked high to greet the Sabbath.

That evening we gathered by the Shabbat River and sang psalms to welcome the Sabbath. The flow of the river slowed with the setting sun until it stopped. I explained to the women that this was the Shabbat River. Every Shabbat the river current ceased. Hence, the name.

The singing of psalms gave way to a simple meal of fish, bread and vegetables. I took one loaf and walked to the fishpond. I finished that perfect loaf with divine satisfaction and laid alongside the field to dreams of bread; the bread of the garden where I was created.

***

Adam and I walked the garden and took from every tree that Father permitted. We knew delight. We knew nothing else. Ah, but we understood there was nothing but Him. None, no higher that man can aspire to reach, but I demanded to change the situation. I would separate by partaking of the impermissible—that tree and its fruit: *bread*. And now, men shall thank me for eating bread through their toil.

***

A warm hand stroked my face. The eyes peering into mine in the fading afternoon light were Mara's. She smiled and asked if I wanted to come lay inside on a bed. Sleep had overtaken me for almost a full day. I sat up and spoke.

"Mara, the wheat of this village grows without toil. There is nothing but Him. Who would not want to live here, to bask in His glory? All His colors reach this valley, this kingdom, in purity.

I am glad to have brought you and the others to this village. The Sabbath is departing but every day in this village is a single day, an eternal Sabbath. Please do not speak. My departure is soon."

I strode the valley while drinking the dusk of the last Sabbath I would know, and *understand*, in this village, in this garden. Once the stars were visible, I went to the grain room and grabbed a handful of wheat, which I placed in a satchel.

I said my goodbyes and moved across the bridge of the Sabbath River with my horse. When I reached the other side of the bridge, planted firmly on the ground of Adam, I turned around and waved to Mara. Mara stared back at me while I took the wheat from the satchel and cast it onto the bridge. The stones of the bridge crumbled under the weight of the wheat of Chava. The bridge was no more. None shall traverse the raging river during the six days, and none would dare cross and desecrate the Sabbath when its flow ceased. They made their choice. They stay now.

***

I destroyed the bridge and rode from the east into darkness. The big green-eyed wolf with pure animal soul walked alongside my skittish horse that first night. With the first perceptible rays of dawn she diverted north. As soon as she departed, I dismounted to rest my tired horse. I laid by a stream and began to dream as the horse grazed nearby.

I dreamed of Sarah and her husband Abraham the blacksmith. The two have settled in Ur Kasdim. Yes, they went to the land of Terach.

Abraham feeds the fiery forge and fashions burnished swords while Sarah prays for children. I recall how I scolded Abraham throughout our journey and shed futile tears of frustration in ridiculous yearning that Abraham could be like Abraham, but he never understood, and I never even called him by his name.

I dream of Barak. He sits crossed leg under the shade of a fig tree with my staff straddled across his lap. A young and attentive Amos sits in front of Barak under a mighty fig tree of Tekoa. Amos will pioneer a new age of prophecy. All these machinations were for Amos who shall carry the message of His indestructible truth.

My soul rests with Sarah, clothed in knowledge.

My soul rests with Mara, clothed in understanding.

Adam's soul dwells in Joseph's garden and Abraham's workshop.

Lilith, Jezebel, and Atalaya are no more.

My dream takes me back to the garden. I dream of the tree. No, not the tree of knowledge, of good and evil, but the *tree of life* that the Almighty gave unto me. I synthesize Wisdom and Understanding into Knowledge. I ate and live yet.

Being a created being, born to be palpably—grazing the edge between spiritual and material—with physical resolve, a carnal yearn of finite majesty, I chose for me; or was it He?

You go now.